PLANET USTINOV

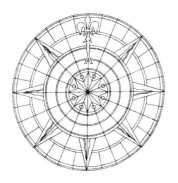

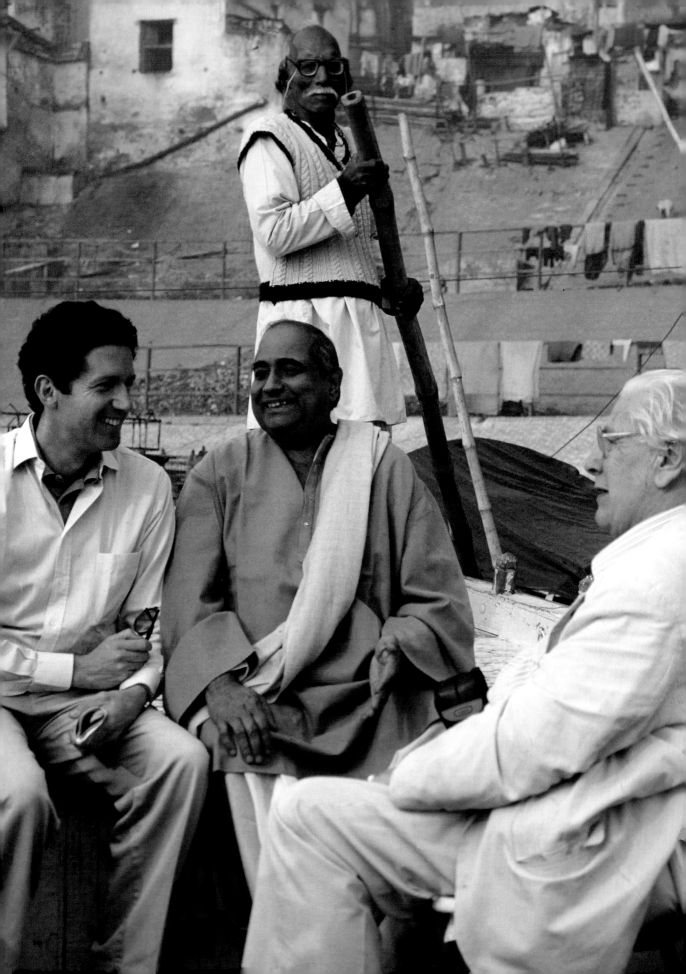

PLANET USTINOV

FOLLOWING THE
EQUATOR
WITH SIR PETER USTINOV

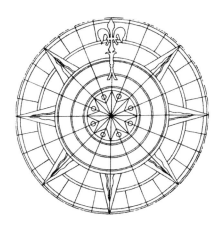

Michael Waldman

SIMON & SCHUSTER
A VIACOM COMPANY

First published in Great Britain by Simon & Schuster UK Ltd, 1998
A Viacom company

Text copyright © Granada Media Group Ltd, 1998
Planet Ustinov series copyright © Granada TV Ltd, 1998

1 3 5 7 9 10 8 6 4 2

Simon & Schuster UK Ltd
Africa House
64-78 Kingsway
London WC2B 6AH

Simon & Schuster Australia
Sydney

A CIP catalogue record for this book is available from the British Library

ISBN 0-684-81975-9

Designed by Design 23
Printed and bound in Great Britain by The Bath Press, Bath

For George

ACKNOWLEDGEMENTS

There are many who have been involved in this book, but one person's contribution has been fundamental. Without Maria Malone the book could not have been written, and it has been a continuous pleasure to work with her on its writing.

Sir Peter Ustinov's voice is of course to be found throughout the book. His generosity of spirit while filming the television series on which it is based was a privilege to experience, his extraordinary company a constant delight. A great bonus was the occasional presence of his wife, Lady Ustinov, who combined unobtrusiveness with charm whenever she joined us. I feel sure she will forgive my lighthearted and affectionate references to her suitcases.

The two associate producers on the series, Toby Follett (Hawaii, Fiji and India) and Pratap Rughani (Australia, New Zealand and South Africa) not only proved to be stimulating travelling companions but also fine photographers; evidence of their work is to be found throughout these pages. Back at base, production coordinator Sharon Thomas sustained her wonderful sense of humour despite innumerable provocations and illegible faxes from the Front.

On the road, cameramen Mike Fox and Chris Cox, assistants Matthew Fox and Nemone Mercer, sound recordists Mike Lax and Alastair Widgery, and in London film editor Charles Davies, were all towers of strength. Providing support and encouragement, executive producer Bill Jones, who originated the project, has been a joy to work with. The same is true of his colleagues at Granada TV, controller of factual programmes Charles Tremayne and the then director of programmes Peter Salmon and, at Channel Four, commissioning editor Peter Grimsdale. At WCA Licensing, Elaine Collins skillfully saw the book through its earliest stages and at publishers Simon & Schuster, editors Gillian Holmes and Sally Partington have made the challenging process of getting it to the printers on time surprisingly painless. And a final thank you to Sam, Rosie and Alex . . .

CONTENTS

Be good + you will be lonesome.

Mark Twain

First Things First...

It was not perhaps the most auspicious of beginnings.

A journey which had already taken me halfway round the world. London to Honolulu via Los Angeles. Honolulu to Fiji. A tortuous five hour flight on a small and not very robust aircraft to Kiribati, a country made up of dozens of islands scattered across thousands of miles of the Pacific Ocean.

All this to reach the equator. I was not even altogether sure what to expect once I arrived at this familiar reference point, since the equator is a peculiar thing. Easy enough to pinpoint on a map, to trace the countries it passes through as it neatly slices the world in two. But it is also invisible. There but not there.

I was on the trail of suitable stories and locations for a series of films in which Sir Peter Ustinov would journey around the world. A series about people first and foremost, but one in which the equator would also play its part. A century before, the writer Mark Twain had undertaken his own epic journey, chronicling his experiences in the aptly-named *Following the Equator*. A well-thumbed copy lay in my luggage. This was to be our inspiration, although it was never the intention to follow slavishly in Twain's footsteps. Indeed he never visited Kiribati, which lies so far off the beaten track that only the most determined of travellers is likely to find it.

What brought me to the capital, Tarawa, a narrow strip of coral just a few miles long, was the knowledge that Kiribati straddles the equator – and, as it happens, the International Date Line (but that was to be another story). Early research had indicated that there were stories to be told on two of the country's islands, Aranuka and Abemama, which conveniently lay on opposite sides of the invisible line. We could take a small ferry from one to the next, a trip of less than five hours, and on our way cross what Twain had described as 'a blue ribbon stretched across the ocean'. It seemed ideal. Too ideal, perhaps.

Just twenty-four hours later, marooned in the rather depressing Otintaai Hotel on the edge of the Tarawa lagoon, I found myself contemplating some unexpected and mildly disturbing news: the equator was in the wrong place.

Despite previous assurances from my local guide, close scrutiny of a seafarers' chart now revealed that both Aranuka and Abemama lay inconveniently to the north of the equator. It seemed impossible, yet confusion over the exact whereabouts of these two tiny islands was entirely understandable. Kiribati is a mass of islands and atolls and several hundred dots on a map can be very misleading.

Reassuringly, the positioning of Abemama and Aranuka turned out to be less critical than it might first have appeared. There was nothing to stop us from sailing from one to the next and crossing the equator on the way, even if it meant a slight detour. Seven hours in the ferry instead of five. Surely the locals wouldn't mind?

Not ideal perhaps, but short of moving the equator, our best option.

The blue horizon of the Pacific: the seductive tropical vision that has lured western travellers ever since Captain Cook first sailed these seas.

Opposite: The frontespiece to the original 1897 edition of Following the Equator.

It is easy to make plans in this world; even a cat can do it; and when one is out in these remote oceans it is noticeable that a cat's plans and a man's are worth about the same. There is much the same shrinkage in both, in the matter of values.

MARK TWAIN, *FOLLOWING THE EQUATOR*

◆

ON ANY GREAT JOURNEY it is advisable to expect the unexpected. However precise the planning, no matter how carefully everything has been arranged, there are, inevitably, surprises. When you are not simply travelling but making a series of films along the way even more complications are certain to arise. Our journey would take in destinations all around the world, beginning in Hawaii and the South Pacific, moving on to Australia and New Zealand, then India, and finally to Mauritius and South Africa. An arduous schedule by any standards, covering thousands of miles by air, sea and land, zig-zagging across time zones, going back and forth across the International Date Line, which was not exactly in the wrong place (unlike the equator) but had certainly shifted.

It was useful in some respects to be retracing the footsteps of another traveller, yet the intervening hundred years had wrought so many changes it was clear that Twain's difficulties and our own would at times be very different. This struck us with force on the eve of our filming when a thoroughly modern obstacle presented itself. Twain had journeyed by sea from Vancouver to Hawaii, his first destination. He had already visited what were then the Sandwich Islands many years previously and had been thoroughly smitten. Hawaii was Twain's idea of paradise. On his arrival in 1897, however, an outbreak of cholera on the islands meant he was unable to land and was forced instead to gaze on Honolulu, the Hawaiian capital, from the deck of his ship, which remained anchored a mile offshore. It was this which prompted him to comment on the futility of making plans. A century later we found ourselves in considerable sympathy with his sentiments.

While we were reasonably confident there would be no cholera epidemic to prevent us from making it to Hawaii, we failed to anticipate the bureaucratic web in which we were about to become entangled just days before we were due to set off. Without explanation the American Embassy refused the necessary work visas for Sir Peter and two members of the film crew. Their applications were rejected, without so much as a hint as to how we might rapidly overturn the decision. Indeed we were told to wait fourteen days before making any appeal. Bearing in mind our planned departure was a mere seventy-two hours away this was not encouraging news. Attached to the applications was nothing more than a standard letter and a telephone number for enquiries.

Dialling the number it crossed my mind that it would be fairly tricky to make a film in Hawaii – or anywhere else for that matter – in which Sir Peter Ustinov was meant to feature prominently, while Sir Peter remained stranded in London. Moments later I was listening to a recorded message which offered a number of options, one of which was, thankfully, to be connected to a real person rather than an answering machine. My hopes soared briefly until it became clear that I was not through to a member of the Embassy staff after all, but to an agent acting on their behalf. No, he said, he was unable to explain the rejection. No, he was unable to put me through to the Embassy's visa section – and he was expressly forbidden from giving out their direct number. All telephone visa enquiries came through his office, or in writing. Politely but firmly he made it clear he was unable to help. It was like beating one's head against a solid wall. I hung up and contemplated our next move. With time ticking away there were few avenues open. I rang the Embassy Press Office and told them of our plight. They were nominally sympathetic but indicated there was little they could do. They also refused to allow me to speak directly to the visa decision-makers but said they would try to follow it up. The hours ticked by. As the office day was coming to an end I rang again and

Everybody smile: the visas have arrived.

calmly informed them I was about to call the Secretary of State in Washington. This seemed to have the desired effect. Suddenly cracks began to appear in the very wall which had seemed so impenetrable just moments earlier.

It seemed there would be no need to appeal directly to Madeleine Albright after all. In the space of a few hours the missing visas were issued and the Hawaii shoot – with Sir Peter – was on. We breathed a collective sigh of relief and finished packing.

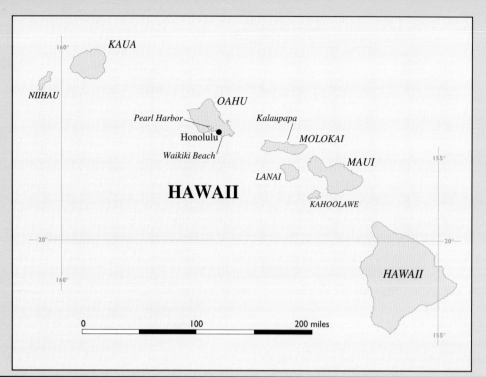

KAUA

NIIHAU

OAHU

Pearl Harbor

Kalaupapa

Honolulu

MOLOKAI

Waikiki Beach

MAUI

LANAI

KAHOOLAWE

HAWAII

HAWAII

0   100   200 miles

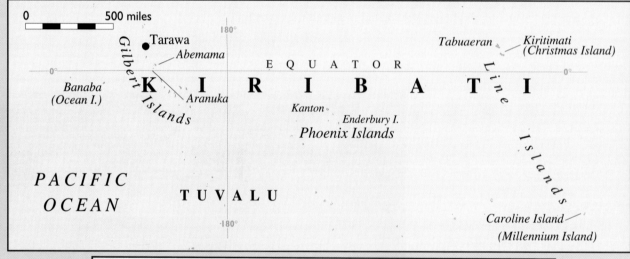

0   500 miles

180°

Tarawa

Tabuaeran

Kiritimati
(Christmas Island)

Gilbert Islands

Abemama

E Q U A T O R

0°

0°

Banaba
(Ocean I.)

K I R I B A T I

Line Islands

Aranuka

Kanton

Enderbury I.

Phoenix Islands

**PACIFIC
OCEAN**

T U V A L U

-180°

Caroline Island
(Millennium Island)

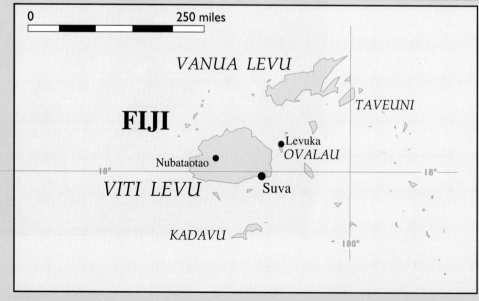

0   250 miles

VANUA LEVU

TAVEUNI

FIJI

Levuka

OVALAU

Nubataotao

18°

18°

VITI LEVU

Suva

KADAVU

180°

PART ONE

HAWAII

·

KIRIBATI

·

FIJI

HAWAII

In my time it was a beautiful little town, made up of snow white wooden cottages deliciously smothered in tropical vines and flowers and trees and shrubs; and its coral roads and street were hard and smooth, and as white as the houses.
MARK TWAIN, FOLLOWING THE EQUATOR

The town was buried under a mat of foliage that looked like a cushion of moss. The silky mountains were clothed in soft, rich splendors of melting color, and some of the cliffs were veiled in slanting mists. I recognized it all. It was just as I had seen it long before, with nothing of its beauty lost, nothing of its charm wanting.
MARK TWAIN, FOLLOWING THE EQUATOR

◆

HONOLULU TODAY IS A VERY different place from the unspoiled paradise which Twain visited in the late 1800s. High-rise buildings dominate the once pristine shoreline. The beaches throb with surfers and holidaymakers wearing oversized shirts in bright, splashy cotton prints. Hawaiian shirts, no less. Honolulu itself is a busy, noisy metropolis which merges into Waikiki Beach with its massive hotels. In some respects it is very much like any other American city. Yet somehow Hawaii manages to hang on to its image as an island paradise.

This is the land of hula and grass skirts, where visitors are greeted with flower garlands and a simple *hello* is transformed into an exotic *aloha*. None of this is accidental. Hawaii has built its tourist industry as much on the successful marketing of its folklore as its beaches and climate. You know you're in Hawaii from the moment you arrive.

Indeed it is practically impossible to slip quietly into Honolulu even if your plane lands after midnight and, having travelled for eighteen hours, your greatest wish is to take your jet-lagged body off to bed quietly. I know. I tried. Somewhat surreally, the airport public address system booms out *aloha* in welcome. Garlands – *leis* – appear

Skyscrapers and tourists compete for space on crowded and cosmopolitan Waikiki Beach.

almost magically and coil themselves about the necks of new arrivals. There are only two possibilities. Either you are dreaming or you are in Hawaii.

Yet there is another side to these paradise islands. Scratch the surface and beneath lies a community which takes seriously its separate identity, which celebrates its culture with dignity, and which resents the manner in which the folklore of the islands has been corrupted to make it more palatable for tourists. It was this, the 'real' Hawaii, which held a fascination for us. We were anxious to learn more about its people, to find out what it is to be Hawaiian.

With perfect timing we had arrived in Honolulu as preparations were underway for the Fourth of July, Independence Day. Quite whether the fiftieth state would be prepared to throw itself as wholeheartedly into the celebrations as the rest of America remained to be seen. On a crowded Waikiki Beach we met with one of Hawaii's more vocal radicals, who watched uneasily as American fighter jets swooped overhead in a showy display which left plumes of white smoke trailing across the sky. The beachfront aerobatics had Lilikala Kame'eleihiwa, Deputy Director of the Center for Hawaiian Studies, shaking her head in irritation. 'This is why people go hungry in America, to pay for this,' she remarked, nodding at the jets.

Four aircraft roared past with casual grace. Beneath them oarsmen in traditional canoes raced expertly across the ocean. Lilikala frowned. Like many native Hawaiians she resents the presence of the United States on the islands. If she had her way tourists would be discouraged from Waikiki and Hawaii would regain its sovereignty. 'I want my country back,' she told us. 'I don't want to be part of America.'

Independence is a complicated matter in Hawaii. This may well be the only American state where some of the citizens mark the Fourth of July by protesting their annexation a century ago to the Superpower. It is certainly the only American state with a royal palace.

Outside the Iolani Palace in Honolulu that morning a costume drama had been played out in which there was much talk of liberty being trampled by outsiders since the islands had lost their independence. Throughout the proceedings banners calling for a restoration of Hawaiian sovereignty were held aloft. *Ku'o Ko'a*, they said. Independence. Some islanders truly believe that separation from the United States is the only solution. Yet America's influence is everywhere. And while the Americanisation of the islands may have brought an identity crisis for some, it has bestowed massive material benefits at the same time. To separate one from the other would appear impossible. For radicals like Lilikala, however, questions of identity will always be more important than superficial prosperity. 'We would give up the refrigerators and TVs, the cars and the freeways, the apartment buildings, to have our country and to live peacefully,' she insists.

The island of Oahu is home to several US military bases. To activists like Lilikala Kame'eleihiwa (below) their presence is an increasing source of resentment. Occasions such as the 1997 Fourth of July celebrations, which was marked by a US Airforce fly-past over Waikiki Beach (right, above) and displays at the nearby bases of US military might (right, below), have done little to ease their disquiet.

This proud Hawaiian flagbearer was taking part in a historical reenactment of the overthrow of the last Queen of Hawaii. It is ironic that while the USA celebrates the anniversary of its independence from Britain, the Hawiian sovereignty movement uses the occasion to protest what some Hawaiians regard as the loss of their own independence to the USA. At the same time they celebrate the memory of their national heroes (below).

On my first visit to Hawaii some weeks earlier I had journeyed into the hills above Honolulu to meet an activist who pursues his quest for sovereignty with a quiet passion.

It was then, while driving out of the city, that I first became aware of the true beauty of Hawaii with its lush tropical greenery and dramatic landscape. All around were huge, bulbous blooms in brilliant colours. A bright yellow flower shaped like the head of an exotic bird caught my eye. In Honolulu it is all too easy to have one's vision blurred by the profusion of high-rise buildings which crowd together along the shoreline and dominate the view.

Here, away from the bustle of the city, I met Dr Kekuni Blaisdell. At first sight Dr Blaisdell, a slight, softly-spoken man, appeared very much the conventional academic, an image appropriate to his work as Professor of Medicine in the Haematology Department at the University of Hawaii. Yet as he showed me into his home I found the floor strewn with boxes, each one containing neatly-filed documents relating to political activism.

In his own quiet way Kekuni Blaisdell wants to see Hawaii achieve independence. 'We're a colony of the United States and of course colonialism is an international crime barred by the UN, so we're seeking self-determination for our own homeland. And that's shaking up the colonial establishment,' he said. As things stand now, he believes the islands and their native people are massively disadvantaged. He lists a depressing catalogue of ills – homelessness, delinquency, lack of education.

As a doctor, he's particularly concerned about the serious health problems, cancer and heart disease among them, to which the local people are especially susceptible. Hawaiians have a long history of poor health. Ever since the arrival of the first outsiders on the islands more than two hundred years ago the native people have been vulnerable to sickness. Tragically, just fifty years after Captain Cook sailed to Hawaii in 1778 ninety per cent of the local population had been wiped out by diseases brought from the outside world. As Sir Peter later put it, what the European explorers brought to the islands was not so much civilisation as 'syphilisation'.

It was apparent almost at once that Kekuni Blaisdell could be an interesting subject for our series. Charming and articulate, there was something extremely persuasive in the quiet manner in which he expressed himself. It seemed especially fortuitous to find a haematologist who was also a radical, since issues of ancestry and bloodlines are of enormous importance in Hawaii, for reasons which are both practical and financial.

Under a government scheme land is available for just a dollar a year to islanders who can prove they are fifty per cent Hawaiian. This is not as easy as it sounds, since the native population is in serious decline. Only an estimated 5,000 locals out of a population of 200,000 native Hawaiians can today claim pure Hawaiian ancestry. Some experts believe even those figures are optimistic. And many of those who believe

themselves to be Hawaiian fail the state's stringent blood quantum test. To fall short of the magical fifty per cent – even by the most frustratingly small of margins – is to be deemed ineligible for this land.

Like most Hawaiians, Kekuni Blaisdell is of mixed ancestry. He is among those who do not qualify. Nonetheless, he possesses a keen sense of his own identity which cannot be measured in percentage points. He defines himself simply as *kanakamali*, the Hawaiian for a true person.

Some weeks after our first meeting we returned to find him hard at work in his laboratory at the University of Hawaii, every inch the doctor and academic, huddled over a microscope in a spotless white lab coat and a pair of seriously large spectacles. The previous afternoon Sir Peter had spent a trying few hours at the offices of the homelands trust trying to fathom out precisely how one goes about satisfying the government's criteria on what it is to be Hawaiian. He had pored over detailed forms and seen for himself the disappointment on the faces of those whose applications were rejected. The blood quantum test is a bit like negotiating a particularly tricky obstacle course. Many, if not all of those who apply, have no doubt that they are as authentically Hawaiian as it is possible to be. Unfortunately, that in itself is not enough. 'Why do we need to prove who we are when this is our birthright?' asked one woman.

Having witnessed first hand the complexities which surround the issue of blood quantum, Sir Peter wanted to know if it is possible to apply mathematics to the business of being Hawaiian. Surely identity is an emotional matter?

Intriguingly, Kekuni Blaisdell boasts two distinct and separate personas, and can switch expertly from one to the other depending on the circumstances in which he finds himself. He carries two business cards, one brown, one white, which he hands out selectively. The white card bears the name Dr Richard Blaisdell, together with his professional and academic qualifications. The brown card is in the name of Kekuni Blaisdell, Convenor for the Pro-Kanaka Maoli Independence Working Group.

He handed us one of each. 'The brown card is because I'm a brown man,' he said. 'But I also live in a white man's world and have to survive in it, so I have a white man's card.'

As we prepared to leave him a storm broke darkly over a distant hill. 'You see,' he said, as the rain fell in great sheets. 'That's my father god giving his semen to mother earth.'

His choice of words was not in the least self-conscious. He was simply describing what he saw in terms of the ancient symbolism passed down from his ancestors. As we stood and watched nature at work, his words made perfect sense. The heavens were indeed inseminating the earth.

The two identities of Dr Blaisdell: (top) in traditional Hawaiian mode and (below) in western guise as Professor of Medicine at the University of Hawaii, with his two different business cards.

◆

WE ARE IN A LARGE, BARE ROOM. Sunlight streams in through the
open sides of the building. At one end of the room is a stage on which
a young Hawaiian girl performs traditional *hula* with confidence and
grace beyond her years. She is barefoot, dressed in a simple tee-shirt and
skirt. There is a subtlety about her which is compelling as she moves in
a manner taught by her ancestors and passed down through generations.
The story she tells is of ancient kings. This is not the *hula* beloved of
tourists who expect – and get – a Hollywood version of a dance which
is steeped in culture and tradition. What we are seeing is the real thing.

The girl is Punihei. Her mother is Lilikala, Deputy Director of the
Center for Hawaiian Studies. While her daughter dances Lilikala sits
cross-legged on the floor softly drumming, an exotic figure in a scarlet
wrap and a *lei*, glossy black hair trailing over bare shoulders. On stage
with Punihei is Sir Peter, dressed appropriately in a floral patterned
shirt, a *lei* around his neck, attempting to *hula* in his stockinged feet.

'Bend your knees,' Punihei instructs.

'This is getting awfully like Cossack dancing and I can't do that,' Sir
Peter replies.

For native Hawaiians the *hula* has a sacred quality. It is a celebration
of their culture, an expression of joy. It is also deeply erotic, which is
why it was so intensely disliked by the Calvinist missionaries who came
to the islands in the nineteenth century. The sight of native men and
women dancing in such a gloriously sexy manner must have caused
enormous consternation. The Calvinists made it their business to stamp
out the *hula*. They might well have thought they had succeeded too but
the Hawaiians were an ingenious lot. Forbidden from dancing in their
customary manner they simply came up with a version of the *hula*
which could be performed sitting down. So discreet was their body
language that the watching missionaries were oblivious to the sensual
messages being passed from person to person right under their noses.

While they danced they chanted too. Had an interpreter been present
the missionaries would have been deeply shocked. The chanting was all
to do with the splendid genitals of their ancestors. While the natives
sang sweetly of the exploits of a king known as 'Long, Strong and Wide',
the missionaries remained oblivious. Little wonder that genital chanting

Punihei (left) and Lilikala.

At the hula class at the Center for Hawaiian Studies, where men as well as women practise their national dance, accompanied by the rhythm of traditional gourd drums, and watched by (below) by Sir Peter and Punihei.

is a popular class at the Centre for Hawaiian Studies today. And, far from being banned, the *hula* is once more booming. Regular *hula hulau*, or dance groups, are well-attended. Not a grass skirt in sight, but plenty of teenagers, their baseball caps worn back to front, having a good time. *Hula,* authentic *hula* anyway, is definitely cool.

It's not something the tourists to Hawaii are likely to find in the beachfront clubs and hotels. What they see are commercial floorshows, pretty girls in bras made from coconut shells and hip-skimming grass skirts. There's every chance the dancers aren't even Hawaiian, since many locals find it all highly embarrassing. Inevitably, however, there are occasions when principles must be compromised for hard cash.

Kau'i Delire is a political activist. She believes wholeheartedly in Hawaiian culture and tradition. She also dances the *hula* – the Hollywood *hula* – at The New Tokyo restaurant in Waikiki. It is a job she hates. '*Hula* is so spiritual, so sacred,' she explains. 'It tells us stories of our rulers, of our people, our history, our genealogy. This is how we teach our kids about ourselves and our identity – through the *hula*. The

Puunana ka Manu i Haili la
The birds are nesting at Haili

Puunana ka Manu i Haili la
The birds are nesting at Haili

Ka nu'a lehua i Mokaulele la
*The blossoms are carpeting the ground
of Mokaulele*

Aia kou ma'i i lehua ea
There is your ma'i in the lehua blossom

Ka wai huna o ka Pao'o la ea
There the hidden waters of the Pao'o fish

He ma'i, i kaaa'ika'iku, i ka'ika'iku,
a ho'olale
*This is a ma'i that leads against the will,
fits into tight spots until ejaculation*

'A'ohe ho'olale a koe aku
Don't come yet, there is more

*This is a genital chant for King
Kamehameha and told of a love
affair he had in Hilo. Our translator,
Lilikala, pointed out that the chief's
genital name – Kunuiakea – means
Long, Strong and Wide.*

kind of dancing they do in Waikiki is not hula at all.' *Hula* dancing Waikiki-style is, she says bluntly, a prostitution of the Hawaiian culture.

It is not easy for Kau'i Delire to put on a revealing costume and face an audience to perform a dance she despises. It's practically sacrilege. But she needs the money. It is a matter of survival. 'Dancing in Waikiki is a difficult thing for me because of what I believe in. What I do there is not authentic hula. The costumes we wear are very skimpy. They show more of your body and attention is given more to the body than the dance itself,' she says. 'But it's a means of supporting the family. I am torn between surviving and taking care of traditional values.'

Shortly after arriving in Hawaii we had gone to a tourist *hula* show at one of the big hotels on Waikiki Beach to see first-hand what constituted 'traditional' entertainment. It turned out to be a fairly mixed bag of Polynesian singing and dancing. The audience, mostly Japanese with a few Americans, seemed to like what it saw. Two young girls seated next to the stage watched open-mouthed as a male dancer wearing very little swayed seductively just inches away. The compere played to the house, switching smoothly between English and Japanese, a technique which brought bursts of enthusiastic applause. An enormously fat man sang falsetto in the Hawaiian style. Some of the dancing was indeed impressive, although whether it was authentically Hawaiian was open to debate. It was too glamorous to be convincing somehow. In the end the overall effect was rather tacky. I can remember thinking, uncharitably perhaps, that the evening definitely constituted work and not pleasure. My heart went out to Kau'i Delire.

*At night they feasted and the girls danced the lascivious hula-hula — a dance that
is said to exhibit the very perfection of educated motion of limb and arm, hand,
head and body, and the exactest uniformity of movement and accuracy of 'time'. . .
It was performed by a circle of girls with no raiment on them to speak of, who
went through an infinite variety of motions and figures without prompting and yet
so true was their 'time' and in such perfect concert did they move that when they
were placed in a straight line, hands, arms, bodies, limbs and heads waved, swayed,
gesticulated, bowed, stooped, whirled, squirmed, twisted and undulated as if it were
part and parcel of a single individual; and it was difficult to believe they were not
moved in a body by some exquisite piece of mechanism.*
MARK TWAIN, *ROUGHING IT*

Presently we came to a place where no grass grew — a wide expanse of deep sand. They said it was an old battle ground. All around everywhere, not three feet apart, the bleached bones of men gleamed white in the moonlight.

MARK TWAIN, ROUGHING IT

♦

WE CALLED THEM THE BURIAL BOYS, since that was what they were. Three impressively large individuals in wraparound shades and shorts. Kala'au Wahilani, Kana'i and Kai. Not like any gravediggers we had ever seen before. Then again, they were not in the business of conventional burials.

In the past Hawaiians would bury their dead wherever they felt the remains would be safe. Consequently, old, forgotten graves litter the islands. Since burial was a private matter, rarely marked by anything so formal as a headstone, no one even knows where the ancestors lie. Inevitably, as more and more land is developed, these ancient burial

The sensitivity with which the Burial Boys carry out their appointed task belies their somewhat fearsome appearance.

grounds are being unearthed. Bones secreted hundreds of years ago are surfacing once more. Until recently, no one knew quite what to do about this. For some the solution was simply to shovel up the dead and dump them somewhere else. It was hardly satisfactory. When the remains of 1,000 people were unceremoniously moved to make way for a hotel complex on Maui, Hawaiians were incensed.

In recent years a law has come into effect to protect the dead. And it is the Burial Boys who make sure their ancestors are treated with respect. They have become the guardians of the dead. When graves are disturbed this formidable trio have formal powers to stop building work and arrange for a suitable burial on another site. It is a job which demands considerable tact and sensitivity. Despite their brawny appearance, the Burial Boys have an abundance of both.

On the day we met them they were preparing for a burial at sea. We gathered in Honolulu Harbour and boarded a powerboat for the short trip out into the bay. On board was a small reed basket containing the bones of a woman whose sandy grave had been washed away by the ocean. Tourists had stumbled upon her remains on one of the beaches. There were no clues to her identity. Kala'au Wahilani, one of the Burial Boys, told us, 'We don't know who she is, but it's our responsibility to take care of her on behalf of her family who may have lived two or three hundred years ago.' Our trip takes us out into the ocean where a short prayer is offered and the casket gently lowered into the ocean. Flowers are scattered in its wake. The ceremony is short, solemn, and quietly moving in its simplicity.

For native Hawaiians there are all kinds of ancient beliefs bound up in burial. The bones of the ancestors have a special significance, and must be protected since therein lies *iwi*, the source of spiritual power. According to Hawaiian culture the essence of a person – their manna – is to be found in their bones.

Kana'i explained. 'We plant our ancestors' *iwi* in the ground and it becomes part of the land. When we plant food it receives its nourishment from the bones of the ancestors. Then later when we harvest those foods our succeeding generations receive their sustenance from their ancestry. This is why *iwi* is very important.'

In the past the bones of enemies would be used to make fish-hooks or arrowheads as a means of desecration. No native Hawaiian wants to think of the bones of their ancestors being desecrated, which is why a proper burial means so much.

His colleague, Kala'au Wahilani, told us, 'The Hawaiian people were always spiritual people, and from generation to generation we are taught to uphold the honour and the spirit and dignity of our ancestors. By doing this it helps show others the things we hold true. In this environment where everything is so commercial and developed we strive every day to keep the essence of who we are alive.'

The Burial Boys seem ideally suited to their work. All three of these gentle giants chose to abandon more conventional careers in order to join the State Archeology Department. One worked in Hawaii's booming tourist industry, one was an academic, the third was an attorney. Kai said, 'My parents told me, *Go to law school so you won't have to be a gravedigger*. I went to law school and now I'm a gravedigger and I'm as happy as I can be. It's something we all find very spiritually rewarding for ourselves as Hawaiians. None of us can think of any other job we'd rather be doing.'

Indeed their work is of enormous importance to a people for whom the past and the present are so bound up. 'You cannot know where you're going if you don't know where you've been,' is how Kana'i neatly sums it up. 'For us, for Hawaiians as a whole, when you take care of your ancestors it gives you a cultural foundation upon which to build as an

Opposite: The Burial Boys do not only handle the remains of native Hawaiians. Here, observed by a Chinese priest (below), they carefully reinterr what are thought to be Chinese bones in a specially consecrated site adjacent to the new building under which they were discovered.

We all know about Father Damien, the French priest who voluntarily forsook the world and went to the leper island of Molokai to labor among its population of sorrowful exiles who wait there, in slow-consuming misery, for death to come and release them from their troubles; and we know that the thing which he knew beforehand would happen, did happen: that he became a leper himself and died of that horrible disease.
MARK TWAIN, FOLLOWING THE EQUATOR

◆

Father Damien, who did so much to relieve the suffering of the original nineteenth-century leper colony on the island of Molokai.

acknowledgement of the connection between you and the past.'

IT IS BRIGHT AND SUNNY the day we board an Island Air propeller plane for our short flight to Molokai. This is one destination which is not to be found on the average tourist map. In the past a part of Molokai was a dumping ground for the sick. Those who came here were suffering from leprosy, a disease which made them outcasts. By law they were forcibly separated from their families and loved ones for the remainder of their lives.

The first patients were shipped out to Kalaupapa, an inaccessible peninsula of the island, in 1866. Fear of leprosy was running so high that some of the ships transporting patients simply anchored offshore. The sick were thrown overboard and told to swim. In all, around 8,000 people were brought to Molokai. In the absence of any effective treatment for their condition they simply waited to die.

It was in 1873 that Father Damien, a Catholic priest from Belgium, came to the island to offer spiritual succour to the abandoned people of the Kalaupapa Settlement. Father Damien soon became a controversial figure. His work frequently brought him into conflict with his superiors. But he is remembered today for his unfailing kindness. The unorthodox priest is well on his way to becoming a saint. His church at Kalaupapa stands as a memorial to his work.

WHEN OUR PLANE touched down at Kalaupapa Airport the weather had turned grim. It was raining hard and the sky was a dull grey. Airport staff ran back and forth across the tarmac to the tiny terminal building, shielding passengers from the downpour under large, brightly coloured umbrellas. Waiting to meet us was Richard Marks, who has lived on Molokai for forty-one years and is Sheriff of Kalaupapa. His association with the place runs deep. Five members of his family, including his father and brother, were brought here and are buried in the graveyard on the edge of the Pacific Ocean. Richard, a gentle and humorous individual, also suffers from leprosy. He led us to a big old bus with Damien's Tours emblazoned on the front and side. Kalaupapa still has its

leper colony, although the seventy or so people who live here today do so by choice. And attitudes to the disease have changed so much that the residents now run guided tours for curious visitors.

With Richard behind the wheel we set off for the cemetery where thousands of lepers lie buried in unmarked graves. There were burials all over Kalaupapa, although this is the biggest graveyard, a jumble of weathered, lopsided headstones, some in pieces. It lies on the edge of the ocean surrounded by tall, gawky palm trees. Clouds obscure the top of a nearby mountain. The wind whips about us, the palms bend, and the cries of sea birds break the silence. Rain threatens.

It is amazing to think that no one knows exactly who lies buried here since the identities of most of those who came to Molokai are a mystery. So great was the shame of having leprosy that often those brought to the island would change their name to protect the family they had left behind. Indeed this was encouraged. For this reason Richard Marks's father took on his mother's maiden name.

'If you were declared a leper you were entitled to a name change, including a new birth certificate and everything else,' he tells us. 'This was to avoid embarrassing your relatives, not to protect you.' Now, however, the dead are being repossessed. It is all to do with claiming entitlement to land. Hawaiians desperate to prove their ancestry are coming to Molokai in search of long lost relatives. Finding them is another matter. To trace someone whose name has changed to who knows what and who has been dead for many years is in most cases impossible. Still, there are those who feel it is at least worth the effort to try.

Richard Marks for one knows his family history. A simple cross marks his brother's recent grave. The inscription reads 'Edward Marks', in bold

The atmospheric Kalaupapa graveyard, in which yet another member of Richard Marks's family has recently been buried.

Richard Marks makes a relaxed and genial Sheriff of Kalaupapa. In a place with few roads and only a handful of vehicles, he turns a blind eye in particular to modern US traffic laws. Under his jurisdiction, many drivers still use their old original licences, issued before Hawaii became an American state in 1959.

black letters against a white background. 'I am not ashamed,' he says. 'I have never been ashamed.' He is one of the few people on the island who has not adopted the new and more politically correct term for leprosy, Hansen's Disease.

From early childhood Richard Marks grew up in the shadow of a disease which brought disgrace and broke up families. He was nine when his father was taken to Molokai. The following year his five-year-old sister was locked away for almost two years on the island as a 'suspect' before the authorities released her. Even though she never contracted the disease the experience blighted her life. Children would not play with her. She was bullied at school. Out of desperation her mother sent her to Honolulu where she was brought up by an aunt. In the end she left the islands.

'We were constantly having physicals, every month,' Richard recalled, 'so I knew what to look for.' When he spotted the first signs of the disease on his arms more than forty years ago he was determined not to end up on Molokai. But when he visited the island to see his father the medical authorities were tipped off – ironically by his mother – and he was locked up.

'She wanted me to get treatment, so she told the doctors I was there. I was at my father's house when they caught me.' He managed to escape from Molokai, but his leprosy became worse. Eventually, in need of medical help, he returned voluntarily to the island and has been there ever since.

Over the years society has become more understanding of a disease which in Father Damien's day led to the widespread persecution of sufferers. In the past it was branded 'unclean', a disease visited upon sinners. The physical symptoms provoked panic and revulsion. Leprosy patients were sent away in the misguided belief that isolation was the only means to halt the spread of the disease. Yet more than 1,100 people came to Molokai to work with the sick over a 120-year period and only one contracted the disease:. Father Damien.

What made this Belgian priest so special was that he chose to be with a community which was otherwise ostracised. Damien built a church on the island, a small and relatively spartan building where the patients could attend mass. Only a few were Catholic, but most were grateful for any form of religious worship.

During his time on Molokai the priest had numerous run-ins with his superiors. Father Damien's compassionate response to leprosy was frowned upon. Walking around his church today one comes across holes cut in the floor at various points. These served a practical purpose, enabling patients in the last stages of the disease to come to mass. Once leprosy was advanced the throat and nasal passages would become blocked, forcing patients to spit in order to clear the airways. Since most believed it was sacrilege to spit during a service they would not attend mass. Damien came up with a controversial solution: spittoons. His Bishop was not impressed.

As we walked around the church Richard Marks spoke to us about the rebel priest. 'Damien was a very practical man,' he said. 'He never worked a miracle, never cured a leper, never walked on clouds, nothing like that. But these were people who had lost everything. They were dragged in here, they were made to feel ashamed. They sat around and just waited to die. And here was this guy from a country they had never even heard of who came among them and held their hands while they were dying. Promised them a decent burial. This is what Damien did. Not some fancy miracles, just a man on the spot when they died who would make sure they got a decent burial. This is what makes him special to the Hawaiians.'

Leprosy whipped up enormous fear in Hawaii, yet it was by no means the worst disease to afflict the islands. It claimed around 8,000 lives, a small number compared with the tens of thousands wiped out by tuberculosis. Even measles killed six times as many people as leprosy.

But leprosy was unique in its day. Richard Marks compared it to AIDS. 'Fear without understanding,' he says. In 1907, almost twenty years after Father Damien died, Jack London visited the leper colony at Kalaupapa. He wrote later, 'The chief horror of leprosy obtains in the minds of those who do not know anything about the disease.'

Had he still been alive, Damien might well have said Amen to that.

MOT? What MOT. . . ? Under the benign regime of Sheriff Marks, long-time Kalaupapa resident Clarence doesn't even require a door for his car.

————————◆————————

Would you expect to find in that awful Leper Settlement a custom worthy to be transplanted to your own country? They have one such, and it is inexpressibly touching and beautiful. When death sets open the prison-door of life there, the band salutes the freed soul with a burst of glad music!
MARK TWAIN, FOLLOWING THE EQUATOR

It is extraordinary when you see this vast expanse of water. Even without battleships it looks vulnerable. This is exactly the kind of balmy climate and huge open spaces and ordered coastline which seems to invite trouble.
SIR PETER USTINOV

WE JOIN A GROUP OF TOURISTS for a guided tour of Pearl Harbor. Everyone else is Japanese. It feels slightly strange to be tagging along with a tour group from the very country responsible for inflicting the greatest ever disaster on the US Navy in its history, yet no one seems to mind. Indeed it is difficult to connect the events of 7 December 1941 with the people around us in their shorts and tee-shirts, carrying the latest in photographic equipment. We file into a building dedicated to the warship *Arizona*, which was sunk with the loss of all 1,177 crew during the air raid on Pearl Harbor. In a small theatre the lights are dimmed and a scratchy black and white film takes us back to that fateful day.

The commentary asks, 'How shall we remember them, those that died? Mourn the dead, remember the battle, understand the tragedy, honour their memory.' What is striking is the measured tone of the narrator, who takes care to give an account of events which is as conciliatory as possible. Not easy, all things considered, yet somehow the facts are relayed in a neutral, blameless manner.

In the darkness we are reminded how, in the space of two hours, Japanese warplanes left more than 2,400 dead and another 1,200 wounded. How twenty-one vessels were sunk or left crippled and 170 aircraft destroyed. For the United States, utterly unprepared for such an attack, it was an appalling episode. Today, however, Hawaii must balance the tragedy of Pearl Harbor with a determination not to alienate its Japanese visitors, of whom there are many. The absence of rancour in the recounting of the air raid is striking.

As one moves about Honolulu the extent to which Japanese influence has taken hold is clear. Many of the businesses and hotels are Japanese owned. Sushi bars, restaurants and foreign exchange bureaux, all boasting signage in Japanese, abound. Everywhere, there are huge numbers of Japanese tourists. The yen is definitely a force to be reckoned with. Even our tour of Pearl Harbor is conducted in Japanese, courtesy of Hiromi Kirihari, a Japanese-Hawaiian and retired US soldier. He fought on the side of the Allies during the war and later worked as an interpreter for US military intelligence, interrogating Japanese prisoners of war. This is not something he is prepared to share with his tour group, however, who may find his twin loyalties rather bemusing.

We follow Hiromi on board a boat which takes us out into Pearl

Hiromi Kirihari – self-styled Yankee Samurai – is a Japanese Hawaiian who fought in the US Army in the Second World War.

Harbor to the USS *Arizona* Memorial, a sixties structure in white concrete which sits on the water where its namesake went down. The American flag flutters proudly high above the monument. When the *Arizona* was hit the bomb went right through her deck, igniting thousands of tons of ammunition. Within moments the entire crew was lost.

Our party gathers round to hear details of the fate of the ship. We hang back, wishing we had at least a smattering of Japanese. Later Hiromi explains his complicated background, how his parents left Japan to settle in Hawaii in the early 1900s, and how he grew up feeling himself to be both Japanese and American. He calls himself a Yankee Samurai. 'I was born in the United States and raised in the United States but my parents came from Japan. I had to join the US Army and wear the uniform because I didn't have Japanese citizenship. It was a very complicated situation,' he tells us.

Above the wreck of the USS *Arizona*, a group of Japanese tourists listens attentively as Hiromi gives a blow-by-blow account of the events of Pearl Harbor.

Joining the army was a way of reinforcing his allegiance to the country of his birth. It was something his parents strongly opposed, in view of the discrimination experienced by the US citizens of Japanese descent at the time. Like many Japanese-Americans he fought hard for his country. It was a way of proving loyalty. Later, stationed in Tokyo, the sight of Hiromi, a Japanese soldier in US khakis, drew plenty of comments. He said, 'The Japanese people could not understand that. All pointing the finger at us and saying, *How come you are in an American uniform?*

Hiromi's experience prompted Sir Peter to recall how he served in the British Army, despite having a German passport. It was only when the war was nearly over that he learned that the Germans would have shot him as a deserter had he ever fallen into their hands. 'Luckily I found out too late to be frightened,' he said.

After thirty-eight years in the military, Hiromi Kirihari has adapted well to his civilian role. His job helps keep alive the story of Pearl Harbor in the minds of a new generation of Japanese tourists. And perhaps they listen all the harder to a story told in their own language by someone who looks every bit as Japanese as themselves.

Sir Peter and Hiromi quickly found that their wartime experiences gave them a common bond.

We had a sunset of a very fine sort. The vast plain of the sea was marked
off in bands of sharply-contrasted colors: great stretches of dark blue, others
of purple, others of polished bronze; the billowy mountains showed all
sorts of dainty browns and greens, blues and purples and blacks, and the
rounded velvety backs of certain of them made one want to stroke them, as
one would the sleek back of a cat.
MARK TWAIN, FOLLOWING THE EQUATOR

◆

OUR STAY IN HAWAII would not have been complete without heading out to sea on a sailing ship to gaze on Honolulu as Twain had done. With this in mind we joined passengers for a sunset cruise on the *Windjammer.* Not quite a vessel in the style of Twain's, but nonetheless the closest we could find. The process of boarding was held up as each passenger paused to be photographed flanked by a young Hawaiian couple appropriately dressed in very little: she in a grass skirt and coconut bra, he bare-chested in shorts and a dazzling smile. To relieve the tedium as we shuffled forward in single file, Sir Peter began to *hula.* The passenger in front gave

The Windjammer rides majestically at anchor in Honolulu harbour.

him a strange look, no doubt unaware that this was probably the most authentic *hula* he would see on his visit to Hawaii.

It was a beautiful evening as the *Windjammer* prepared to ease out of her mooring. Sir Peter settled himself in the deserted restaurant in anticipation of dinner. 'Only another eight hundred and sixty-three passengers, then we're off,' he said bleakly.

We were hardly sailing in the true sense of the word, but we were at least at sea. Our view of Hawaii with its high-rise buildings, however, was very different to the one enjoyed by Twain. In the dining room a band played something vaguely Hawaiian. Inevitably there was a hula show. Now that we were in a position to tell the difference we instantly recognised it as Hollywood *hula.* Three girls gyrating energetically to a drumbeat. Sir Peter retired to the deck, a copy of *Following the Equator* in his hands, looking impressively like the cover photograph of Twain himself, snapped in 1897.

Since arriving in Hawaii we had become well aware of the large US military presence on the islands. First the fighter planes over Waikiki Beach on Independence Day. Then Pearl Harbor. There are thousands of American military personnel stationed on the islands; whole communities of servicemen and women. It might seem like a tropical paradise if you're from Texas or Oklahoma, but Hawaii can be an uncomfortable posting. We sought the opinion of John Trail, a Chief Petty Officer in the US Navy and part-time crew member on the *Windjammer*. His experiences of serving in the fiftieth state are not entirely happy. Hawaii, 2,500 miles off the coast of California, is a long way from home.

'Sometimes you feel that it's not America,' he said. 'You've got the dollar bill and you've got all the American foods and all the conveniences but sometimes you feel ostracised.'

On more than one occasion John Trail has been made to feel distinctly unwelcome. 'They call you *haoli*. In the Hawaiian vernacular that's supposed to mean *foreigner*. When you have friends who call you *haoli* you really don't take offence. But when they put another word in front of it that starts with an F . . .'

He has little sympathy with the radicals. 'We have a lot of movements here that want to bring the monarchy back. They preach about the past, the way it was, and how beautiful it was before Captain Cook came here in 1778, and they're not being real. Back then the local Hawaiians didn't have a sense of property, they had different ways of dealing with life. If a woman was menstruating she had to stay apart from everybody, if a baby was born deformed they put it to death. When they fought battles there were no prisoners taken – they slaughtered all the other men. I wouldn't want to go back to that and I don't think most of the people here would either, but they have fantasy a past they look back to.'

At that moment our fantasy was to transport ourselves back in time too, to Twain's day. As the sun went down and we gazed out into the Pacific it could well have been 1897. What gave the game away was the drumming which thumped away relentlessly below deck. We imagined a time when there was no cabaret, no drums. Just the sun sinking slowly over the water, the boat rocking gently with the motion of the sea, and a game of shuffleboard on deck for those feeling energetic. For a moment we reflected on this before Sir Peter interrupted the sound of guitars and drums. 'Lucky, lucky Twain,' he said.

It isn't only tourists who gravitate to Waikiki Beach. The beach is just as much the hub of social activity for the everyday inhabitants of Honolulu. Bronzed Waikiki boys mingle alongside off-duty GIs, while groups of laughing girls watch crews of fiercely competitive canoe racers power their sleek craft through the surf.

KIRIBATI

*Closing in on the equator this noon. A sailor explained to a young girl
that the ship's speed is poor because we are climbing up the bulge toward
the center of the globe; but that when we should once get over, at the
equator, and start downhill, we should fly.*
MARK TWAIN, FOLLOWING THE EQUATOR

◆

THERE WE WERE ON A TINY ISLAND in the middle of the South Pacific
looking for pigs. At least I was. Bizarre though it may seem, there was
some logic to this.

The island was Aranuka, a few miles long, barely a hundred metres across,
and with a population of around 1,000. From here we would take a ferry
to neighbouring Abemama, crossing the equator on the way. Seven hours
in all. I had made up my mind there would be pigs on that ferry with us
and had broadcast a number of radio appeals asking local people to turn
up for the trip – with their animals in tow. The broadcast made it clear
that pigs had been accorded special status and would therefore travel free.

It was some weeks earlier that I had first come to Kiribati and seen the
local ferry with its cargo of people and livestock. On that occasion five
pigs, protesting noisily as they were made to board, had lent an air of chaos
and colour to the proceedings. I knew from that moment that it was
imperative that we also had pigs. Needless to say, on the appointed day we
were out of luck. It seemed no one wanted to transport their pigs to
Abemama, despite our inducement. Refusing to accept defeat, I went in

*There are no hotels on the unspoilt
islands of Aranuka and Abemama.
This is about as sophisticated as
accommodation gets.*

For centuries breadfruit – the cargo carried by Captain Bligh on the fateful final journey of the Bounty – has been the staple harvest of the South Seas.

search of our desired cargo, appealing directly to the islanders – whether or not they wished to travel – to join us on the crossing. In the end our guide and I succeeded in rustling up some rather bemused folk and, more importantly, two reluctant pigs.

Aranuka is part of the Republic of Kiribati, which lies hidden away in the South Pacific. Despite its spelling, Kiribati is pronounced *Kiribas*. When the missionaries came here and began keeping a written record of the local language there was no letter s on their printing press. Ingeniously they improvised using the letters *ti*, as in na*ti*on. And so we have Kiribati. Or Kiribas. In the same vein, the local spelling of Christmas Island, which is also part of Kiribati, is *Kiritimati*. That's *Kirisimas*. And the country's President Tito is, as you would expect, actually President *Sito*. There is great potential for confusion until you get into the habit of saying s whenever you see the letters *ti*.

President Tito governs what must rank as one of the most unwieldy countries on earth. Kiribati, with a population of 80,000, is made up of a string of islands scattered across thousands of miles of the Pacific Ocean. To travel from one end of the country to another is a lengthy, convoluted matter which requires visas for two other countries and takes several days. On a recent thirteen-day trip the President spent just six days engaged in meetings with his fellow countrymen. The rest of the time he was in transit. To get to Christmas Island, in the extreme east of the country, means flights via the Marshall Islands and Honolulu. Kiribati itself does not possess an aircraft capable of undertaking such a long haul flight direct.

Kiribati straddles the equator and, until recently, straddled the International Date Line too. From an administrative point of view this proved a major headache, with different parts of the country operating on different days. While Christmas Island in the far east was enjoying Sunday it was already Monday in Tarawa, the capital. In 1995 the President tackled the problem head-on by simply shifting the Date Line so that it no longer swept through his country. An interesting side-effect of this was to pitch Caroline Island, which lies in the far east of the country, to the forefront of millennium celebrations. It is here that dawn will break first on 1 January 2000. Caroline, hastily renamed Millennium Island, is revelling in this stroke of good fortune. Tonga, which now comes a poor second, is pretty furious.

WE FLEW TO ARANUKA from Tarawa, braving torrential rain for a bumpy fifty-minute flight on a fifteen-seater aircraft. Just before take-off our female pilot sheltered under the wing of the plane as the rain lashed down. I had encountered a similar storm on my previous visit. On that occasion the pilot had simply refused to take off and we were turned away. This time, however, we managed to get airborne. Travelling with us was a prison officer from Tarawa on his way to collect two offenders, and the MP for Aranuka, who must have one of the smallest constituencies in the world.

We landed on an airstrip made of flattened coral where children played unconcerned at the end of the runway. One of the island's two trucks (there were no cars) was waiting to meet us. We looked doubtfully at the bald tyres as we loaded our gear, but decided we would have to be exceptionally unlucky to collide with the only other vehicle on the island.

Off we went, moving carefully along a dusty coral road, tooting now and then to disperse dogs and people in our path, finally pulling up outside a low building with a sloping tin roof and open sides. From inside the sound of singing and chanting reached us. A crowd of solemn-faced children appeared and watched with open curiosity as we ducked inside to find the place filled with local people squatting on the hard earth. In their midst were dancers led by two small girls in elaborate costumes, their arms covered in bright objects which bobbed and shook like exotic pom-poms. On their heads they wore scarlet and gold crowns. All around the villagers swayed and clapped and sang. We had arrived as the island's annual dance competition was underway. It was a dazzling and energetic affair.

Having dipped into the folklore of Hawaii and seen the extent to which the culture of those islands has become commercialised, Aranuka felt somehow more real. Sir Peter called it 'refreshingly authentic. These people are not spoiled like so many of us from the outside world are,' he said. 'They're not at all affected by tourism. This is like a breath of fresh air, or should I say a rinse of sea water.'

I hoped he would feel the same after a night on the island. Peaceful and unspoiled it might be, but Aranuka is an austere place for those of us accustomed to the comforts of the outside world. There are no hotels. No electricity even. Just a Government Rest House, a small shack on the edge of the ocean with little more than a place to lay your head. There was at least a shower, although not a terribly good one. It had crossed my mind more than once that Sir Peter might find the limited facilities trying. When I looked at the room he had been given I practically shuddered. It was hardly what a knighted, Oscar-winning actor was used to. However, as we relaxed that evening looking out at the Pacific, I silently prayed that the tranquillity of our surroundings would compensate for the limitations of the accommodation.

Before turning in we filmed one last sequence with Sir Peter sitting on the verandah of the rest house, recording his impressions of Aranuka. 'I'm absolutely convinced we'll spend a very good night here,' he announced cheerfully. 'We're under mosquito nets which don't fit properly, but this is a voyage of discovery and one is compelled not to show that one is disappointed, which one isn't. If you forget for a moment all the convenience of pressing a switch and an electric light comes on, or the air conditioning or the fridge . . . well, what did they do beforehand? So we are back to fundamentals.' We were indeed. His closing worlds were, 'I'll tell you what it was like tomorrow.'

My own room was on the oceanfront and when I woke the next

Visitors to the remoter parts of Kiribati are rare, and consequently we were a focus of shy curiosity.

A perfect end to the day on Aranuka: a typically glorious sunset bathes the entire lagoon in gold.

morning at dawn I was in good spirits. I pulled on some shorts, grabbed a towel, and went for a shower. It was not yet 5 a.m. and I wasn't expecting to run into anyone. However, there in the kitchen was Sir Peter, already dressed and wearing the expression of a man who had not slept. I wondered how long he had been sitting there. It was probably not a good time to ask if his prediction of a good night had been realised. Unwisely, that's exactly what I did.

'Did you sleep well?'

He looked at me as if I had gone completely mad. 'Are you joking?'

It was apparent he was in extreme discomfort. Guilt flooded through me. I felt entirely responsible. I guessed he was beyond anger, although not so much with me as with the world and his situation. It had been, he said, the worst night of his life. I didn't doubt it. For hours he had lain awake on his hard bed cursing the mosquito net which had utterly failed to prevent the insects from feasting on him throughout the night. By now the intriguingly-named film crew – Mike Fox, Mike Lax and Matthew Fox – had assembled. They too had been bitten to pieces and a general bonding process of shared misery began. I was itching to start filming, to capture some of this, but sensed it might be a bad move. Instead I decided to wait a little until the general mood had improved, which it did fairly rapidly.

When Sir Peter returned to his room to pack we followed, camera running. By then he was starting to see the funny side of his dreadful experience. He started to sing a mournful spiritual. 'I'm feeling a little homesick,' he said. 'It's been one of the longest nights I've ever experienced. This mosquito net, it's very much like a ladies' bustle dress of the last century. Getting under it takes so long it lets about fifty mosquitoes in to become prisoner inside. Of course I'm bitten all over.

'And the poultry here get everything wrong. They start crowing at one o'clock in the morning and the eight hundred dogs tell them to shut up and we're all awake. I woke up at four-thirty and decided to have a shower, but the shower knob came off in my hand and I had to try to get it back and it wasn't very successful. I didn't have a shower. I haven't shaved. I won't, either; because, after all, you can't shave very easily without a mirror and a drop of water and certainly no electricity. And the loo . . . well, I won't go into that, and I would advise you not to either.'

He held up his bag. 'I'm ready. Is someone going to help me with this? I'm very old, you know.'

Old perhaps, but certainly not defeated.

Approaching the equator on a long slant. Those of us who have never seen the equator are a good deal excited. I think I would rather see it than any other thing in the world.
MARK TWAIN, FOLLOWING THE EQUATOR

---◆---

THERE WAS AN AIR OF EXCITEMENT as we boarded the decrepit old boat that served as the ferry which would take us to the equator. When Twain had crossed the invisible line a hundred years earlier he had waxed lyrical about the 'blue ribbon stretched across the ocean. Several passengers kodak'd it.' Indeed in *Following the Equator* there is a photograph, allegedly of this blue ribbon. We were all sceptical. Still, we hoped we might at least be moved by a sense of occasion as we crossed from north to south.

Pigs and passengers aboard, the ferry chugged out to sea, leaving Aranuka behind. We settled down in the shade to await the momentous event. Sir Peter said, 'I must have crossed the equator many times but

One stretch of ocean looks much like another. This, however, is the equator as 'kodak'd' by one of Twain's fellow passengers in 1897.

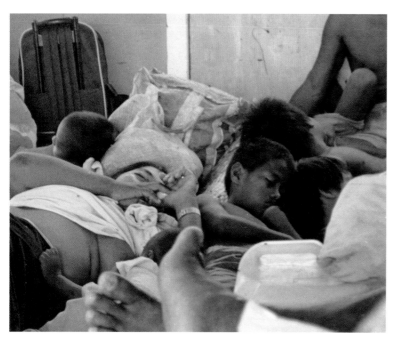

For these young islanders asleep on the local ferry, crossing the equator is clearly no big deal.

I've never known when. I've mostly been asleep on an airliner. They never come and wake you up to say, *Oh, we're crossing the equator now, and would you like another canapé, by the way?'*

The sea beneath us had turned a deep sapphire. Sun sparkled on the water. Not far away on our port side two smallish whales swam, occasionally breaking the surface of the ocean. Estimates as to how long it would take us to reach the equator varied between twenty minutes and two hours. 'Of course,' Sir Peter noted drily, 'time is a very fluid thing here.'

As we drew nearer to the invisible line almost everyone else on the boat was sleeping. The deck was strewn with bodies slumped in a peaceful jumble. Our pigs dozed side by side, a piece of sacking protecting them from the fierce heat. Clearly, to the people of Kiribati the equator is not a magical, mythical entity at all but simply another bit of ocean. Meanwhile we craned our necks to keep an eye on the readout on the Global Positioning System which exactly pinpointed our whereabouts. Our captain, weatherbeaten and toothless, seemed entirely bemused by the proceedings. We crossed the equator not once but twice, so that we could film all we needed. The captain, increasingly confused, obliged uncertainly, steering his boat erratically across the open sea.

As we watched the GPS take us in fractions of a degree to the magical zero degrees, Sir Peter gave a short cheer. He gazed solemnly at the camera. 'We're on the equator and I felt nothing at all,' he announced.

Heading north once more, we continued on our way to Abemama. Lots more open ocean before we sighted land. Another coral island very similar in appearance to the one we had left that morning. It was late afternoon by the time the ferry anchored and a smaller craft took us ashore. Sir Peter, his trousers rolled up to his knees, waded on to the beach.

We had been lured to Abemama by the promise of two fascinating characters. Firstly a man named Eric Bailey, an eighty-year-old Brit who had settled on the island many years ago and was married to a local woman. After our miserable night on Aranuka we were intrigued to know how he had adapted to his circumstances. Secondly, we had an appointment with a native Abemaman who claimed to be king of the tiny island. We had high expectations, having read an account of Robert Louis Stevenson's visit to Abemama and his encounter with the then monarch. Subsequently, he had enthused about what a fine and eloquent fellow he was.

The following morning we were up and about early, anxious to begin filming and acutely aware that our only way off the island was the charter plane we had arranged to pick us up at 10 a.m. We had to be back in Tarawa that afternoon for an interview with President Tito. It took longer than anticipated to pack and check out of the government rest house, since individual accounts were drawn up for each room and each meal – and the only person with authority to take payment, the island's treasurer, had to be fetched from her home. Finally, having settled the bundle of bills – which together came to very little – we set off, by now running late, to find the king. He was waiting for us on a bench shaded by a sheet of corrugated iron, sipping tea from a plastic mug. For a king he was dressed informally in a pale pink polo shirt and casual grey trousers. Kittens played at his feet. The setting could hardly have been less grand.

We had no idea whether he would live up to his ancestor's fiery and tempestuous image, as described by Stevenson, but we hoped we would end up with an interesting interview in any event. It was not to be. The self-proclaimed King of Abemama, pleasant and hospitable though he was, was not much given to conversation. For half an hour Sir Peter struggled gamely to gently coax small snippets of information from him. For half an hour the king remained cheerfully unforthcoming. We were at our wits' end. Time and again the interview would shudder to a halt and we would try another approach. Failure. Another attempt. Failure again. It was in one sense frustrating but at the same time strangely funny. We continued until we felt we had wrung every last word from his majesty.

'You are the king of Abemama,' Sir Peter said.

'Yes,' said the king.

'It's an historical thing, evidently, dating from when?'

'Seventeen-something,' the king recalled.

'Oh, I think that's safe enough. But you are still the king?'

'Yes.'

'How does that fit in with the new independence of Kiribati?'

The king looked blank for a moment. Sir Peter pressed him. 'You have some official functions still?'

Smiling. 'Oh yes.'

'Ah, I see. So you exercise a function in the government?'

The king appeared bemused. 'No.'

Sir Peter makes the crossing of the equator in somewhat less comfortable circumstances than his predecessor. Mind you, even on his journey Twain, just like Sir Peter, was obliged to take with him everywhere his own folding chair.

And so it went on. By the time we gave up it felt as if we had been interrogating a subject who was never likely to crack however many times he was faced with the same, relentless questioning. Sir Peter, courteous to the end, wound up the interview by thanking the king for his hospitality. 'I think you're the least frightening king I have ever come across,' he told the king. 'Do you agree?'

'Oh yes,' said the king cheerfully.

Clearly, things had been different in Robert Louis Stevenson's day.

We packed our things and went to find Eric Bailey.

By now time was against us. Our plane was due to leave in twenty minutes. Our guide was despatched to send a radio message to the airport to say we were delayed and to push back our departure time. While I was concerned not to hold things up too long, I was equally determined not to make our meeting with Eric Bailey a rushed affair. Nor was I too worried about delaying our flight. After all, we had chartered the plane. It seemed a small matter to request a slightly later take-off than originally planned.

We approached Eric Bailey's home along a narrow coral path. Even though it was still early the sun was beating down with an intensity that was exhausting. As we drew close to the house a tanned figure appeared, managing somehow to appear elegant in only a pair of spotless white shorts. Eric Bailey looked a good deal younger than his eighty years. Fit and lean, he was a wonderful advertisement for his unorthodox lifestyle.

Eric Bailey was born in England but has spent most of his life roving around the world. At just twenty-one he left home to serve as a police officer in Palestine. Six years later he returned briefly to London but by then was too restless to settle. He moved to Africa, spending twenty happy years in Malawi. In 1973, by then in his mid-fifties, he was on the move again, this time to Abemama where he lives in more or less the same style as the local people. To put it bluntly, he has gone native.

As he showed us into his home it was clear he had long since come to terms with the practical limitations of island life. In the absence of electricity he had devised a rudimentary form of air conditioning; an open living area which allowed a breeze to waft through. 'It's designed so that air can flow,' he told us. 'That's from African experience, really.'

His is clearly a simple life with few pressures. He stays fit by doing plenty of manual labour. In the days before we arrived he had been hard at work in the garden

The modest and unassuming King of Abemama . . .

. . . and one of his 'subjects', Eric Bailey, an archetypal Englishman if ever there was one.

digging a deep trench round a lemon tree which stubbornly refused to bear fruit.

'That's very good for the stomach muscles,' Sir Peter observed.

Eric offered a word of caution. 'I wouldn't recommend it to you,' he said. 'I think you've left it a bit late.'

Sir Peter laughed. 'I think you're right.'

As we chatted we came to the conclusion that Eric Bailey had made a fine life for himself, although it was nothing like that of the conventional ex-pat. Abemama has no golf club where he can mingle with other like-minded souls over a gin and tonic. There is nothing. And no one. Still, he is happy enough. Between his radio and regular copy of the *Guardian* each week he stays in touch with world events. Considering his relative isolation, that in itself is a considerable achievement.

There isn't much he misses about England, only his family. His children and his grandchildren are there. One day in the not too distant future he hopes to join them. 'I expect to be back there in time for the millennium. A lot of people are rushing out here. They have this incredible idea that there's something special in seeing the sun come over the horizon on the zero meridian. The whole thing is completely artificial. I mean we made it. We said it was there. We've even bent it to make it more convenient for certain countries.' In the unlikely event of a rush of visitors to Abemama seeking that special millennium experience, Eric Bailey intends to be safely on the other side of the world.

Above all it is his advancing years that have convinced him his days on Abemama are numbered. 'We're a long way from hospitals here and as the years flick by one gets a bit apprehensive,' he told us. 'Health problems beset us all the time, don't they?' A thought crosses his mind. 'Incidentally, you've been wandering about a bit here. There's a loo if you want to make use of it.'

Sir Peter shakes his head. 'Don't mention the word, because it makes me agitated and want to go at once. I've reached that time . . . well, you must know.' 'Yes, I have that problem and I think I would be up all night, but I use one of those hospital bottles,' our host offers helpfully. No good, Sir Peter tells him. 'We're travelling light and there's no room for an extra hospital bottle.'

As we prepared to leave, our guide was gazing anxiously at his watch, concerned we were cutting it rather fine if we intended to catch our flight. We still had a thirty-minute drive on a coral road to reach the other end of the island and the airport. Our driver did his best to put his foot down but our battered old truck wasn't built for speed and the bumpy roads didn't help. As we lurched along it started to rain, soaking those of us huddled in the back of the open vehicle. Still some minutes from the airport we heard what sounded like an aircraft. Surely not our plane? We took comfort from the thought that a charter flight would never leave without its passengers. Yet when we finally reached the airport we found it eerily quiet. Three nuns waiting for a scheduled flight – the only scheduled flight – due later in the day confirmed our worst fears. Our plane had indeed returned to Tarawa without us.

Leaving Sir Peter and the crew in the half-built hut which served as the terminal building I went off with our guide to see what could be done to remedy the situation. I had visions of failing to keep our appointment with President Tito who was expecting us a few hours later. We had to get off the island. At the local Post Office we pleaded with the radio operator to send a message to Air Kiribati. He refused. Radio channels on Abemama are restricted. From 11 a.m. the island is incommunicado. We were too late. I pleaded an emergency, told him about our impending interview with the President. He remained unmoved. At the root of this lack of cooperation lay a real fear of what might happen if he broke a cardinal rule and radioed outside his allotted time. Finally I begged him to open a channel to Air Kiribati so that I could speak to the operator at the other end. He could remain silent at my side. Reluctantly he agreed, no doubt against his better judgement.

From Tarawa the radio operator told me our plane had left because we were too late for the flight. But it was a charter, I said. Surely it might have waited? As I spoke I was aware that the previous week the Kiribati Cabinet had pilloried the airline for its poor time-keeping. We had fallen victim to a move by Air Kiribati to clean up its act and run its flights – even charter flights – on time. For several minutes I wrangled over whether they would send another plane and how much it would cost. All the while time was ticking away and our interview with the President looking less likely. Finally, Air Kiribati agreed to despatch another aircraft. All we could do was sit and wait.

Myself and our guide went in search of food. We were in luck. A funeral was about to take place and a feast had been prepared for the mourners. Under normal circumstances I would never gatecrash a funeral but the situation was desperate. I approached a woman who smiled sympathetically at our plight. She was more than happy to provide us with food. Grateful, I insisted on paying her despite her protestations, and returned to the airport where Sir Peter, the crew, and the three nuns were waiting patiently. They were pleased and amused when they saw what I was carrying – five loaves and two fishes. We all tucked in.

And then we must drop out a day – lose a day of our lives, a day never
to be found again. We shall all die one day earlier than from the
beginning of time we were foreordained to die. We shall be a day
behindhand through eternity. We shall always be saying to the other
angels, 'Fine day today', and they shall always be retorting, 'But it isn't
today, it's tomorrow.' We shall be in a state of confusion all the time and
shall never know what true happiness is.
MARK TWAIN (ON THE INTERNATIONAL DATE LINE),
FOLLOWING THE EQUATOR

WHEN WE ARRIVED BACK in Tarawa we were already several hours too late for our meeting with the President. I put on a shirt and tie, and went to his office to offer our apologies and try to rearrange the interview. As I crept up the stairs, hoping to run into one of the Presidential aides, I encountered the man himself. President Tito is a most amenable character. He is also extremely busy. However, when he heard our story he agreed to come into the office the following morning, a Saturday, to meet with Sir Peter.

We turned up the next day in our smartest clothes, to be greeted by a barefoot assistant in shorts. It should, after all, have been his day off.

It was in 1979 that Kiribati, formerly part of the Gilbert and Ellice Islands, gained independence and became a democratic republic. The country now comprises the old Gilbert Islands together with the Phoenix and Line Islands. From end to end Kiribati measures more than

3,000 miles; a string of tiny islands, thirty-three of them inhabited, and hundreds of small atolls. Its economy is fishing. Tales of fishermen who get into difficulties far out in the ocean and end up drifting in tiny open vessels, often for months on end, surviving on the fish they catch and drinking shark's blood, are part of the popular culture.

Kiribati also has a tradition of training its young men to work as merchant seamen all over the world. Two hundred students at a time, from all over Kiribati, embark on a rigorous fifteen-month course at a specialised school on Tarawa. The institution, dubbed the Monastery because of its rigid disciplinary code, is funded by a group of German shipping companies. At its helm is a no-nonsense Hamburger, Henning Bussman. 'No alcohol, no shore leave, no ladies,' is his motto. Discipline is so strict that, on the weekend day that we film, there are dozens of trainees working – all on punishment duty. Herr Bussman sometimes despairs of their very un-Germanic lack of self-control but is unstinting in his praise of one particular ability of theirs – to sing. A group of four have been set methodically to remove every last out-of-place leaf from a path and, as naturally as a well-trained barbershop quartet, sing the while in beautifully controlled harmony.

For much of its history Kiribati has enjoyed a degree of obscurity. The world has largely left it in peace, although during the Second World War Tarawa saw fierce fighting. Hundreds of allied troops lost their lives in a battle with the Japanese for control of an island just a few miles long and a few hundred yards wide.

Having dramatically kinked the International Date Line, however, Kiribati is now at the centre of millennial controversy. The President is unperturbed. 'We're pleased we're going to lead the millennium, because we're going to tell the world that we have something they have lost,' he

On the shores of Kiribati there are still Japanese gun emplacements left over from the Battle of Tarawa in the Second World War, when the islands took a brief dramatic role on the world stage.

told us. 'I think what we have is the virtue and good of humanity. We say that because we're still intact as families, as communities.'

In contrast to Hawaii, the extent to which Kiribati is unspoiled is striking. Not a single high-rise building and only three foreign embassies in Tarawa – Australia, New Zealand and China. 'We are lucky that we have been able to stay away from most of the external influences that other countries have had to go through. And therefore we are evolving at our own pace and in our own way more than other Pacific island countries, and we quite enjoy that,' said President Tito. 'We're watching other countries make mistakes, and as we walk behind them, we know where the potholes are, so we tend to know our way around these things much better than some of these countries who are ahead of us.'

When we left the President's office there was still the quarrel over the charter flight with Air Kiribati to be resolved. Although Tarawa is a small place, getting around can be tricky. The local travel agent, Susan Bareti (pronounced *Bairess*) – whose main clients were shipping companies getting their workers back to the Philippines – had helped arrange our trip. I felt it might be useful to have her along as moral support when I tackled the airline representative. To reach her exquisite house, which stood on stilts on the other side of the lagoon, meant hiring a boat (it could be walked to only when the tide was out). The round trip took nearly three hours. Back on dry land, our man from the airline was being elusive. We turned up at his home only to find he was no longer living there. After going from house to house and being directed here and there, along roads now lit only by a half moon, we finally managed to track him down. I can't say he was delighted to see us.

A long and difficult process of negotiation followed. He wanted us to pay for two charter flights. I wanted to pay for one. We talked round in circles for what seemed like hours before coming to an arrangement which was acceptable to both of us. The next morning we were back at the airport for a flight, a scheduled one this time, en route from the Marshall Islands, to Fiji. We had been promised our tickets would be there awaiting collection. Of course they weren't. It was a Sunday and there was no one about. I had visions of another plane leaving without us. By some stroke of good fortune we managed to raise the airline's marketing manager at his home in the Marshall Islands – another country, almost 1,000 miles to the north. My final memory of leaving Kiribati was of Sir Peter boarding the aircraft followed by two Mormons, while I knelt on the runway frantically signing travellers' cheques to pay for the trip. It was the height of chaos and more or less par for the course.

FIJI

*In the old times the Fijians were fierce fighters; they were very religious,
and worshipped idols; the big chiefs were proud and haughty, and they
were men of style.*

MARK TWAIN, *FOLLOWING THE EQUATOR*

———————————◆———————————

WE FLEW TO FIJI WITH A SHORT stopover on the island of Tuvalu. Two
flights a week connect this tiny country with the outside world. It appears
entirely unspoiled. At the airport, passengers are given transit cards made
from polished coconut-palm. There is an old-fashioned charm about the
place. Yet, bizarrely, Tuvalu earns a good living as a central exchange for
telephone sex lines. Other countries route their calls through this remote
tropical island. It's a profitable business, accounting, at the last count, for
eight per cent of Tuvalu's gross national product. Quite how a quaint little
place like Tuvalu found itself at the heart of the telephone sex industry is
not entirely clear, but there it is. Perhaps nowhere is quite what it seems at
first sight.

On to Suva, the capital of Fiji. We head straight for the local market with
just one item on our shopping list. Sir Peter leads the way, weaving around
stalls piled high with local produce.

Leaving behind colourful displays of fruit and vegetables we take a flight
of stairs, following a sign which reads 'Grog Sales'. We have come to buy
kava, a local plant root noted for its narcotic effects. Since ancient times
Fijians have dried the root, ground it to a powder and turned it into a
drink. Native people would consume kava as part of a daily rite bound up
in their religious beliefs. The practice, known as the *yangona* ritual, is still
popular today. To give and receive kava remains an important aspect of life
in Fiji. We were about to pay our respects to the chief of an old cannibal
village deep in the interior, and had been advised that a gift of high-grade
kava was an essential calling card.

Our stallholder assured us his stock was the best available. We were in no
position to argue. One kilogram at 22 Fijian dollars (around £9.00) was
duly weighed and wrapped. In its raw state kava is a strange-looking
substance. Long, grey woody roots with nodules. Sir Peter looked dubious.
'Are you sure the chief will expect to receive it like this?' The stallholder
was adamant as he lashed the roots together with a length of twine,
carefully making them taper to a point like an exotic wig. 'This is the
normal way of doing things,' he assured us. Again, we took his word.

There was something mildly disconcerting about the sight of Sir Peter

A helicopter is often the only practical way to travel to the more inaccessible regions – the one tiny road to our destination of Nubutaotao was wiped out by a flood in 1997. Our Fijian guide, Aminiashi Ngaidabou (right), was returning to his home village for the first time in five years.

It doesn't do to offend the ancestral spirits. Strange goings-on in the National Museum in Suva had almost convinced us of their presence.

leaving the market with a kilo of narcotics in a carrier bag. Thankfully, in Fiji kava is perfectly legal.

Nubutaotao is an isolated settlement deep in the heart of Fiji's main island, Viti Levu. Around fifty people live quietly in this remote spot hidden away in the mountains. On the face of it there is nothing exceptional about the village. But one extraordinary incident more than a hundred years ago has put it on the map forever. It was here that a Methodist missionary, newly arrived in what were then known as the Cannibal Isles, was killed and eaten by local people.

The Reverend Thomas Baker arrived in Nubutaotao in 1867 in search of converts. While staying in the village he committed such a flagrant breach of protocol that it cost him his life. All that remains of the missionary today are the tattered soles of his shoes, preserved for posterity in the National Museum in Suva.

Even today protocol is carefully observed in Fiji, although you're unlikely to be thrown into the cooking pot if you get it wrong. It was the great grandfather of the present chief, Filmoni Nawawabalavu, who wielded the axe which brought the Reverend Baker's life to an untimely end. As we planned our own trip to the village we were at pains to know how to behave once we got there. Bearing in mind the missionary's experience, we were anxious not to offend the chief.

We turned to our guide, Aminiashi Ngiadabou, who grew up in Nubutaotao, for advice on appropriate behaviour. Some weeks before, he had taken me and assistant producer Toby Follett on a reconnaissance trip to the village to meet the chief. It took six hours from Suva, along roads which only a four-wheel drive vehicle could manage. Eventually, the road became impassable and we covered the last hour-long stretch on foot, descending a mountain into the village.

Despite their fearsome reputation the local people greeted us warmly, offering us a bit of floor space in the main thatched hut for the night. We were glad of their offer of blankets since the temperature had dropped considerably the higher into the mountains we climbed. That evening a wonderful meal of yams and chicken was presented to us. In our honour, sandwiches made of white bread with the corners cut off – far from typical fare in Nubutaotao – were also produced. After the feast came the *yangona* session. We had watched the preparations, the root being ground in a stone basin and strained through what might well have been an old sock to produce a muddy liquid. Both Toby and I sipped cautiously. Kava is definitely an acquired taste. Aminiashi, back among his people for the first time in five years, partook with enthusiasm. By the end of the night he was well and truly drunk, staggering around the hut cheerfully inebriated.

When we returned to film in Nubutaotao we went by helicopter, flying low over the densely forested areas of central Fiji on our way. The issue of protocol remained uppermost in all our minds. A new concern had arisen, too. We were wary of offending the local people's ancestral spirits. Just the previous day, while filming in the National Museum, a series of mysterious problems had beset our sound recording gear. Each time we tried to film beside a display case containing the Reverend Baker's shoes, something went wrong. We were all perplexed. The curator, however, was not. It was simply the spirits making their presence felt. She told us, 'Strange things happen here all the time.'

Aminiashi outlined some essential dos and don'ts as we prepared to land in the village. No hands in pockets, no singing or whistling. No hats, no bags. We were to remove our shoes and sit cross-legged on the floor in the presence of the chief. We should keep our heads bowed as a sign of respect. We were to clap when offered a bowl of kava and again after taking a drink. There seemed an awful lot to remember. Most importantly, under no circumstances were we to touch the head of the chief. This had been the undoing of the Reverend Baker.

When we arrived, the village appeared eerily quiet. Since there was not even two-way radio contact, we had to broadcast on the local radio station to confirm to them that we would be coming, but had no way of knowing if the message had been received. We threaded our way through the thatched huts to a building known as the *bure*, or meeting place, where the chief was waiting for us flanked by a dozen or so young men. Slipping off our shoes we went inside to find a *yangona* ceremony underway. On the floor was a large bowl, a *tanoa*, containing kava. The men sat smoking as smaller bowls were passed among them, clapping their hands in unison each time a drink was given and received. We kept one eye on Aminiashi. When he clapped, we did too. The atmosphere in the room was distinctly formal.

At Aminiashi's signal we presented our bundle of kava root and thanked the chief for his hospitality. In the past, kava was consumed only by chiefs and priests in religious ceremonies. They would kneel on the floor and drink from a bowl which was considered sacred. However, Aminiashi had advised us that modern protocol demanded we all drink the kava when it was offered. Sir Peter accepted a bowl and sipped at the grey liquid. 'It's very good,' he declared. All eyes were on him. 'Do I have to drink it all?' The chief nodded. It seemed he did. Bravely, he raised the bowl once more to his lips. 'They've given me an awful lot,' he said.

Only the chief abstained, ironically for religious reasons of his own. He later told us that as a Seventh Day Adventist he is not permitted to drink! Aminiashi explained that for all the other men in the village their 'Fijianness' trumped their Seventh Day Adventism, so that their religious prohibition was simply ignored when it came to kava.

After the *yangona* ceremony Chief Nawawabalavu walked us to the site on

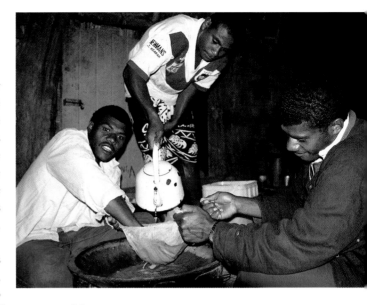

Preparing the kava for a yangona session is only the first step of a complex and time-honoured ritual.

The morning after the night before. Chief Filimoni Nawawabalavu of Nubutaotao leads our still heavily intoxicated guide.

This is the very axe with which the Chief's great grandfather killed the Reverend Thomas Baker in 1867.

Outwardly, the so-called 'cannibal village' has changed hardly at all since the missionaries first came here 130 years ago.

the edge of the village where the Reverend Baker is buried. He tends the grave himself. A simple plaque marks the spot. With Aminiashi acting as interpreter the chief explained that it was a dispute over a comb which had led to the missionary's death. Hearing the story today it may seem a trivial matter, but to Fijians a century ago death was the only possible outcome. Protocol had been breached beyond repair.

It seemed the reverend had loaned the chief his comb. The chief, never having seen such a thing, was much taken by it and placed it decoratively in his hair. The reverend, however, had not intended his comb as a gift. Unwisely, he tried to retrieve it. 'The Reverend Baker should have known better,' said Aminiashi. 'When you touch a chief's head you are requesting death.'

Even today Fijians believe that the head is sacred, a source of *manna*, or power. It would still be considered disrespectful to touch someone's head. In 1867 it was unthinkable. 'When the sun sets tomorrow you will not be here to see it,' the chief told the missionary.

Indeed he wasn't. That night he met his maker. His body was cut into pieces and shared among the neighbouring villagers, who pronounced him delicious. Only his leather shoes proved inedible. As the chief recounted the story with considerable jollity, he leaned on the very axe, an awesome-looking weapon, used by his great grandfather in the execution of the cleric.

It was quite a relief to know our own visit had passed without any disastrous incidents. Later, however, we discovered we had unwittingly offended Fijian protocol even before we set off for Nubutaotao. 'When we were in the restaurant at the hotel last night the crew were throwing food around,' Aminiashi admonished. 'In Fijian society it's very disrespectful to throw food at people.' Sir Peter nodded gravely. 'I'll talk to them,' he promised. 'I'll threaten them with death.'

A hundred and thirty years on, the villagers of Nubutaotao have mixed feelings about their reputation as the people who killed and ate a missionary. While they take some pleasure from the notoriety they also believe the village has been blighted by the Baker incident. Had it not been for this one unfortunate episode in their history, they feel sure Nubutaotao would have benefited from development by now, that access roads and services would have been improved.

As it is, they see themselves as an abandoned people. And they believe it is no coincidence that the government, led by a Methodist Prime Minister, has largely left this community of Seventh Day Adventists to their own devices.

The children of Nubutaotao would prefer to look forward to the future rather than dwell on the past.

There is a noble and beautiful view of ocean and islands and castellated peaks from the governor's high placed house and its immediate surroundings lie drowsing in that dreamy repose and serenity which are the charm of life in the Pacific Islands.
MARK TWAIN, FOLLOWING THE EQUATOR

WE HAD ARRIVED IN FIJI just as the new constitution was about to be signed, marking a turning point in the country's recent troubled history. Seven years earlier the constitution had been redrawn against a background of hostility towards the country's massive Indian population. Official resentment towards the Indian community was about to be replaced by a new spirit of reconciliation.

It was a hundred years ago that the first Indians arrived in Fiji, brought by the British to work the sugar plantations. They settled and prospered. Now they make up almost half the population of the islands. After the General Election of 1987 there was a real chance that this non-indigenous community would assume political control. For some the idea was unthinkable. Under the leadership of Colonel Sitiveni Rabuka, a persuasive and charismatic figure, the armed forces revolted.

In the wake of the coup the Indian community suffered. Faced with an uncertain future and a constitution which openly discriminated against them, many fled the country. Now the same man who led the coup is the country's Prime Minister. And, in a remarkable *volte face*, Mr Rabuka now sees his task as being to unite rather than divide his people under a new constitution which offers a fairer deal to all Fiji's citizens.

In many respects issues of identity are as perplexing to the people of Fiji as they are to those in Hawaii. In a theatre on the campus of the University of the South Pacific in Suva, two actresses run through their lines for a performance of a play about what it is to be Fijian. We called them the Benetton Girls. Their message is simple: appearances can be deceptive.

Opposite, top right: Plaques high on a rock outside the village tell Nubutaotao's story. One in English and one in Fijian, they read: 'OBEDIENCE ALL THE WAY TO DEATH. The Reverend Thomas Baker and his Fijian assistants met their death in this very place on the morning of 21 July 1867 during a missionary tour of the interior of Viti Levu'. The boy on the far right of this group is the son of the present Chief.

Mountains, palm trees and fertile plains: the Island of Viti Levu includes all the ingredients of paradise.

Asela was born in Fiji and speaks Fijian, but she looks decidedly European. Her very light skin can be a handicap. 'I hear people talk about me all the time,' she says. 'If I'm in the market and trying to pick vegetables or coconuts the way a Fijian would I'll hear people saying, *What does she know about it?* They see me and think I'm a white woman.'

On stage her character declares, 'My father's European and my mother is Fijian. We used to be called part-European but now it is very trendy to be called part-Fijian.'

Chantelle was also born in Fiji. She is an Indo-Fijian but her skin is black. She stands alongside Alesa at the front of the stage. 'My mother is Fijian and my father is Indian. I was never sure what to call myself, an Indian or a Fijian. My mother is a Christian and my father is Hindu. They have these arguments sometimes and I listen to them with my brother. They sometimes forget we exist, but when they do remember they realise that we are caught in the middle. Instead of having the best of both worlds we have lost out. We feel we belong nowhere.'

The play was written by Larry Thomas, a lecturer at the university who has wrestled with his own identity at times. He is an exotic mix of Fijian and Welsh. 'It's wonderful to be able to have a wide family of Fijians and Indians and Europeans,' he says. 'The problem here is that some people look down on that. Because you're not pure you don't belong here, or you shouldn't be here, and because you're not pure Fijian you can't claim a right to the land.'

Sir Peter briefly sketches his own family history. Half Russian; an Ethiopian great grandmother. Some French, Italian, Swiss and German thrown in. 'I am intensely proud of all that,' he tells Larry. 'I don't feel I belong nowhere. I feel I belong everywhere.'

Imrana Jalal is a fourth generation Fijian whose ancestors were brought to the islands from India by the British a century ago. Despite the divisions between the Fijian and Indian communities ,Imrana, a lawyer and human rights campaigner, is in no doubt: she is Fijian through and through.

Like many Fijians of Indian descent, at the time of the military coup, Imrana was faced with a difficult decision. The threat to the Indian community had prompted an exodus. Hundreds of people poured out of the country every month. Her mother left, taking her youngest child with her. In time the entire family followed. Imrana stayed. 'I felt I was so tangled up in what was happening here,' she said. 'I really love Fiji. I felt that I had a place here and I was going to stay and struggle for a better Fiji.'

It's not all politics . . . Imrana Jalal may be a vocal campaigner on behalf of Fiji's Indian population but she can be as entertaining as she is formidable.

Now she detects a mood of optimism in the country. There are signs that slowly but surely Fiji will transform itself into the multiracial society many wish it to be. 'We still have a long way to go. Our cultures have existed side by side but quite separate. The younger generation, they mix more inter-racially. They make more friendships in other races, but my parents' generation did not do that. Things are changing, but there is still a lot of wariness and suspicion by the bulk of Indians and the bulk of Fijians.'

The problems are more acute in the urban areas where the communities live in their own ethnic enclaves. It was a practice encouraged by the British when they brought the first Indian labourers to the islands. Some Fijians favour separate and distinct communities even today. Imrana's own experience is of growing up in a family intent on keeping its culture and religion intact. She was urged to marry within her ethnic group.

'My father said to his four daughters, "Do not marry out of your race or your religion." Most Indians don't want their children to marry out of their race.' Only one of Imrana's sisters found a husband who is a mixture of Fijian, Indian, Chinese and Samoan, in defiance of her father. 'There is very little intermarriage with the Fijians and the Indians,' Imrana tells us. 'Yet if you intermarry you form ties and allegiances immediately. How can you commit a coup against people in your own family?'

In her work Imrana Jalal runs training seminars designed to change attitudes among Fiji's influential figures. Unless those attitudes change, she feels, the country will remain stuck in its old and damaging ways. We

Fiji is working towards a fully integrated police force with equal opportunities for both men and women, Fijians and Indians alike. Behind this group is the thatched lecture hall in which Imrana conducted her seminar.

eavesdrop on a workshop attended by some of Fiji's top police officers. They are tackling a difficult and sensitive subject; rape. Imrana wants them to examine the assumptions they make about women and to question how the law treats rape victims.

Fiji has a long history of dealing with crime through customary law rather than by recourse to the official authorities. Traditionally, village elders meet to seek compensation for the crime, in return for which the perpetrator is forgiven. For generations this has been an accepted means of resolving even the most serious crimes and keeping the peace in the village. Now it's up to the police to persuade communities that customary law alone is not enough.

'As police officers, every day you're having to face the old culture, the Indian culture and the Fijian culture, and then here is this modern life intruding on the way we've traditionally dealt with things,' says Imrana. One of the officers mentions a recent case where a teenage girl was abducted and raped by six men. Villagers kept the incident from the authorities for three days while they attempted to find a means of reconciling things themselves. 'Is that really solving the problem?' Imrana asks. 'What about the victim?' Round the table the officers agree. Customary law may well heal rifts within communities, but takes little account of the plight of the individual.

Under their new constitution, Fijians are going to have to conduct a delicate balancing act if they want to retain the traditions they value within the framework of a modern society. 'As Fijians we face a dilemma,' says Imrana. 'We want to retain our customs and our culture, we want the customary law to be observed as far as if should be, but we also want our individual rights.'

It is up to the country's law enforcers to reach an acceptable compromise. 'Our job is to carry out the law under the constitution in a proper way. We have to unlearn our prejudices and not make assumptions about people simply because they don't fulfil a particular expectation.' The new spirit of tolerance on the part of Prime Minister Rabuka is a source of great encouragement to her. 'I think the Prime Minister has gone through a process of change, an evolutionary one rather than a revolutionary one,' she says. 'And he has realised that there is a very close link between a stable political system and economic benefits.'

For the country to prosper, she believes that ordinary Fijians must be assisted. Not just by the government but by the more successful business elements within the Indian community. She tells us, 'I think that one of the keys to multiracialism in this country is that the average Fijian must at the end of the day have money in his pocket to feed his children. They must have a larger slice of the economic pie. And the Indians must help them to do this.'

An outspoken firebrand in his earlier career, Fiji's Prime Minister Rabuka has come to be regarded as a politician of genuine vision and stature.

IT IS THE MORNING of the State Opening of Parliament. Prime Minister Rabuka is at his desk signing letters. We are shown into his office and seated.

'My word, these are impressive,' Sir Peter remarks as he settles himself into a large and comfortable chair.

'Made of coconut timber,' says the PM with a wry smile. 'Too heavy to take with you when you lose office.' Mr Rabuka – his name means fire – has mellowed considerably since he seized power back in 1987 and plunged Fiji into chaos. At the time he favoured positive discrimination for indigenous Fijians. Today he is more understanding of their Indian neighbours. 'We still have two sides but we are one side as far as our vision and objective for Fiji is concerned,' says the man who once referred to the coup as 'a mission that God has given me.'

The Prime Minister is an impressive and controversial figure. As a Fijian UN soldier he

was awarded the French Legion D'Honneur for an act of bravery in Lebanon. As a young man he played rugby for his country. As a politician he called on army chaplains to convert Indians to Christianity. Now the man who burst into parliament and kidnapped the entire government in the space of four minutes has a more diplomatic way of doing things. Following the coup Fiji was expelled from the Commonwealth. Mr Rabuka is negotiating peacefully for her readmission.

Sir Peter accompanies the Prime Minister to parliament in his official car. The limousine, registration PM 001, was a gift from Malaysia where Fijian troops fought in the early 1950s. As the car sweeps through the streets of Suva the PM turns to Sir Peter. 'Are you related to the former Russian Defence Minister?' he says, referring to the late Dmitry Ustinov.

Sir Peter chuckles. 'Gorbachev told me, I don't think you're related to him, he's got very little humour. But you never know.'

The State Opening is an impressive affair. Soldiers in ceremonial dress drill on the lawn in front of the parliament building. MPs wearing traditional *sulus* – wrapover skirts – somewhat incongruously topped with jacket and tie, pack the house to hear the President, His Excellency The Right Honourable Ratu Sir Kamisese Mara, outline the objectives of the new constitution.

President Ratu Sir Kamisese Mara (above, right) is wearing a formal and businesslike version of the traditional Fijian sulu. The sulus of the military band (below) at the State Opening of Parliament are altogether more flamboyant.

On the day the new constitution is to be signed we gather at the President's residence. It is raining heavily and in the garden a police band, sheltering under a small tarpaulin, plays a soothing medley of what might well be love songs.

The signing itself is a formal affair in the presence of forty or so dignitaries. Afterwards we adjourn for refreshments. The ample figure of the bishop who blessed at some length the formal ceremony is the first to plunge heartily into the cucumber sandwiches. Liveried waiters in red jackets and white *sulu* 'skirts' move discreetly among the guests. They have a look about them of warriors or rugby players rather than conventional waiters. One, pouring tea from an elegant silver pot, has an intricate spider's web tattooed across the back of his hand. We suspect that pouring tea and passing round sandwiches is something they do infrequently in their spare time.

Away from the lunch party the President shows us round his home, which was previously the official residence of the Governor General. The building, a relic of Fiji's colonial past, is a copy of a museum in Sri Lanka, which a previous Governor General had seen and liked – and so ordered one of his own. It sits high above Suva and in fine weather the view is terrific. Unfortunately, Suva is noted for its rainy climate. We stand gazing through the drizzle into a blanket of mist. 'On a good day you can see a lovely range of mountains. Unfortunately this is unseasonable,' the President comments with an apologetic smile.

As for the new mood in parliament, he observes the change with quiet satisfaction. 'I lost the election in 1987 because the Fijians thought I was giving away what adhered to them. I said at the time that development is not only about land, it's about money – how to make money and how to use money wisely. And that involves other races as well as Fijians.

'The Indians have succeeded in building up the big business houses that you see in our capital. They know how to do it.'

The conversation continues in a civilised way, as the president of a country expelled from the Commonwealth for its military coup sits somewhat bizarrely surrounded by portraits of the British Royal Family, including a particularly fetching one of Princess Margaret.

The President, attended by the Prime Minister and the Acting Secretary General of Parliament, officially signs the new constitution. Sir Peter's name is among the list of witnesses.

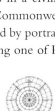

◆

ANOTHER TINY PLANE, this time for our journey from Suva to the island of Ovalau. Its main town, Levuka, was once the capital of Fiji, and it was here that the country was ceded to the British in 1874. It was also here that Prince Charles handed it back less than a hundred years later once independence was declared. Levuka today is a sleepy little place, still relatively undiscovered by tourists. Its main street is distinguished by a few basic shops and even fewer people. Even so, word of our arrival had spread. As we swept past the general store a local man held up a banner. *Welcome to Levuka, Sir Peter,* it read.

We were on our way to meet Duncan Crichton, a Scotsman now settled on the island. More than thirty years have passed since Duncan

The town of Levuka clings tenaciously to Ovalau's precipitous shoreline.

left his native Edinburgh to travel the world. His journey took him to the Middle East, the Far East, through India and on to Australia and New Zealand before bringing him to Fiji. After half a lifetime of searching, he had finally found his paradise.

It was too much to expect that such an adventurer would settle for an ordinary house in a quiet street. Instead Duncan had found himself a place halfway up a mountain high above Levuka. There was no road; just a steep, stone staircase connecting him to civilisation. We stood at the foot of the mountain contemplating a gruelling climb up 199 steps. It was not an ordeal I was prepared to inflict on Sir Peter. On the reconnaissance trip I had decided that there was only one thing for it. We would revive an old Fijian custom and have him carried off up the mountain by a team of bearers in the style of the ancient tribal chiefs.

We had turned to the Mayor of Levuka, who had promised to round up six strapping bodybuilders for us. On the morning in question we hung around at the foot of the staircase for some time while the Mayor dashed about. Bad news. The bodybuilders had, at the last minute, come over all shy. They had not turned up.

Desperate to find replacements, the Mayor pulled rank. Half a dozen local authority workers were volunteered. They appeared in their overalls. It was not quite the effect we had been hoping for. However, within minutes they had transformed themselves into an impressive crew sporting colourful sulus, their bare chests glistening with coconut oil. A chair decorated with exotic flowers was produced. Sir Peter appeared doubtful but sat in it. He was hoisted in the air and carried off up the mountain, the rest of us trailing breathlessly behind. 'I feel like

The modern end of Levuka's high street bears a disconcerting resemblance to a typical one-horse town of the American midwest.

The council workers who found themselves suddenly dragooned into replacing our missing bodybuilders nevertheless put on an impressively oiled display.

Fiji's misty mountains remind Duncan Creighton daily of his native Scottish highlands.

I'm in a Popemobile,' he announced.

When we reached the top, Duncan, resplendent in a kilt and talking nineteen to the dozen in a broad Scottish accent, ushered us into the house. We could see at once why he had fallen in love with the place.

The view was spectacular. To the east was the vastness of the South Sea. To the west lay mist-covered mountains, a daily reminder of his beloved Scotland. 'Each time I open these shutters I never walk away without looking at all this,' he told us, gazing out to sea. 'It never ceases to amaze and astonish me.'

Duncan, a well-preserved fifty-something with steely grey hair and piercing blue eyes, lives alone in his mountainside retreat. For company he has two iguanas – in a shade of green which exactly matches his kilt – and a parrot called Polly who spent her formative years with an Indian couple and speaks only Hindi. Duncan chatters to her endlessly in the hope that one day she may respond in something resembling an Edinburgh accent.

He leafs through a stack of vinyl LPs and selects some background music before settling into a chair. Suddenly the air is filled with sounds vaguely evocative of the South Seas. Closer inspection reveals that Duncan's record collection comprises Kenneth McKellar or Pacific maidens wailing, with nothing in between.

All around the house are Scottish artefacts. A tablecloth emblazoned with *The Tradition of Scotland*. A tartan rug on the floor. Even Polly is learning to enjoy porridge. There can be no mistaking Duncan's deep love of his homeland, yet since leaving as a teenager he has been back to Scotland just once.

After an absence of more than twenty years, Duncan wrote to his family saying he was planning to fly back from New Zealand. He didn't have precise dates for his trip and ended up arriving in Edinburgh unannounced. Suitcases in hand, he walked into his brother's shop, thinking he would surprise him. He did. Duncan's brother gazed blankly at the tanned stranger grinning at him. He had no idea who he was. Duncan had been gone too long.

'I suppose it's a blend of highland and island,' he said, summing up his surroundings. 'I think somewhere along the line all of us want to escape from where we are and go to some new place, some exotic, romantic place. You go out to look for it and most times you don't succeed in finding what it is you're looking for. But if you're lucky to come to a place like this, all of a sudden here's a little Brigadoon in Levuka . . . It's almost as if you step through a kind of time warp to the nineteenth century, and once you're living here you become a part of it.'

A splendidly surrealistic scene: in his lush tropical garden Duncan coaches his charges in the intricate steps of traditional Scottish reels.

It is six years since Duncan landed in Levuka and he appears utterly contented. Yet he knows that one day he is likely to pack up and move on. 'The only disadvantage to being a traveller is that you must keep travelling,' he says. 'Every so often you get this urge to move again. And this is at the back of your mind. When will the urge strike?' He pauses briefly. 'It would take a lot to beat this place, that's for sure.'

In the meantime, if Duncan won't go to Scotland he can at least bring a tiny corner of the highlands to his paradise island. Unlikely though it may seem, Duncan is teaching Scottish dancing – with some success – to local children. We adjourn to the garden where a group of girls and boys are waiting to demonstrate their newly-acquired dance steps. A tape recorder belts out a Scottish reel. The girls are in white, a swathe of tartan across their shoulders. The boys are in the local equivalent of a kilt, knee-length *sulus*. In amongst the coconut palms and the tropical plants they trot and skip in a surreal display. 'Arms in the air, boys,' Duncan instructs. 'Like antlers, don't forget.'

WE TIP-TOE AWAY, leaving Duncan in mid-reel, to keep our next appointment at the local primary school where we are about to witness something more

traditional to Levuka. The children are learning about blackbirding, a practice in which natives from neighbouring islands were captured and brought to Fiji to work the plantations.

Blackbirding began in the late 1800s when European farmers came to the islands expecting to find plentiful cheap labour. Instead they met with resistance from local chiefs who refused to allow their villagers to work for the settlers. Labour was then brought in from the nearby Solomon Islands and New Hebrides. Locals, tricked into boarding ships for Fiji, found themselves lined up in the harbour and sold. Often women, separated from their husbands and sons, would follow on voluntarily. Some of the so-called blackbirds were released at the end of a five-year period and allowed to return home. Others were not. They married into the local population and their influence can still be seen among their descendants on the island.

The children, wearing grass skirts and leafy garlands round their necks and wrists, troop into the playground to sing a Fijian song which tells the story of a child captured as part of the feared labour traffic.

This page and opposite:
We were as entranced by the children of Levuka Primary School as they were intrigued by us. No matter how many times their teacher tried to persuade them to stand neatly in line to welcome us, their excitement and their natural exuberance invariably got the better of them.

I took a walk to the beach
The ships appeared
And they rowed the smaller boats to the shore
The white men took hold of me
They tied me with a rope
I started crying
They put me in a sack
They took me to the boat.

One way and another most of our day in Levuka seemed to have been taken up with singing and dancing. With a mixture of Duncan's Scottish reel and the primary school pupils' blackbirding song still ringing in our ears, we longed for a quiet evening. It was not to be. There was one more job to be done before we could call it a day. A hundred years after the unfortunate demise of the Reverend Baker at the hands of cannibals, a new breed of missionaries is at work in Fiji. They could not be more different from the Englishman who brought Christianity to the islands more than a century ago. Today it is an American evangelical movement, the Everyhome Crusade, which is moving among the people. Founded in 1984, the movement has grown at a phenomenal rate. Its crusaders favour fiery rhetoric over gentle persuasion. They are attracting converts at such a rate they can't build churches fast enough to accommodate them.

Our curiosity aroused, we joined an Everyhome gathering at Levuka's Queen Victoria Hall. When we arrived the meeting was already underway. A young man played loud electric guitar and led the worshippers in a hymn which seemed to be endless. 'One people, one nation, praising the Lord', they sang, in a style more American gospel than English traditional. The pastor sat among his congregation, a young Fijian in casual clothes. As we chatted to him he appeared to be the gentlest of souls, a mild, sweet-natured man. He had spent a spell in prison, he said, and was now a reformed character. It was difficult to picture him as a rousing evangelical

preacher. When he rose to address his people, however, that is exactly what he became. His sermon was nothing less than a breathtaking rant. The congregation murmured and clapped in approval. On the walls above them portraits of the British Royal Family, including the matriarchal Victoria, cast a stern eye over the proceedings.

The pastor gave thanks for the first missionaries who came to Fiji from England. 'The great missionaries,' he bellowed, 'the early missionaries, they left their comfortable homes, they left their nation – England. They left their kingdom, they left their forefathers, their loved ones, and they obeyed God.' Leaving behind the life they knew, these pioneers of Christianity came willingly to the other side of the world, to a place which was known as the Cannibal Isles. Our pastor fixed his congregation with a zealous eye. 'They dared to bring the Gospel to this land. We are the great witness to what they've done. And I want to thank God for them . . . People coming into this nation now, they cannot believe we were cannibals, that we were eating human flesh. They see the change in us. Now we know how to smile, we teach them to smile.'

Religion plays a major role in Fijian life, whether in Muslim mosques or Hindu temples or Evangelical Christian churches.

Quite what the Reverend Baker would have thought had he known he was blazing a trail for the new evangelists is anyone's guess. He would no doubt be comforted, however, to know that missionaries venturing into the heartland of Viti Levu today no longer run the risk of being eaten, however badly they behave.

It was too late to catch a flight back to Suva that night. We had booked into the finest hotel in Levuka, The Royal. Sir Peter and I were given the best rooms, two recently-built wooden structures in the hotel grounds, each of which had its own private shower and toilet. That night Sir Peter was on good form. He was probably relieved to be in a hotel which not only had power at the flick of a switch but running water too, and an indoor loo. He had become used to much less.

The keys to our rooms were engraved with the names of the owners of the place, an un-Fijian sounding couple called Derek and Edna. For the duration of the evening Sir Peter adopted for himself the persona of Derek. I became Edna.

Some hours later Derek and Edna retired to their rooms. Since I had no alarm clock I asked Sir Peter to give me a knock the next morning. As dawn broke I heard the crisp tones of a newsreader coming from the room next door. Sir Peter, who never goes anywhere without his shortwave radio, had tuned in to the BBC World Service. I lay there listening to a story about Northern Ireland. Then I heard a loud crowing. It was Sir Peter doing a convincing impersonation of a cockerel. Moments later he called, 'Edna!' at the top of his voice. It was time to get up.

These two typify the energy and the spontaneity we found everywhere in Fiji.

Well, this is odd. You're one of those sort they call eccentrics,
I judge.
MARK TWAIN, FOLLOWING THE EQUATOR

───────── ◆ ─────────

IT WAS AN UNLIKELY SETTING for the keeper of the secret of the universe. A dilapidated wooden shack well off the beaten track an hour's drive from Suva. A hand-painted sign hammered into the ground offered shells for sale. The place appeared tumbledown and deserted. I and my colleague Toby Follet trudged across a soggy piece of ground to reach a creaking wooden staircase at the side of the building. At the foot of the stairs lay a coffin, the wood going rotten.

We had been directed to this isolated spot by locals who spoke of an eccentric old man with a fabulous collection of shells. In the end, however, it was not the shells which captured our imagination. It was the man himself.

The shell man turned out to be a well-preserved 86-year-old. He was an Indian whose parents had travelled from Calcutta to Durban in South Africa – where he was born – and then on to Fiji. At first he seemed suspicious of us but was soon sufficiently at ease to be entertaining us with a selection of his own compositions played on a tiny, wheezing, hand-powered organ. It was slightly surreal, but we listened politely.

Suddenly he announced he had written a book, and produced two bound exercise books in which his story had been recorded. It was handwritten in capital letters using a leaky biro. The middle section of the book – Chapter Eleven – was off-limits. Two heavy bulldog clips held the pages firmly together. Here, within this sealed chapter, lay the secret of the universe.

'Do you know why men have nipples?' the shell man demanded.

Toby and I exchanged glances. We had to admit we didn't.

'Well, there you are!' came the triumphant response.

By now our curiosity was aroused. The shell man told us it would cost $1 million just to see the secret scribbled on those few clamped pages. There would be a further fee of $10 million for anyone wishing to publish. Neither Toby nor I had that kind of money on us. Instead we spent $16 on a few exquisite shells and left, mildly intrigued by our encounter.

At the foot of the stairs the shell man called out, 'That's my coffin. I made it ten years ago – it has died before me!'

By now I had decided it would be a good idea to return with Sir Peter and the crew to record an interview. Toby was not convinced of the wisdom of this. He felt the shell man's eccentricity made him less than reliable. I knew it was high-risk but felt it could turn out to be interesting. At least he was both articulate and comprehensible which, remembering the King of Abemama, is not always the case.

Some weeks later we were back. Toby had returned in between times to make sure that everything was arranged. Even so, it was with a sense of foreboding that we set off from Suva on the appointed day. When we arrived the shell man was not pleased to see us. It seemed someone had offered to buy the book which would reveal the secret of the universe. (Since the so-called 'purchase' involved the shell man paying for the printing, it was clearly a case of vanity publishing.) But for some reason he had convinced himself that talking to us about the book, even in general terms, would result in the deal falling through.

I tried to persuade him. Perhaps if we could just film him holding the book, without, of course, giving away its contents . . . He was adamant. We most certainly could not. In any event it had been sent to Nadi, 160 kilometres away, for the manuscript to be typed. I had hoped to record Sir Peter in conversation with the shell man, negotiating to buy his secret, in the end unable to afford the millions of dollars required and leaving empty-handed. It was not to be.

Perhaps we could just do a small piece on the shell collection? No, definitely not. It emerged that the shells had also gone. A collector had turned up and bought the lot. I appealed to Sir Peter to try and salvage the situation. Perhaps he could use his influence to persuade our man to let us film a brief interview. But to no avail. The shell man was polite, getting his pretty granddaughter to bring us endless cups of tea. He would not be drawn on anything, however – not his book, his shells, or even his music.

I was unprepared for such a scenario. I had suspected he might not be there when we arrived to film. Or that his interview might prove so eccentric as to be unusable. Not for a moment had I imagined he would be at home but would stubbornly refuse to be interviewed or filmed. He would not even be photographed. In the end we were forced to admit defeat at the hands of his magnificent obsession. He was not willing even to hint at what the secret of the universe might be. We left Fiji none the wiser.

Levukan fisherwomen paddle their home-made boat off the coast of Ovalau.

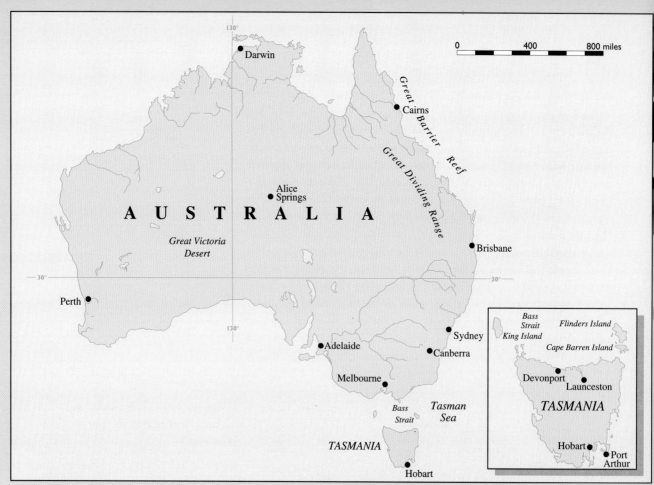

0   400   800 miles

130°

Darwin

Cairns

Great Barrier Reef

Great Dividing Range

Alice
Springs

A U S T R A L I A

*Great Victoria
Desert*

Brisbane

30°

Perth

130°

Sydney

Adelaide

Canberra

Melbourne

*Bass
Strait*

*Tasman
Sea*

TASMANIA

Hobart

*Bass
Strait*

Flinders Island

King Island

Cape Barren Island

Devonport

Launceston

TASMANIA

Hobart

Port
Arthur

Kaipara

Auckland

NORTH ISLAND

Rotorua

170°

40°

Cook Strait

Picton

Wellington

NEW ZEALAND

Kaikoura

Christchurch

Milford Sound

▲ *Mitre Peak*

SOUTH ISLAND

170°

0   200 miles

PART TWO

NEW ZEALAND

·

AUSTRALIA

A lovely summer morning; brilliant blue sky . . . passed through vast level green expanses snowed over with sheep. Fine to see. The green, deep and very vivid sometimes; at other times less so, but delicate and lovely. A passenger reminds me that I am in 'the England of the Far South'.
MARK TWAIN, FOLLOWING THE EQUATOR

◆

LONDON. A SUITCASE lies open on the bed, an assortment of clothes in a heap beside it. Packing yet again, this time for the trip to New Zealand to film the next stage of the series. New Zealand seems so far away. It is. Thirteen thousand miles. A twenty-six-hour flight. A lost day as we cross the International Date Line.

Arriving in Auckland at dawn the following morning all the luggage from the flight is held up for an inspection by sniffer dogs trained to identify contraband goods. What is surprising is the kind of illicit items they're after. Not, as you might expect, drugs; but food. Thankfully, there was nothing edible in my suitcase.

Later that morning I find myself on board the *Pride of Auckland* for a trip round the harbour with assistant producer, Pratap Rughani. It is a chance to run through the schedule before Sir Peter and the crew arrive. Every day will be packed with filming and travel from one location to the next. It is at some point during this trip that a worrying realisation hits me. The intensity of the filming – all the travelling and being nice to new people – is making me uncharacteristically anti-social. Instinctively, I have started seeking out quiet places and avoiding as much contact with other people as possible. Sitting on an aircraft with an empty seat beside me has become a cause for celebration.

At 4.45 a.m. the next day we are at the airport awaiting the arrival of Sir Peter and the film crew from LA. Despite the early hour, Sir Peter is on good form. His journey has brought him from his home in Geneva to London and then on to LA and Auckland. It seems he has had bizarre but entertaining encounters en route with the porters who have taken charge of his wheelchairs at both Heathrow and LAX.

In London he found himself trapped in a lift at Terminal 2 with a jolly Irish porter who didn't know which terminal Air New Zealand fly from. On arrival at LAX he was entrusted to a Filipino lady who spoke little English and seemed unfamiliar with the layout of the airport. It was a miracle that he finally arrived at the correct gate for his onward flight to Auckland. It occurs to me that Sir Peter and airport wheelchairs might make a good sequence . . . although not before he has a chance to catch up on some sleep after his long journey.

In the early days things went well enough. The natives sold land without clearly understanding the terms of exchange, and the whites bought it without being much disturbed about the native's confusion of mind. By and by the Maori began to comprehend that he was being wronged; then there was trouble, for he was not the man to swallow a wrong and go aside and cry about it.

MARK TWAIN, FOLLOWING THE EQUATOR

———————————◆———————————

SUITABLY REFRESHED, we set off in a rental car, heading for the town of Kaipara on the west coast, some two hours north of Auckland. Sir Peter is at the wheel, trying to keep one eye on the road while distracted by spectacular scenery all around.

'What an extraordinarily clean country,' he remarks. 'One has the impression the countryside has been washed together with the smalls and everything else this morning.'

He is right. New Zealand has a freshly scrubbed quality about it. An emptiness too. We seem to be the only ones on the road. Miles go by before before we see another vehicle. So much space, so few people. We round a bend to find the sea suddenly sparkling in front of us. 'That's probably the best view we've seen so far in New Zealand,' says Sir Peter as he drives on. There is a twinkle in his eye. 'When the car overturns you'll get a different angle on it.'

It makes a pleasant change to be travelling by road instead of the dizzying succession of planes – some of which have felt barely bigger than our rental car – throughout our journey so far. No airport check-in. No mislaid tickets. No harrowing flight through tropical rain. To our tired bodies, disorientated from the many miles covered so far, it is a welcome respite.

We arrive at the remote Brynderwyn Motel, where judging from the name, we anticipate a welcome in Welsh. In fact the owner has no knowledge of the Welsh language and is unaccustomed to knighted guests. He seems thrown by this posse which has taken over all six rooms of his establishment. Since the Brynderwyn has no restaurant I dash off up a hill to a garage – which also happens to be the nearest catering establishment – in search of breakfast. It proves a wise move. Sir Peter, relaxing in the sun, a pot of fragrant lavender on one side, a plate of hot buttered toast on the other, has the appearance of being utterly content in his new surroundings.

Next morning we arrive at Kaipara, where the Maori people are engaged in a dispute with the New Zealand government over land and fishing rights. Their battle is representative of a process taking place throughout the country, as Maoris try to reclaim territory they believe has fallen into government hands by unfair means.

Kaipara is buzzing. The small community has been temporarily swollen by the arrival of an official tribunal, which has taken over local hotels and set itself up in the *marae*, a meeting place held sacred by Maori people. The Waitangi Tribunal has been hearing the claims of disaffected Maoris since 1975. Although its role is merely advisory, in its short history its recommendations have come to carry considerable weight. When the tribunal rules in favour of a particular claim the government tends to follow suit, sometimes at great expense. To date the New Zealand government has settled some impressive claims, including one payout of NZ$150 million (about £62 million).

To outsiders like ourselves, there appears a genuine sense that the country's authorities are seeking to make amends for past injustices perpetrated on the Maori people. It is a rare attitude, and it is more than simply reconciliation. There is restitution at work here too. It is all a far cry from what we had seen in Hawaii.

Somehow, remarkably, the Maoris struck a deal with the settlers who began arriving in their land with the first missionaries in 1814. Local chiefs met with representatives of Queen Victoria in 1840 to draw up a unique treaty which acknowledged the rights of the indigenous people of New Zealand. Under the Treaty of Waitangi the Maoris acceded to British rule. In return, their rights, culture and heritage were to be protected. Before long, however, the treaty was being violated. In the years that followed much of the land traditionally in the hands of the Maoris ended up under white ownership. Now the indigenous people want it back. Organised and eloquent, the Maoris have become a persuasive force, possessing a keen sense of what is theirs, coupled with a steely determination to prove their point.

Open-air tea break. We take advantage of an interval in the proceedings of the Waitangi Tribunal to interview Dame Augusta Wallace.

At Kaipara the tribunal is to hear claims relating to land and fishing rights. Its chairman is a retired judge, Dame Augusta Wallace, well-liked and respected both by the Maoris and the *Pakeha* – the whites. We had first met her some weeks earlier on a reconnaissance trip when she had treated us to lunch in her Auckland club. It was all terribly formal and smart. White-jacketed waiters and starched tablecloths. I remember ordering local green oysters at her insistence and secretly thinking it was

Inside the marae the bust of Queen Victoria is draped in a Maori cloak, while behind her Dame Augusta presides over the tribunal, watched over by portraits of past leaders of the Maori people.

probably a bad idea, since I had a flight back to London later that day. As it turned out the oysters were both safe and delicious.

Dame Augusta, a tiny figure in a smart business suit and, somewhat incongruously, bright orange socks, is a dynamo with a wonderful sense of humour and a sharp legal brain. Ideal for the job and living proof that it is no disadvantage to be diminutive. Dame Augusta believes she owes her life to her stature. Some years previously, a prisoner she was about to sentence leapt from the dock and lunged at her with a machete he had cunningly concealed in his trousers. The blade struck her a severe blow, but when the assailant struck a second time he missed. She is convinced she was simply too small to make a decent target.

She laughs as she tells us, 'Those who know me would say it is not surprising that at his subsequent trial for my attempted murder, he was found not guilty on the grounds of insanity.'

Dame Augusta describes the Waitangi Tribunal hearings as 'a pathway to solutions'. The proceedings are not intended to be adversarial. They are an opportunity for grievances to be aired.

As the Tribunal prepared to begin we waited with the visiting officials outside the hall. Someone rushed past carrying a bust of Queen Victoria, hurriedly installing it inside. Before we could enter the *marae* there was a strict code of etiquette to be observed. Four Maori women approached, greeting everyone present in song. Slowly, accompanied by this simple chorus, the procession moved forward. At the entrance to the hall we all slipped off our shoes and left them among the dozens of pairs already discarded.

Once inside, Sir Peter was formally welcomed. Inspired by the Maori women, he got to his feet and delivered, impressively, a few lines in German from *The Magic Flute*. A sea of faces beamed up at him in delight. After a few bars he continued the melody without text.

'I haven't forgotten the words,' he told the gathering. 'I never knew them. But the ones I do know mean, *In these hallowed halls there can be no disagreement.*'

It seemed an appropriate sentiment.

'I know you're streets ahead of most countries, as far as being able to listen is concerned,' he went on. 'Many countries have the gift of the gab but if you're going to reach any conclusions you simply have to listen.'

Much rubbing of noses followed, with Dame Augusta leading Sir Peter down a line of local people stretching the length of the building for this traditional Maori greeting. A man whispered encouragingly as he approached a line of women, *'They're all widows!'* Sir Peter gazed at an elderly woman. 'You look exactly like my grandmother,' he told her. 'Alarming!'

A large lady approached me. 'Bring those lovely lips here,' she commanded. I was strangely flattered!

Rubbing noses is still the traditional Maori greeting.

Unless you happen to be fluent in Maori, the opening rituals of the Waitangi Tribunal can become a rather confusing affair. One by one the claimants rise to express their demands. This is not simply a question of identifying a piece of land and asking for it back. What they do is run through their family history, going back hundreds of years to when the first Polynesians landed their canoes on the shores of New Zealand. This is known as *Whakapapa* – a spoken family tree. Who they are and where they come from is central to their claim.

The whole thing takes a great deal of time. The ritualistic language has an almost biblical feel. So-and-so begat so-and-so. And so on. Watching this procedure it is impossible not to be impressed at the depth of knowledge each person demonstrates about their ancestry, not to mention the confidence and ease with which they reel off the most complicated of family trees.

For all the formality of the tribunal there is a lightness to the proceedings too. We might not get the jokes – the few words of Maori we have managed to pick up are not enough – but the good-natured banter between claimants and officials is unmistakable. Throughout the day there are moments when the *marae* is filled with infectious laughter.

At the close of the day's business we catch up with Dame Augusta. Despite the good-humoured nature of the proceedings she admits the tribunal has its critics. 'There are some non-Maori who say the Maori are trying to take things they're not entitled to,' she says. 'And there are some Maori who in the ultimate extreme would say to everyone who is not Maori – *Go and live somewhere else.'*

Sir Peter nods. 'Such people exist everywhere. You can't avoid them. But what is remarkable from an outsider's point of view is the very equitable and even humorous atmosphere which exists in your tribunal.'

'Everyone is very relaxed about this procedure,' she says. 'I think if people are relaxed they are more likely to be able to say what they want. And then it's possible to direct their minds towards solutions.'

IT WAS SHORTLY AFTER 7 A.M., slipping off my watch and carefully placing it on top of my clothing, that I stepped into a thermal bath in the New Zealand spa of Whakarewarewa, in Rotorua. In less than two hours I had to catch a flight back to Auckland, but this was one bathing experience I was not prepared to miss, even if it meant a last-minute dash to the airport (nothing unusual about that). Steam billowed into the chill morning air as I lowered myself into the hot water. All around were men, women and children, all bathing without a trace of embarrassment. Everyone, myself included, was completely naked.

This was the Hirere Bath, reserved for the exclusive use of the Maori villagers. As an outsider I felt deeply privileged to be sharing in their bathing ritual. I was slightly surprised too that my presence – the only stranger among them – had failed to cause the slightest stir. This nonchalant acceptance was undoubtedly due to the fact that I was a guest of Emily Schuster, a seventy-year-old village elder. If it was okay with Emily then it was fine with the rest of the community.

As I basked in the soothing water I knew this was something I wanted Sir Peter to experience. When I mentioned it some weeks later, however, he appeared reluctant. For all my enthusiasm, the idea of stripping off and sharing a bath with a mixed group of strangers did not immediately appeal to him. We reached a compromise. I promised he could keep on his boxer shorts and that the filming would be discreet. He agreed, although somewhat hesitantly.

Whakarewarewa – pronounced fakareywa-reywa – is a remarkable place in the heart of New Zealand's volcanic region. Remarkable not only for the many thermal pools and geysers all around the town, but also for having what may well rank as one of the longest place names in the world.

Whakarewarewa is short for Te Whakarewarewatangaoteopetauaa-wahio, which in Maori means, 'the gathering together of the war forces of Wahio'. There have been Maoris here for as long as anyone can remember. Now the people inhabit what is known as a Living Village. Theirs is a model community and a major tourist attraction. Thousands of visitors stroll through the village each year. The Hirere Bath, however, is strictly off-limits.

On our way to film at Rotorua we stopped for lunch at Shirley's Café, a fish and chip place about sixty kilometres from our final

destination. The menu offered a dish called 'inbetween fish', which turned out to be surprisingly good. There was also a fish none of us had heard of, called Angostino. It might have been named after an Italian tenor. Sir Peter ordered an extraordinarily pink milkshake. 'It's so bad I have to keep drinking it out of fascination,' he said.

Over lunch I tried to explain once again what a rare honour it was to be invited to take part in the Hirere bathing ritual. Sir Peter, sipping his flamingo-tinted milkshake through a straw, remained unmoved. Communal bathing was without doubt one of the strangest things I had asked him to do thus far. I could well imagine why he might feel uncomfortable conducting an interview while sitting up to his chest in warm water surrounded by naked people. It is all credit to him that when the moment came he handled it with dignity. If he was embarrassed it didn't show.

As he slipped into the water a small child splashed about nearby. A woman soaped herself. A man balanced a mirror on the side of the pool and shaved himself. No one paid much attention to anyone else.

'The thing today with the Maori people is that we still respect and hold fast to our traditions, yet we live in a modern society,' said Emily Schuster, submerged up to her neck in the water alongside Sir Peter. 'Here in the village we have grown comfortable in two worlds. So here we are, sharing our community life with you.'

Emily, her long grey hair tamed in neat braids, waded off to the other side of the bath to stand under a pipe from which a stream of hot water

Sir Peter was persuaded to experience the invigorating waters of Whakarewarewa's thermal pool with village elder Emily Schuster. Around them the everyday business of life is conducted in the waters: (opposite, above) a mother bathes her children while (below) a man shaves in the steam.

The Living Village is a vibrant working community, and remarkable proof that traditional customs and modern society can function side by side.

gushed. 'I've got a bad neck,' she explained as the water cascaded down on her. 'This might be the cure.'

'Oh yes,' Sir Peter said with some sympathy. 'I've had a bad neck for the past seventy-six years.'

In some repects it is amazing that the Maori tradition of communal bathing has survived. When the missionaries arrived in New Zealand they were shocked by the more uninhibited aspects of the native people's culture.

'I suppose we were lucky in a way, in that we capitalised on the mistakes of other indigenous people. Our grandparents said that we have to learn to live in a western society but we don't have to lose our traditions or our identity,' said Emily.

Later, we went with her to the public areas of the Living Village. The presence of the underground springs creates an unearthly atmosphere. The whole village is swathed in a warm, white mist, which obscures whole buildings. There is an eeriness about the way in which people step into a pocket of mist and vanish. The Living Village is a remarkable example of a community combining modern living with the best of their old ways. Dotted throughout are natural steam cookers – simple pits in the ground in which meat and vegetables are left to slow-cook. As Emily lifted the lid off one for us, a figure emerged like a spectre from the mist with an armful of foil-wrapped food which he deposited into the pit. He would be back two hours later to collect his lunch.

'Is there ever any confusion about whose food it is?' Sir Peter wanted to know. 'Don't you have to mark it?'

Emily shook her head. 'No. Everybody knows who it belongs to. They only take what they put in.'

'Maori logic,' said Sir Peter.

'That's it. Maori logic.'

Despite the presence of tourists and the inevitable souvenir shops, Whakarewarewa remains a real village populated by a real community. Perhaps it is because the steam so cleverly swallows up the visitors, making their presence less obvious.

'You live completely normally, as if no one was passing through your back yard,' observed Sir Peter. 'Usually when you get such places they're like an empty zoo.'

'The important thing for us is the culture we're preserving,' said Emily. 'We bathe as a community, we cook as a community, we use the hot water here for washing as a community. It doesn't mean to say we don't have the microwave back home or the automatic washing machine, but we live with the culture of the old alongside the comforts of the new.'

New Zealand's Maoris now account for around 500,000 of the country's population of 3.5 million. Many, like Emily, are of mixed race, but today it is not so much the purity of their ancestry which matters as the fact that they remain true to the ideals of their culture.

'There is no purity in any case,' said Sir Peter. 'It's an ideal, which can be an intellectual idea, but it doesn't work in practice. What's really important in my mind is the Maori culture – the people who feel it and who live it.'

Emily Schuster demonstrates one of the communal geothermal cookers. Simply deposit your parcel of food in the steaming chamber and collect it when it is done.

WHEN THE MAORI PEOPLE first discovered Rotorua it was the unusual beauty of the landscape that seduced them. There is something other-worldly about the place. All around steam hisses from craters in the ground. There are great bubbling pools of thick, cloying mud that plop and pop. The very earth beneath your feet is a living, breathing thing. It gasps and splutters, shifts and sinks. There is an overpowering smell of sulphur in the air. Some of the locals call it 'Sulphur City'.

At the region's Waitapu Thermal Park tourists gather each day to see one of New Zealand's most famous sights – the Lady Knox Geyser in full flow. In her quiet moments Lady Knox appears tame and quite unspectacular, a small innocuous crater in the earth. It is a mistake to underestimate her true potential, however. When roused, she is a force to be reckoned with.

One cold winter morning we waited amongst a crowd of tourists from all over the world to watch Lady Knox blow her top. Our guide, a Maori called Wiki, leaned confidently on the rim of the crater and talked us through her history. It is around a hundred years since the powerful properties of the geyser were first recorded by a group of prison labourers who had been toiling nearby. They were bathing and soaping themselves in what they believed to be a thermal pool when suddenly an ominous rumbling began beneath them. We tried to imagine how they must have felt when their soothing bath transformed itself into a jacuzzi of volcanic proportions and thirty thousand litres of boiling water hurtled skywards with tremendous force.

Today, for the benefit of the tourists, Lady Knox is less prone to sudden outbursts. She erupts to order at precisely 10.15 each morning, helped along by Wiki. Several bars of soap slipped into the crater bring the geyser to life. Within minutes, as the soap breaks down the surface tension of the water, an almighty eruption occurs. As we watch and wait a low throaty rumble starts up below the surface. Then water begins to spurt skywards, gently at first. Seconds later a jet of boiling water is dancing fifteen metres above our heads. It is quite a display.

The extraordinary qualities of Rotorua led the first Maoris who arrived there in the fourteenth century to believe they were on holy ground. The name Waitapu means sacred waters. Almost at once, however, they started dying, poisoned by the water from the thermal springs.

'It's toxic?' said Sir Peter.

'It has traces of arsenic in it and it's quite acid,' said Wiki.

Sir Peter appeared mildly shocked. 'My God, thanks for telling me. I was going to take a drink when no one was looking.'

Even today the landscape has a dangerous and unpredictable quality about it. Visitors are warned not to stray from designated pathways while strolling around the park. Wander off the beaten track and the landscape might swallow you up. Every now and then the earth unexpectedly opens, like a great, hungry mouth, and devours whatever happens to be

'. . . a jacuzzi of volcanic proportions'. The Lady Knox (left) is the most spectacular of Waitupu's many geysers.

Wiki was our guide to Waitupu. Although half European, he regards himself as Maori, and his Maori ancestry is unmistakable. The question of identity is more complex, however, for his quarter-Maori son, who has inherited his European forebears' blue eyes and blond hair.

there. Only recently a house was gobbled up in this way.

We sit down with Wiki on what we hope is solid ground at a safe enough distance from the puffing geysers. It is evident from his bearing and his manner that Wiki, who describes himself as half-Maori, takes pride in his ancestry. Yet he is among a minority of Maoris who believe that the grievances of the native people should now be buried and forgotten. Wiki takes the unfashionable view that it is time for history to move on.

'The Maoris always seem to go to the Treaty of Waitangi,' he told us. 'I personally believe that the treaty should be scrapped and the whole issue of New Zealand politics reborn. I think the Maoris are treated more fairly than any other ethnic group in the world, I really do, and I think they should sort themselves out.' A moment or two after this brave speech he grins awkwardly. 'I'll probably get my head cut off for saying that.'

Wiki has first-hand experience of discrimination – although, ironically, not at the hands of the white population. His eleven-year-old son has inherited the European genes of his ancestors and is consequently blond-haired and blue-eyed. He could not look less like a traditional Maori and he knows it. As a small child he wanted to dye his hair black to be like his father. At school he is taunted by the dark-skinned children who call him *honky* and *maggot*, derisive terms for a white boy.

'He came home in tears,' recalled Wiki. 'His mother and I sat him down and told him that he is Maori and in any case to feel proud of what he is.'

Sir Peter nodded gravely. 'Let him know he has the support of a 76-year-old maggot with an Ethiopian great grandmother,' he said.

Left to our own devices we explored the thermal park, carefully sticking to the footpaths at all times. Sir Peter stared morosely into a mud pool which burped and spat at him. We found the antics of the pool amusing – its noise akin to a particularly violent manifestation of indigestion. Sir Peter, however, was not amused. He was suffering from a real bout of stomach ache and all my efforts to get him to say something humorous about the mud pools fell on deaf ears.

'To make this exciting for me I think you'd suddenly have to sight a periscope; a German, for a change, who didn't know the war was over,' he remarked, glumly.

Mud pools belch and bubble constantly into odd formations.

Beyond the call of duty: the two Foxes, cameraman Mike and assistant cameraman Matthew (below, with tripod) watch anxiously while sound recordist Mike Lax leans precariously into the vent to catch the sound of steam.

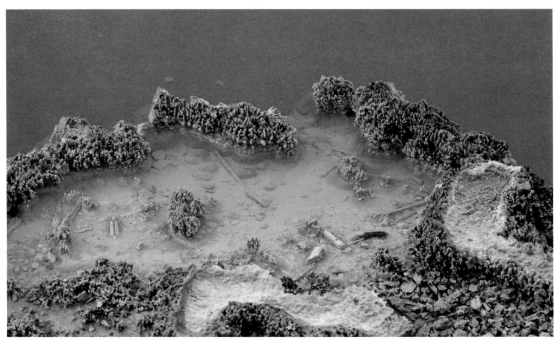

Wellington . . . It is a fine city and nobly situated. A busy place, and
full of life and movement. Have spent the three days partly in
walking about, partly in enjoying social privileges, and largely in
idling around the magnificent garden at Hutt, a little distance away,
around the shore.
MARK TWAIN, FOLLOWING THE EQUATOR

◆

WE LEFT ROTORUA on a wet and wintry morning, well wrapped up against the bitter south-easterly wind that whipped about us as we crossed the tarmac to board a small plane for the forty-five-minute flight to Wellington, the capital.

On arrival, a wheelchair was awaiting Sir Peter. 'How did you enjoy your flight?' said the airline lady as she steered him towards the terminal building.

'Very much,' he replied. 'Didn't see much, didn't feel much and slept quite soundly.'

A photographer from the local *Evening Post* was waiting to meet us. Sir Peter brandished his cane as he was propelled towards the camera, a flash bulb popping in his face. 'I'm in my war canoe,' he announced, using the cane as an oar. The presence of the local press wherever we filmed was to become a regular feature of the trip. Such is Sir Peter's renown in both New Zealand and Australia, having toured both countries in the past, that we became accustomed to impromptu press conferences in unlikely locations.

Our first stop in Wellington was the parliament building, where we were to meet the government chief whip, John Carter. He was amongst a number of people we would encounter – all, as it happens, involved in politics – for whom the temptation to assume an alter ego had proved irresistible. Two years previously, Carter had telephoned a local radio show and duped the host – fellow MP and Tourism Minister John Banks – into believing he was an unemployed Maori surviving on state benefits. 'I've been having a free trip all my life,' he declared provocatively before ringing off.

His idea of a joke did not amuse his government colleagues and he was swiftly relegated to the back benches in disgrace. Now, apparently rehabilitated, he has been given his old job back.

In the deserted parliamentary chamber, an elegant building filled with caramel wood and thick green carpet, he recalled his infamous radio broadcast.

'A lot of people weren't prepared to accept that a senior politician in the New Zealand parliament would be so uncouth as to take off an unemployed Maori,' he said.

Opposite: Sulphurous pools and hot volcanic rocks lend the Waitapu Thermal Park its unearthly yellow colours.

With novelist Fiona Kidman on the Massey Memorial. Despite the tales she told us of murder, mayhem and madness, she and Sir Peter are clearly having fun.

We tried very hard to get our hands on a tape of the offending broadcast but drew a complete blank, although we had the impression John Carter would not have minded in the least. Despite his fall from grace he remained cheerfully irreverent, his sombre suit set off with a tie emblazoned with the cartoon character Snoopy.

'While we do take things seriously and understand that politics is a serious business, we can often cope better if we apply some humour,' he said.

As we discovered, however, New Zealand's habitual humour is occasionally overshadowed by its dark side. It was during an encounter with the novelist Fiona Kidman, high on a hilltop overlooking Wellington, that we learned of the country's murderous history. On the reconnaissance trip the location for our meeting, with its uninterrupted views across the bay, had appeared ideal. However, on the appointed day for filming, it was cold and windy and we were, as ever, pressed for time. To reach the location, a memorial dedicated to the former New Zealand Prime Minister William Massey, we faced a steep climb up a difficult gravel path. I had arranged a wheelchair for Sir Peter and began pushing him up the slithery slope. It was quite a hike. When we finally reached the summit it was – in my case, at least – in a state of severe breathlessness.

Fiona Kidman, wrapped up against the elements, spoke of the grim passions which lurk beneath the surface of New Zealand society. Sir Peter expressed surprise. 'This seems to me such a moderate kind of country most of the time,' he said.

'There is quite a lot of passion left around in places,' said Fiona.

'Is there?'

'I think so. Some quite strange, dark passions actually. And I think it's reflected in some of the history we have.'

Like many settlers, Fiona Kidman's ancestors were lured to New Zealand by the promise of cheap land. They arrived with high expectations of prosperity and success, yet for many the reality was disappointment. 'We come from missionary stock,' she explained. 'From a race of people who expected to inherit the earth when they came here.'

The frustrations of the European immigrants have manifested themselves in some fairly gruesome killings over the years. 'We've done a lot of boiling up of bodies in back yards and so forth and chopping people up and shoving them in the burner. Quite innovative,' she told us. 'When I'm talking about a country I really love I find it difficult to have to contemplate this rather dark strain, but our writers write about it. Our novels are full of people who have had bleak, puritanical childhoods that have driven people to murder.'

Would-be emigrants, be warned.

There is nothing of the savage in the faces; nothing could be finer than these men's features, nothing more intellectual than these faces, nothing more masculine, nothing nobler than their aspect. The Aboriginals of Australia looked savage but these chiefs looked like Roman patricians. The tattooing in these portraits ought to suggest the savage, of course, but it does not. The designs are so flowing and graceful and beautiful that they are a most satisfactory decoration. It takes but fifteen minutes to get reconciled to the tattooing, and but fifteen more to perceive that it is just the thing. After that, the undecorated European face is unpleasant and ignoble.
MARK TWAIN, *FOLLOWING THE EQUATOR*

◆

WE MAKE OUR WAY across town to one of the poorer suburbs of Wellington, to watch a ritual which has been part of Maori culture for generations. The small house is packed with friends and relatives of Geoff Karena, a student and Maori activist whose face bears the traditional *Moko* – a swirling tattoo which stretches from his forehead to his chin. Only his cheeks remain unadorned, and he is about to remedy that.

Geoff, his long hair fastened in a ponytail and his face bearing the permanent expression of a warrior, leads his family in a formal prayer before submitting himself to the needle. Meanwhile, in the front room tattooist Rangi Skipper has set up a makeshift studio where he will complete the intricate *Moko* design. At one time the *Moko* was widely adopted by the Maori people – both men and women. It was an affirmation of identity as well as a sign of beauty. To the white settlers arriving in New Zealand, however, it was the mark of the savage. Yet Mark Twain, poring over a private collection of Maori portraits in Dunedin a century ago, recorded his admiration for the strength and character of these tattooed faces. Few whites shared his opinion, and the *Moko* gradually faded from fashion. Over the past hundred years it has lain dormant. Now it is enjoying a revival, principally among the young searching for a link with the cultural traditions of their ancestors.

The tattooing is undeniably impressive. The dark, brooding patterns which curl and swirl over the face are bold and arresting. But the effect is to fashion the face into that of the warrior. To wear the *Moko* is to send out a tough, challenging message to white society.

'Since the arrival of the Europeans it was seen as the most proactive statement of being Maori,' said Rangi. 'I suppose you can say now it's closely aligned with the Maori sovereignty movement.'

Rangi, whose own face is so far unmarked by tattoos – 'It will happen,' he tells us, 'I'm just fussy' – prepares to sketch the final elements of the Moko onto Geoff's cheeks. His pen moves steadily in a sweeping

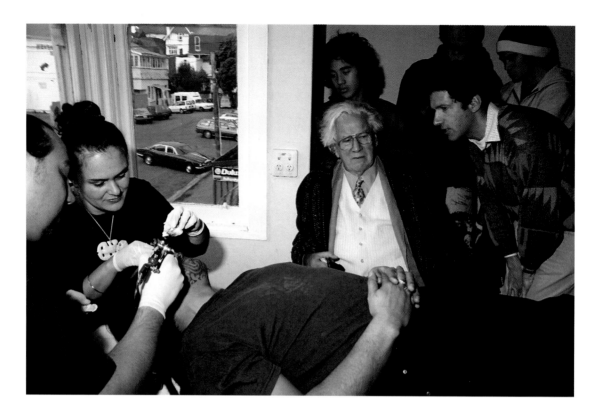

Sir Peter and I look on in fascination as Rangi tattoos the Moko onto Geoff's cheek.

curve from the side of the nose, out beneath the eye, and on towards the hairline. Each *Moko* is an individual and unique work. Rather like a fingerprint, no two are alike.

'When you sit down and talk with the person that's taking on the *Moko,* you try to find out who they are and what they're about,' Rangi explained. 'There will be particular things – like each individual always has something that they see as special to them, or something they have a particular interest in, and so you exploit those and explore them, and encapsulate them into the *Moko.*'

He asks Geoff to sit up so that he can make sure he is happy before committing the design to permanence. Sir Peter is curious. He admits to having shaved off his beard because he felt it made his face less expressive. Geoff, however, had no doubts about his facial tattoo.

'It's my right. My ancestors had the *Moko,* so it just follows that I should have one,' he says.

'Does having the *Moko* affect you at all?'

'Yeah – it means I won't be able to get a job,' says Geoff, to much laughter around the room.

Rangi slips on a pair of surgical gloves and prepares the needle, which makes an ominous buzzing sound. We all wince, although modern methods of applying the *Moko* are a lot less painful than those traditionally used. In the past, deep cuts were made in the skin before pigment was inserted. Serrated and flat blades were used to score the face. Sometimes these gashes were so extreme they went right through the flesh. There are reports of Maoris pausing to puff on a pipe midway through the *Moko* process, and smoke issuing through the open wounds in their cheeks. By comparison the tattooist's needle, for all it looks like a glinting instrument of torture, seems preferable.

Sir Peter spots a tattoo on Geoff's arm. It turns out to have been self-inflicted.

'You did it yourself?' he says, incredulous.

Rangi explains. 'Our people, when they're at school, if they're bored with the subject they grab the compass and . . .' His voice trails off. 'Very artistic group, the Maori people.'

Sir Peter tells him, 'It's an awful hint to the teacher that he's no good – everybody stabbing themselves with the compass.'

We watch, fascinated, as Rangi drags the needle across Geoff's face. Perhaps it sounds worse than it actually is, since Geoff appears remarkably composed. Rangi says, 'It's painful but not unbearable. You could liken it to a piece of broken glass being dragged across your skin.' We digest this piece of information. On reflection it probably is as bad as it looks. Geoff is simply being incredibly brave. Rangi adds, 'You usually come out of this feeling invincible.'

'Watching is different,' Sir Peter tells him. 'I feel I've been to the dentist and it's not over yet.'

The entire process takes just a few minutes. Geoff gets to his feet and goes to find a mirror. Staring back at him is the awesome sight of a warrior whose warpaint can never be erased. His features are masked by the swirling black *Moko*. Whatever his mood, he will forever project an image which to many is unambiguous in its aggression. It is quite a statement to make.

Rangi surveys his handiwork proudly. 'One of the problems he'll be facing from now on is women chasing after him, now I've made him more beautiful than he ever was.'

One of Geoff's sisters steps forward next. She has decided she also wants to have it done in order to express her Maoriness. It is a bold decision. Few women have the *Moko* and she appears nervous as she stretches out on the tattoist's bench.

'For me the most beautiful thing I could see is a woman taking on the *Moko*,' says Rangi as he sets to sketching a dainty scroll on her chin.

Her family gathers round, two sons on each side, gazing at her with extraordinary tenderness. There is something extremely touching in the sight of these streetwise youngsters quietly rallying round their mother, stroking her hands. She smiles bravely as Rangi begins his work. As the needle hums and the ink bleeds into the skin, one of the boys raises her hand to his lips and gently kisses it.

There is something reminiscent of a religious painting in the scene before us. The mother suffering, the children by her side. And the significance of the moment captured in all their faces.

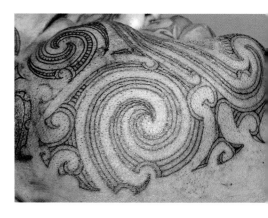

'A most satisfactory decoration'. Once complete, the Moko is a powerful and indelible statement of what it means to be Maori.

*When the vessel got out into the heavy seas and began to pitch and
wallow, the cavern prisoners became immediately sea-sick, and then the
peculiar results that ensued laid all my previous experiences of the kind
well away in the shade. And the wails, the groans, the cries, the shrieks,
the strange ejaculations – it was wonderful.*

MARK TWAIN, *FOLLOWING THE EQUATOR*

◆

IT WAS A FINE MORNING when we left Wellington on board the ferry to Picton, a small port on the north-east tip of New Zealand's South Island. Travelling with us was Sir Tipene O'Regan, a well-to-do businessman and leading campaigner for Maori rights.

Sir Tipene – half-Maori, half-Irish – lobbies relentlessly on behalf of his people. He has fought hard to restore land and fishing rights for his 30,000-strong tribe, the Ngai Tahu. Articulate, determined and genial, with just a hint of self-satisfaction, he has proved extremely effective. He was on his way to his tribal land at Kaikoura, a pretty coastal town situated on a small peninsula around a hundred miles north of Christchurch.

Sir Tipene O'Regan took great delight in pointing out landscape features which in Maori tradition are named for the various body parts they resemble.

According to Maori legend, the Kaikoura peninsula was where the god Mauo sat when he fished New Zealand's North Island out of the depths of the ocean. When Captain Cook sailed past the bay in *Endeavour* in February 1770, he noted in his journal that fifty-seven Maoris in four canoes had sailed towards him, but 'would not be prevail'd upon to put along side.'

Today Kaikoura is New Zealand's whale-watching capital. The deep waters just offshore with their abundance of food draw huge sperm whales. The area is also known for its crayfish. The Maori translation of Kaikoura is 'to eat crayfish'.

Sir Tipene was in buoyant mood. He was about to relay news of a multi-million dollar offer under which the New Zealand government would compensate the Ngai Tahu people for past wrongs relating to land. Not everyone is in favour of compensation, however. There are some for whom battling with the government has become a way of life. For them, money cannot obliterate the injustices perpetrated on their people.

As we passed through the narrow Cook Strait which separates the two main islands, Sir Tipene reflected on the importance of the sea to the Maori people. 'For us it is a god,' he said.

A century earlier Twain had also crossed these straits on an overnight ferry which would eventually take him further south to Lyttleton. His boat had been whipped about by a violent south-easterly gale and when he arrived at his destination he was slightly the worse for wear. Sir Tipene's grandfather – the Irish one – was among those who attended a reception the following evening where Twain, still feeling green, recounted his nightmare crossing.

In contrast our trip was briefer and uneventful. The sun shone and the sea was mercifully calm. We were able to relax and enjoy the view. Along the way, Sir Tipene pointed out various landmarks and explained their cultural significance. Frequently, the placenames adopted by the white settlers have proved wildly – even hilariously – at odds with those traditionally used by the local people.

'We have this famous mountain at Milford Sound down on the south island which is called Mitre Peak,' Sir Tipene told us. 'Its traditional name is nothing to do with a bishop's hat at all. To us the mountain actually represents the engorged penis of the god who created the land.

'It appealed to me that the English came along and started calling it after a bishop's hat. I look at the traditional name and think it has much more force and is capable of engaging the attention of more tourists, if only they knew.'

Sir Peter considered this for a moment. 'Absolutely, but one needs to keep the two apart, otherwise the bishop's mitre becomes a kind of condom, and that's really not what's expected . . .'

It wasn't just Mitre Peak which had earthier connotations for the Maoris. New Zealand is dotted with familiar landmarks named after some or other intimate part of an individual's anatomy. Personal place names were a means of staking a claim to a particular spot, explained Sir Tipene. 'Maoris have always tended to name land features after personal parts of their ancestors – their nose or ear or their genitals – because that was a way of claiming the land for your particular tribal group. So if it was a rock standing up in the water, and it was a valuable fishing rock, it would be named after the upstanding penis of a particular ancestor, and if you were to go and fish there without permission . . .'

'I wouldn't dream of it,' Sir Peter interjected.

'You wouldn't,' said Sir Tipene, 'but to take fish from there and eat it is, in Maori terms, like eating that particular part of someone's ancestor.'

We began to appreciate the effectiveness of the Maori system of laying claim to land.

'To many of us this region is not just beautiful, it's like a reference book to our past and our identity. I think that happens a lot with Maori people. But I think it's equally true that many *Pakeha* (white) people have been in this country long enough in cultural terms to also have

The Maori attitude to sexuality is refreshingly earthy and uninhibited.

that same identity with place,' said Sir Tipene.

'We're looking at a landscape which is in many ways a sort of memorial to our history. Every place name tells another set of stories.'

At Picton we left the ferry and boarded the Coastal Pacific Railway for Kaikoura – no mean feat with twenty-nine pieces of luggage. As we headed south along a rocky coastline Sir Tipene pointed out the cliffs which mark the point at which we would cross the border into his tribal homelands. For five generations his tribe has been battling with the government over land and fishing rights. They first filed a claim back in 1848 and have been engaged in a legal dispute ever since. The settlement he is on his way to present to them is worth around NZ$170 million (about £68 million). It sounds like a vast sum of money, but the Ngai Tahu will have to do some complicated calculations before deciding whether to accept. 'There is certainly an element of our people who don't want to know about settlements', confirmed Sir Tepene 'No amount of money would be satisfactory, because the grievance itself is more precious. It is part of their character, their identity.'

Money in itself, then, is not necessarily a means to an end. There is a delicate balancing act to be done on both sides. After a 150-year battle the Maoris are anxious not to feel they have sold out, while the Government is at pains to ensure they make a fair, although not overly generous, settlement.

On arrival in Kaikoura that night we approach the *marae* (ritual hall) with Sir Tipene for the first in a series of roadshows at which he will address the community and hear their concerns. We walk in slow procession towards the building as his youngest daughter, a striking figure with short, cropped hair, sings a traditional Maori greeting. At some point the tribe will be polled on whether to accept the proposed government settlement, but before then they have some weighty matters to consider. Do they feel they can handle such a large sum of money? Will they make wise investments? Can they guarantee their settlement will grow rather than be whittled away by bad management?

'We've got to do it very, very well and I think it's very difficult,' said Sir Tipene, citing the Alaskans as a sobering example of how things can go easily and rapidly wrong. Seven years after receiving US$13 billion from the US Government they had managed to lose practically everything.

His audience appears anxious. 'Do you honestly think we would be able to develop a skill base that could cope with a hundred-and-seventy-million dollar settlement?' asks one.

'There are no guarantees we won't lose it,' Sir Tipene replies. 'But I think we'd have to be pretty dumb to lose the core capital.'

Despite their concerns, one man sees the money as an opportunity to take control of their own lives. 'We can truly be agents of change, architects of our own destiny,' he says.

As we had already discovered from Dame Augusta at the Waitangi Tribunal hearing in Kaipara, there is a body of opinion – the so-called Rednecks – which resents the huge settlements being made to New Zealand's Maoris. Having spent time with the Maoris, however, it was hard not to accept their point of view and their need to right the wrongs of the past. Some weeks earlier my colleague Pratap Rughani and I had met with Sir Tipene south of Kaikoura. He was working with young Maoris, training them in leadership skills. We spent the night in a *marae* with them, all of us – Sir Tipene included – in our sleeping bags on the floor. It was like being in a particularly raucous dormitory. As the lights went out at the end of a long day all I wanted to do was sleep, but in the darkness, someone started telling jokes – many politically incorrect, most filthy. Suddenly the gags were flying, and in no time at all the building was practically shaking with laughter. It was not the kind of thing you could sleep through. Their infectious hysteria had caught me too.

Next morning I was up early to watch the sun rise over a calm, flat bay and reflect on the extraordinary qualities of New Zealand and its native people.

The fluid swirls and spirals that distinguish the Moko are a recurring and distinctive theme in Maori art.

Perfect summer weather. Large school of whales in the distance. Nothing could be daintier than the puffs of vapor they spout up, when seen against the pink glory of the sinking sun, or against the dark mass of an island reposing in the deep blue shadow of a storm cloud.
MARK TWAIN, FOLLOWING THE EQUATOR

It was porpoises, porpoises aglow with phosphorescent light. They presently collected in a wild and magnificent jumble under the bows, and there they played for an hour, leaping and frollicking and carrying on, turning summersaults in front of the stern or across it and never getting hit, never making a miscalculation, though the stern missed them only about an inch, as a rule.
MARK TWAIN, FOLLOWING THE EQUATOR

◆

The full force of the Southern Ocean breaks uninterrupted onto Kaikoura's sweeping shore.

IT WAS NOT THE WEATHER for whale-watching. Great squally winds howled across the peninsula. The sea had turned an uninviting shade of grey. At the local Whale Watch headquarters all boat trips had been cancelled. For three days we hoped for a breakthrough, but the sea remained choppy and the wind refused to drop. Sir Peter telephoned Whale Watch at regular intervals but the message was always the same; it

was too rough to take out a boat. Looking at the ill-tempered ocean we were almost grateful.

Just the previous evening the weather had appeared more promising. We had ventured into the hills for a view overlooking the town and the bay. In front of us lay rolling green fields, sheep grazing contentedly under a sinking sun which cast a soft orange glow over the magical landscape. Exactly how one imagines New Zealand to be. Even though we all felt weary, the spectacular vista before us succeeded in raising our spirits. As we stood on the hillside our attention was drawn to two bleating lambs, trapped in a small pen. They appeared pathetic and in need of help. We had no way of knowing whether the farmer had put them there for a reason or if they had accidentally got stuck. We hesitated, five grown men, sorely tempted to go to their rescue, but with visions of being pursued down the hill by an angry stockman. In the end we decided with some misgivings to leave well alone.

Although Kaikoura is a tiny place it attracts thousands of tourists each year. They all come to see the whales, which come closer to the shore here than anywhere else in the world. Whale watching was started by four Maori families in the early 1980s and has since become the most successful business there. On a good day, when conditions are favourable, it is possible to manoeuvre a small craft close to these massive forty-ton creatures.

We were not having a good day. There was one more option open to us. I decided to charter a light plane and see if the whales could be spotted from the air.

'I'm rather glad we can't take a boat,' Sir Peter admitted. 'First of all, it's very rough and I can't predict my behaviour on board and, secondly, I am told that sperm whales have a powerful air spout which is irresistable to female whales but deeply repellent to the human nostril.'

We arrived at the airstrip just as the plane was unloading a party of Japanese schoolchildren. No whales had been sighted, but they appeared happy enough anyway, posing for a group photo with the flight crew. Our pilot warned us that conditions were far from ideal. 'We probably have a fifty-fifty chance,' he said. 'Cross your fingers.'

Once airborne all we were able to see was a vast ocean dotted with peaks of white foam. The plane bumped and pitched, and we began to feel very woozy. We flew down the coast, scanning the water for tell-tale water spouts, seeing nothing even vaguely promising. 'What we're actually looking for is the sperm whale, a brown kind of log shape in the water,' announced the pilot. 'Once we are close to it you will actually be able to see the spout, but with the wind conditions here today the spout will only rise about a metre, a metre and a half maximum.'

The odds were stacked against us. Sperm whales spend most of their time underwater hunting for food, surfacing only for five to ten minutes at a time. If there were any whales we couldn't spot them. It was a far

Huge ocean-going sperm whales swim closer to the coast off Kaikoura than anywhere else in the world.

cry from a reconnaissance trip I'd made to Kaikoura a few weeks earlier, when conditions were perfect, and I had not only seen several whales but had also joined a boat trip into the bay to swim with dolphins. It was the most extraordinary experience. Suddenly our boat was right in the middle of a school of more than a hundred of these amazing creatures. I leapt overboard as they flashed by at great speed. Quite what they made of us in our wetsuits and snorkels we can only imagine, although we seemed to arouse their curiosity. I dived under and found myself staring into the face of a dolphin which fixed me with an amused expression. It seemed to be waiting for me to do something so I flipped over in a somersault. It mimicked me, performing an identical manoeuvre, but with considerably more grace. It was actually playing with me.

When the dolphins finally moved on and we returned to the boat, it was with a sense of having experienced something rare, precious and wonderful.

Our pilot made an announcement as he banked the aircraft low over the peninsula one last time. 'It looks like the whales aren't co-operating today. Maybe we'll have better luck tomorrow.' By then, of course, we would be on our way to Sydney.

Back at the airstrip Sir Peter addressed the camera and barked in a thick German accent: 'Well gentlemen, this is an historic day in the history of the Third Reich. Since Professor Waldman gave us a brilliant idea of disguising our U-boats as whales so the spout comes up through the periscope, not one has been identified from the air.'

With that he turned on his heel and goose-stepped away.

A TWO-HOUR DRIVE to Christchurch for our flight to Sydney. At the Air New Zealand check-in desk Sir Peter studied the immigration departure card. 'I suppose you get arrested for fibbing,' he said, a frown creasing his brow.

'*Occupation or job . . .*' he said, reading aloud from the card.

'Good heavens. *Never married, now married, widowed, separated or divorced,*' he mused. 'You have to think so hard about these things. *What is or was your address in New Zealand?* We've been travelling around – I don't know what that would be.

'*How long will you be away from New Zealand?*' He shook his head.

'*Which country will you next live in for twelve months or more?* How can you tell?'

He slipped the card into the back of his passport. 'It's getting worse and worse,' he said. 'The British passport has nothing in it at all about your occupation or job. They don't care what you do so long as you don't stay more than ten minutes.'

It was with some sadness that we prepared to leave New Zealand after a stay of ten days. There is something extremely seductive about this tiny country, so far removed from the rest of the world. Perhaps it is the unspoiled quality of the landscape, the sense that it is too far away from everything to ever become polluted. Or perhaps it is the directness of the people. New Zealanders are charmingly lacking in airs and graces.

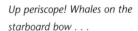
Up periscope! Whales on the starboard bow . . .

AUSTRALIA

*We entered and cast anchor, and in the morning went oh-ing and ah-ing
in admiration up through the crooks and turns of the spacious and
beautiful harbor – a harbor which is the darling of Sydney and the
wonder of the world.*
MARK TWAIN, FOLLOWING THE EQUATOR

◆

SATURDAY MORNING. Arrived in Sydney and went straight to the
Park Hyatt Hotel. Fantastic location overlooking the harbour. Every few
minutes I found myself staring out of my window at the Opera House,
almost hypnotised by this masterpiece of twentieth-century
architecture. It was our first day off since beginning the New Zealand
shoot and we were all pretty exhausted. I spent the morning trying to
make sense of my expenses – which comprised a jumble of bills and
receipts in a confusing combination of currencies – before heading off
to make sure Sir Peter had settled in.

He showed me into his suite. I must have been looking somewhat
more worn out than I had imagined, as he greeted me with a note of
concern. 'You must get some rest,' he said sternly. 'You're going to need
it more than any of us.'

The suite with its commanding view across the harbour was
impressively grand. It even had its own butler, which the hotel no doubt
considered a bonus. However, the benefits of having a butler, who was
maddeningly efficient, had already begun to wear dangerously thin.
Anything left lying around was instantly tidied away. After just a few
hours of this Sir Peter no longer knew where to find anything. He was
practically tearing his hair out. To find even a pair of clean socks would
have required both determination and an element of luck. Worse still,
his precious copy of *Le Monde* had been thrown away before he had
had a chance to read it. It was clear he did not find such feverish and
obsessive neatness at all endearing. As I was leaving he muttered, 'And if
you see the butler on the way out, trip him up!'

After the chill air of New Zealand, Sydney was pleasantly warm. We sat
in the sunshine with the Opera House behind us in the company of the
writer Thomas Keneally, whose novel *Schindler's Ark* inspired the film,
Schindler's List.

Keneally is proud of the way in which his country has grown.
'Australians are in many ways the dregs of Europe,' he tells us, adding
that he himself has convict ancestry. 'It's quite a triumph, having come

from such humble roots, that we have managed to somehow produce all this.' He gestures across the harbour. 'That glorious Opera House over there ... Having begun as a penal colony only a little over two hundred years ago, there is a certain raw energy, raw hope, and informal sophistication to Sydney.'

According to Thomas Keneally, as Australians prepare for the millennium they are wrestling with their sense of place in the world. The close proximity to Asia means stronger trade and diplomatic ties will inevitably develop with that continent. 'Some people are very daunted by coming to terms with our new geographic reality and others are excited by it. I think I belong to the excited hemisphere of the Australian soul,' he says.

Sir Peter nods in agreement. 'It's abundantly clear you can't put an outboard motor on a country and take it somewhere else. You're stuck with where you are.'

Thomas Keneally discusses what goes to make up the Australian soul against a backdrop of Sydney Harbour Bridge.

There is no doubt, says Keneally, that Australia is getting less and less British. He believes the country must soon become a republic.

'We will still be members of the Commonwealth,' he says. 'And we are still willing at regular intervals to humiliate English cricket captains

with the same degree of contemptuous fraternity which operates at the moment!'

However, even in Sydney it is still possible to find the odd monarchist – if you know where to look. And we did. We were anxious to track down a local councillor by the name of Godfrey Bigot, whose reputation for irreverence and outrageous humour had made him something of a minor celebrity. Bigot is not his real name, although he has since adopted it legally by deed poll. In another life he was plain Brad Pedersen. Then he decided to send up Australian politics by standing for election under his new, controversial identity. The amazing thing is that he was elected to a local council.

'I believe he is an attempt to show that political power is fundamentally absurd,' said Thomas Keneally.

Sir Peter was impressed. 'There are characters like that in England, but they never get in, that's the extraordinary thing. They keep losing their deposits at every election,' he said. 'I think the British are still formal enough to consider politics, however corrupt, to be sacrosanct and not to be laughed at too much.'

'I think you would find him enlightening,' Keneally told us. 'His very adoption of the word bigot is whimsy. He is sending up those who are bigoted.'

◆

It seems to me that the occupation of Unbiased Traveler Seeking Information is the pleasantest and most irresponsible trade there is. The traveler can always find out anything he wants to, merely by asking. He can get all the facts, and more. Everybody helps him, nobody hinders him.
MARK TWAIN, FOLLOWING THE EQUATOR

◆

Our search for Godfrey Bigot took us by ferry to Manly, a suburb thus named by the first sailors to land there, after the muscular prowess of its (male) natives. Councillor Bigot was, in theory, to be found at the Town Hall of Manly, which lies on the other side of one of the most spectacular waterways in the world, Sydney Harbour.

Once on board the ferry, Sir Peter settled himself opposite an elderly lady. 'You'll see more if you sit here,' she said, indicating the empty seat beside her. Sir Peter, followed by the film crew, obediently moved. She glanced at the great furry object which sound recordist Mike Lax had thrust in front of Sir Peter. 'What's that?'

'It's a microphone,' he told her. 'It used to be a small dog.'

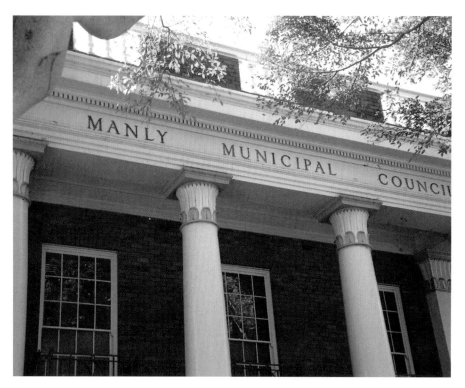

The imposing frontage of Manly Municipal Council, where Brad Pederson's alter ego, Godfrey Bigot, found himself unexpectedly elected to office.

Next the camera caught her eye. 'Why are they taking your photo?'

'We're doing a television programme about Mark Twain who came this way one hundred years ago. We're just seeing how much of the world has changed since then.'

'Oh, that's good, isn't it?'

'I think so,' Sir Peter said.

His newfound friend, June, was not in the least perturbed by the presence of the crew. She was on her way to Manly to visit her brother, a local bank manager. Throughout the short crossing she continued to engage Sir Peter on a number of unrelated topics from talking budgerigars to football. This surreal conversation was to set the tone for what happened next.

Once in Manly I explained to Sir Peter what I wanted him to do. It involved approaching strangers in the street in the style of Twain's Unbiased Traveler Seeking Information, and eliciting opinions on Councillor Bigot. In television these spontaneous interviews are called vox pops. They are normally undertaken by reporters on local news programmes canvassing opinion on anything from soccer to Shakespeare. As far as I know, it is unheard of to ask a knighted, Oscar-winning actor to do vox pops. Sportingly, Sir Peter agreed to have a go.

He hung around outside Liquorland on Manly's main street, looking for suitable subjects.

'Excuse me, Sir,' he began, approaching a man who ignored him and walked briskly on. As he cast about for another victim, a fan approached and requested an autograph.

'Do you know Councillor Bigot?' The fan, an Argentinian called Hugo, shook his head.

Sir Peter then caught the eye of a man in a flat cap and dark glasses. 'Do you know Councillor Bigot?'

'Only by repute. I think he's an excruciating bore,' came the reply.

And so it went on. I urged him to tackle an elderly woman, who beat a hasty retreat as soon as she detected his approach.

'If I ask her I shall be done for harassment,' he complained.

Another man cheerfully gave his view of Councillor Bigot, praising his bizarre plan to straighten Australia's coastline. 'He has novel, revolutionary ideas,' he told us.

By now Sir Peter was no doubt wishing he was back on the set of a movie – any movie – where he would be allowed to rest comfortably in his trailer until it was time to deliver his great oration, after which a chauffeur-driven limousine would whisk him away.

We dodged into a bookshop where the staff were able to provide more insights into the character of Councillor Bigot. 'Very amusing,' said one. 'Extremely flamboyant, a rebel,' said another. They directed us to the council chamber, having first admitted with some embarrassment that they had none of Sir Peter's novels in stock.

At the offices of Manly Council an official showed us into the deserted chamber where Godfrey Bigot's seat was identified by a formal plaque bearing his name. 'Where will we find him?' said Sir Peter.

'I should try his favourite restaurant,' advised the official. In the end, that was indeed where we found the elusive councillor.

I had met Godfrey Bigot once before, on my reconnaissance trip to Australia. Since I was short of time (the usual story), I had arranged to meet him outside a fast food restaurant in the ferry terminal at Manly. All I had to go on was the description he had given me in our brief telephone conversation, during which he had alternated confusingly between Bigot and his alter ego, Brad Pedersen. Arriving at the terminal, I approached two people who roughly fitted the description I had – tall

Brad Pederson plays the unlikely role of Godfrey Bigot to absolute perfection.

and fair, thirty-something. A few yards away Brad Pedersen watched, amused, as I rushed about accosting the wrong people. Finally, he introduced himself and put me out of my misery.

He turned out to be engaging and charming, with an outrageous sense of humour. Wholly irreverent. For all his outspoken right-wing views in the guise of Councillor Bigot, the real Brad Pedersen leaned discernibly to the left. However, on the day we filmed, Brad Pedersen was firmly in Bigot mode. His alter ego had been left safely at home.

Godfrey Bigot is without doubt one of the most reactionary politicians in Australia today. What's more he's proud of his record. He has campaigned vociferously in favour of nuclear energy and atomic weapons. He is unashamedly racist and a fanatical monarchist. He finds vegetarians and republicans equally subversive. Among his hobbies he lists shooting koalas. More than anything he would like to straighten out Australia's wavy coastline, since 'bent beaches are the worst thing for development.' He modestly describes himself as a 'moral beacon'. In real life Brad Pedersen is a nice bloke. In the guise of Godfrey Bigot – 'just call me God' – he is a monster. It was in 1994 that he decided to send up Australian politics by transforming himself into a savage caricature of a right-wing extremist. In the tradition of the British Monster Raving Loony Party he then stood for election. The Australian voters loved him. So much so he polled eighteen per cent of the vote and won a seat on the local council. Quite what that says about the Australian electorate is open to interpretation.

We found him in truculent mood. With his hair darkened and combed to one side in the style favoured by Hitler, he bore no resemblance to the blond, good-humoured bloke I'd met some weeks earlier. He eyed Sir Peter with an expression of undisguised suspicion.

'Ustinov, eh?' he said with a sneer. 'Sounds a bit foreign to me.'

'Yes, pretty foreign,' Sir Peter agreed. 'Pretty foreign everywhere.'

A waiter appeared with tea. Councillor Bigot waved him away. 'I ordered coffee,' he snapped.

Godfrey Bigot plays the part of right-wing extremist with great conviction. Not once did he allow his mask to slip as Sir Peter engaged him on a number of controversial topics. First, Sir Peter broached the subject of immigration. 'Where do you draw the line – you want no foreigners, no Asiatics?'

Councillor Bigot sucked on an unlit cigar which dangled from his lips. 'People often ask me if I'm racist and I say absolutely and unequivocally yes. The problem with these Asians is they're funny looking. And you know why they're funny looking . . .' He paused. Sir Peter appeared perplexed. 'Because they look funny at you?' he ventured.

Councillor Bigot shook his head. 'It's because they're no good. And you know why they're no good? Because they're funny looking.' He sat back in his chair looking pleased with himself. 'That may have a bit of a circular logic to it but if you don't think about it too much it makes a whole lot of sense.'

The waiter returned with a tray of coffee. Councillor Bigot sent it back. 'I ordered tea.'

Sir Peter pressed on. What about Australia's Aboriginals?

'What about them?'

'They were welcoming enough when you arrived.'

'Well, I've always disputed that,' said the councillor. 'I mean I think we were here first. We discovered the place. They came later, that's my view.'

Much of Godfrey Bigot's humour is directed at the Federal MP Pauline Hanson, a champion of the ultra conservative right. Ms Hanson presents herself as a patriot campaigning for equality on behalf of all Australians. She regards the country's Aboriginals as an advantaged minority. It is a long-standing joke that Councillor Bigot and Pauline Hanson are an item.

'I would love to hear about her because I may have to meet her,' said Sir Peter.

'You know, I must say she makes me one proud bigot. I mean, I think she's poised to go global, I really do.'

'Really?'

'I think if we put the right spin on this, Pete, she can be bigger than even the yo-yo. I think we can make a packet.'

Sir Peter nodded. A waiter appeared with tea and was sent away again. 'I wanted coffee,' grumbled Councillor Bigot.

'Do you change your mind very often politically?' inquired Sir Peter.

'No. I don't agree with changing your mind. I mean I've come into this world with a pretty good fixed set of ideas and I've never seen any reason to change any of them.'

Sir Peter remained tactfully silent.

A thought suddenly occurred to the councillor. 'Someone told me you'd been knighted, is that right?'

'Yes, a long time ago now.'

'How much did that cost?'

'Oh, it was extraordinarily cheap. It was just a matter of a tip or two.'

For a fleeting moment an avaricious glint appeared in Godfrey Bigot's eyes. *Sir* Godfrey perhaps, knighted for his services to politics. This being Australia, anything is possible.

◆

AFTER OUR ENCOUNTER with Godfrey Bigot we were looking forward to meeting the MP Pauline Hanson and hearing the views of a politician who takes her right-wing ideals seriously. It took much negotiation with her Press Officer David Oldfield – who happens to serve on Manly Council alongside Godfrey Bigot – before we were granted access. Pauline Hanson has had enough bad press in her time to be cautious about granting interviews. In the end because of tight schedules on both sides we arranged to meet in the VIP lounge at Sydney Airport, where the MP agreed to make a brief stopover en route from Canberra to Brisbane.

In the two years since she first became an MP Pauline Hanson has swiftly established herself as Australia's most controversial politician.

In the short time that Pauline Hanson has served as an MP – she was elected to office at the 1996 election – she has become an extremely controversial figure. She draws much of the support for her One Nation party from poor, white Australians opposed to immigration and what they regard as preferential treatment for the Aboriginals.

The very views which got her elected have also drawn virulent criticism. She is more than merely a target for satirists like Godfrey Bigot. She has also been on the receiving end of death threats. Now, wherever she goes, there is a visible security presence with her. When she arrived for our interview she was flanked by three security people, two men and a woman. As she rather proudly told us, only two other public figures in Australia rate that level of permanent protection – the Prime Minister and the Israeli Ambassador.

Although Pauline Hanson is accustomed to broadcasters, she appeared nervous as she faced Sir Peter, perhaps because he was such a departure from the news and current affairs interviewers she habitually encounters. Sir Peter was his usual courteous self, but found precious little common ground with the MP. She told him, 'I'm proud of Australia, and that's why I wanted to be an Australian politician, so that I can represent my country to the best of my ability. It's only because I saw this country going down the drain, as many millions of other Australians did, that I felt we needed to review the direction we're headed in.'

Pauline Hanson promotes a policy of equality for all which takes no account of the particular needs of Australia's original inhabitants. Indeed, she believes that the Aboriginal people are privileged. The fact that certain government departments target Aboriginals when they advertise job vacancies infuriates her. And she cites other examples such as free health checks, cheap housing loans and free legal advice, which can be available to the Aboriginal community.

'A lot of benefits are given to them which are clearly based on race alone,' she said. 'Does the fact that you're an Aboriginal give you a monopoly on being disadvantaged? I don't think so.'

On the question of immigration Pauline Hanson is clear – no more immigrants until unemployment in Australia is brought down. And then she favours a policy of screening which would exclude criminals – ironic, since modern Australia started life as a penal colony – and anyone likely to be dependent on the welfare system.

And she seems particularly antipathetic to Australia's Asian community. 'I'm Australian, very proud of it, as a lot of other Australians are,' she said. 'I'm proud of my heritage and the culture on which this country was based. I have no problem with people who want to come here but, please, come here to be one of us – to become Australian.'

'Not to be unemployed,' said Sir Peter. 'Not to add to those figures?'

'Not to be unemployed,' said Pauline Hanson, 'and not to want to split this country into a multi-national country. We are Australian.'

Sir Peter listened patiently but remained utterly unconvinced. 'I am of too mixed blood to take patriotism very seriously,' he told her. 'I'm very aware of Dr Johnson who said, *Patriotism, Sir, is the last refuge of the scoundrel*, which was very modern for his time.'

We watched as Pauline Hanson, an elegant figure in a bright pink suit, departed for her flight to Brisbane, her bodyguards in formation around her. Sir Peter turned and, with a wicked glint in his eye, said, 'Now what do you make of that?'

Melbourne spreads around over an immense area of ground. It is a stately city architecturally as well as in magnitude. It has an elaborate system of cable-car services; it has museums, and colleges, and schools, and public gardens, and electricity and gas, and libraries, and theaters, and mining centers, and wool centers, and centers of the arts and sciences, and boards of trade, and ships, and railroads, and a harbor, and social clubs, and a squatter club sumptuously housed and appointed, and as many churches and banks as can make a living.
MARK TWAIN, FOLLOWING THE EQUATOR

◆

IN MELBOURNE WE SPENT a night at the Crown Hotel which, with its attached casino and thirty-five restaurants, takes up an entire block. The Crown was designed to appeal to the gambling crowd. Several floors of the building are given over to enormous luxury suites which cannot be booked. They are for the exclusive – and complimentary – use of the high rollers. Gamblers, mainly wealthy Asians, willing to spend a small fortune on the tables.

By chance we had arrived in Melbourne as the city geared up for a major media event – the opening of a new Planet Hollywood restaurant. Sir Peter was put on a celebrity guest list topped by the actor Sylvester Stallone. Planet Hollywood's publicity machine has perfected the art of generating enormous attention wherever it goes, and Melbourne was no different. The streets around the restaurant had been cordoned off. Crush barriers had been erected along the pavements. Security people in Planet Hollywood tee-shirts paraded about with walkie-talkies. It was a ludicrous amount of razzamatazz, orchestrated with military precision.

We set off for the restaurant in a white stretch limousine with police outriders – blue lights flashing, sirens wailing – alongside. All this for a journey of a few hundred yards. Sir Peter, no great fan of American hype, was apprehensive. Given the choice he would no doubt have preferred a quiet evening in. 'Planet Hollywood,' he said. 'I speak with emotion, being a refugee from Planet Hollywood, a political refugee as much as anything. I've taken sanctuary in places like Kiribati and Fiji, where they still feed on hamburgers made of missionary.'

Spotting a truck at the side of the road, he quipped, 'I think that's Stallone's arrival. I can see a punch-bag inside, which is the kind of architectural feature he would certainly appreciate.' Moments later Sir Peter was mimicking the slow drawl made famous by the star of *Rocky* and its four sequels. 'Hit me,' he instructed cameraman Mike Fox. 'Huh, ya think that hurts?'

The limousine pulled up and we all got out. A man with an umbrella was waiting to shield Sir Peter from the drizzle. Mistakenly, we thought we had arrived at the restaurant, but it was still some way off. A red carpet stretched endlessly before us. We progressed along it slowly as local TV crews clamoured for soundbites. Although we had agreed with the Planet Hollywood people that there would be no lengthy interviews, inevitably, Sir Peter was sucked into the publicity machine before there was time to object.

All this was on the same day that news of the death of Princess Diana had broken. That morning I had sat in my hotel room watching in shock and disbelief as the story of the crash on the other side of the world had unfolded on CNN. The actor Tom Cruise was moved to ring in and protest at the way the paparazzi hound the famous. None of us was in much of a mood to celebrate.

The tragedy had sent the organisers of the Planet Hollywood bash into a spin. They had deliberated about cancelling but in the end decided to go ahead after observing a minute's silence for the Princess. On a small, makeshift stage under the blaze of TV lights and with an audience of teenagers hanging over the crush barriers beneath him, Sir Peter was asked to say a few words about Diana.

'I knew her, but only very briefly, and she certainly made her own way through a particularly dense jungle and made her mark,' he said. 'She had an extraordinary personality, which was troubling at times, but she didn't obey any of the rules, and therefore changed the monarchy in a way.'

As we continued along several hundred yards more of red carpet to the restaurant entrance, Sir Peter was stopped by reporters every few steps. The teenage girls at the front of the barriers screamed obligingly every time they thought they might be caught on camera. We pressed on, wondering how many of these youngsters even knew who the distinguished gentleman passing before them actually was. The whole thing was a mad and chaotic circus, carefully stage-managed to be just that, to give a sense of excitement about nothing.

When we finally made it into Planet Hollywood itself it was of course an anti-climax. Lots of people trying to look glamorous, drinking sparkling wine and shouting above a ludicrous musical din in a vain attempt to make themselves heard. It was not the kind of party any of us enjoyed. I looked at Sir Peter and knew that the only way of salvaging the evening was to leave at once, preferably by a side entrance. We slipped away, just as Sylvester Stallone was arriving. At least we think it was Stallone. We didn't actually stay long enough to see him.

These were wonderful people, the natives. They ought not to have been wasted. They should have been crossed with the Whites. It would have improved the Whites and done the Natives no harm.
MARK TWAIN, FOLLOWING THE EQUATOR

◆

WE LEFT MELBOURNE at dusk the following day on board a giant ferry bound for Tasmania. It was to be an overnight crossing. Almost all the other passengers were driving and we watched a smooth procession of vehicles vanish into the bowels of the ship. For us, foot passengers with an absurd amount of luggage on the quayside, boarding was a trickier affair. Along with all our filming equipment was a small mountain of personal baggage. Sir Peter and Lady Ustinov, who had joined us for the ten-day shoot in Australia, are not accustomed to travelling light. Between them they had seven suitcases, her four all in matching Louis Vuitton. I teased her mercilessly and she took it in good humour. Miraculously, they managed to fit the whole lot into their tiny cabin.

As our vessel, the *Spirit of Tasmania*, began to ease out to sea I went to find Sir Peter. I had an idea about filming him up on the bridge as Melbourne, its darkening skyline dotted with twinkling lights, faded into the distance. Lady Ustinov appeared at the cabin door to tell me her husband was sleeping. I think she had come to regard me as a well-intentioned slave-driver. When we were filming in Honolulu some weeks previously, she had remarked in her charming French accent, 'Michael, I hope you are not trying to kill my husband.' Remembering this, I decided it would be wise to allow Sir Peter his rest. 'I think that is a very good idea,' said Lady Ustinov, politely closing the cabin door on me.

During winter the crossings can be rough and unpleasant, but we were fortunate. The sea was calm as we approached the notorious Bass Strait through which shipping has to pass to reach Devonport on Tasmania's north coast. In the early morning half-light as we eased through the narrow, awkward channel, the sight of the giant ship towering above miniature rows of houses along the shore proved awesome. It sailed ponderously towards its berth, casting a shadow over the neat suburban landscape.

At one point there seemed hardly any clearance either side of the hull. When the weather is bad in this infamous channel, docking is not for the faint-hearted.

'Ninety per cent of the time the Bass Strait is pretty well like you've got it now, calm. But ten per cent of the time it can be one of the wildest and roughest places you can imagine,' the Captain said. 'You

can't believe that this same place can suddenly have five- and six- metre swells.'

We were anxious not to distract him. When Twain had sailed from Vancouver for Sydney a century earlier, his captain was on his final journey and in disgrace. In *Following the Equator* he wrote, 'He had had the ill-luck to lose his bearings and get his ship on the rocks. A matter like this would rank merely as an error with you and me; it ranks as a crime with the directors of steamship companies.'

Fortunately, our captain proved expert at squeezing us into Devonport without incident.

As we left the ship we realised a welcoming party was waiting to greet us. Three local Tasmanian TV crews and a dozen reporters and photographers crowded round Sir Peter. We hastily set up an informal press conference in the cafe at the terminal. As Sir Peter answered questions, Lady Ustinov, splendid in a purple coat and bright green snakeskin handbag, settled herself happily away from the action on a plastic seat with a cup of bad coffee and an old copy of *Le Monde*.

Squeezing into Devonport. So narrow is the channel here that from up on the bridge only land is visible on either side of the ship. The tension of this tight manouevre shows clearly on the faces of the captain (on the left, above) and his crew.

Afterwards, one of the local TV crews took pleasure in filming us as we struggled to load the Louis Vuitton luggage into the back of our vehicle. 'Do you always travel this light?' said the reporter.

'No comment,' I smiled, slamming the back door shut.

Impromptu press conferences had a tendency to pop up wherever we went.

'The Natives . . . sat homesick on their alien crags, and day by day gazed out through their tears over the sea with unappeasable longing towards the hazy bulk which was the specter of what had been their paradise; one by one their hearts broke and they died.'
MARK TWAIN, FOLLOWING THE EQUATOR

WE WERE ON OUR WAY to meet up with Michael Mansell, a lawyer and a Tasmanian Aboriginal. To be a Tasmanian Aboriginal is in itself controversial, since the entire indigenous population of the island was thought to have died out more than a century ago, wiped out in a series of terrible massacres by the British. When Twain visited Tasmania he wrote about the last surviving Aboriginal, a woman named Truganini, who died in 1876. Indeed her picture, captioned 'The Last of Her Race', appears in *Following the Equator.*

The tragedy of Truganini is that she spent the last few years of her life as a curiosity, an example of a people about to become extinct. Consequently, she lived in fear of what would become of her body after her death, insisting she should be cremated and her ashes scattered over her old tribal area. In defiance of her wishes her skeleton was preserved and displayed in a museum in Oxford. It took a hundred years for her remains to be rescued and for the cremation she had requested to take place. Finally, her ashes were scattered at Oyster Cove, a secluded spot not far from Hobart, the Tasmanian capital. Only then did the Aboriginal people accept that her spirit was finally at peace.

Despite the tale of Truganini there are plenty of Aboriginals left in Tasmania. They are of mixed race, that's all.

I had first encountered Michael Mansell at an international convention on reconciliation in Melbourne some weeks before. It was during a reconnaissance trip and I had flown straight from Fiji to attend the conference, not entirely sure what to expect once I got there. Without warning, a middle-aged woman had rushed onto the stage, grabbed the microphone, and begun haranguing the Australian government for its record on Aboriginal issues. Prime Minister John Howard sat through this outburst in some discomfort. When he finally rose to speak, the hostility from the audience was tangible.

They waited for him to offer a formal apology for the way in which successive governments have treated the Aboriginals. When he failed to do so, hundreds of people all around the auditorium got to their feet and turned their backs on him. It was an extraordinary snub. I watched, slightly jet-lagged, but intrigued. A conference I had imagined would be sedate had suddenly erupted before my eyes. It was my first indication of the passion with which the Aboriginal people of Australia are consumed by their cause.

That night I had dinner with Michael Mansell and some of his friends. It was clear that he regarded himself in every sense as a black man. Indeed, he referred to himself as being black throughout the conversation. Yet Michael Mansell is white skinned, with fair hair and blue eyes.

Sir Peter wondered if his western appearance caused much surprise. 'If one drained the humour out of your face – which would be difficult to do – you could be mistaken for an obtuse Colonel of the regular army here,' he told him.

Michael Mansell grinned. 'Well, that's one of the nicest things that's been said to me in a long time,' he said. 'Until I was in my twenties no one ever questioned my Aboriginality. My teachers called me quarter-caste. When I mixed in my own community people called us blacks. Then I stood up on Australian television and said, "I'm a Tasmanian Aboriginal." Suddenly the telephone calls started coming in with people saying, *How can he be Aboriginal – he's got blue eyes?* That stung me because it was the first time anyone had ever questioned it.'

In Hawaii we had met native people prepared to go to extraordinary lengths to prove their identity. They knew precisely how much Hawaiian blood was coursing through their veins and could illustrate in carefully measured percentages the individual elements of their ancestry. Michael Mansell, however, was not the kind of man to pore over a genealogical tree with a calculator. In cold scientific terms he may be only part-Aboriginal, but in his heart that's the bit that counts. 'I'm fully Aboriginal,' he told us. 'I know nothing else, even though there has been

Ethnic cleansing is not a new phenomenon. At her death in 1876, Truganini was the last of Tasmania's indigenous Aboriginal population, all of them either forcibly deported to barren offshore islands or massacred by the European settlers.

mixed marriage in my family for three or four generations.

'I was born to Aboriginal parents, both of whom had a white parent on either side and their grandparents the same, so that explains the fairness of skin and the blue eyes. But being raised in an Aboriginal family we only mixed with the Aboriginal community. Our culture was Aboriginal. Whenever we mixed with whites it was to our disadvantage.'

There were others like him at the Melbourne convention. One woman was a mixture of Irish and Italian with a tiny but significant amount of Tasmanian Aboriginal blood. Yet it was her Aboriginal ancestry with which she most strongly identified. It was more than simply a genetic link. Her awareness of her people's history tugged at her soul. And her Aboriginal roots, however slight, represented a powerful physical connection with the land in which she had grown up.

There are still Aboriginals in Tasmania: they just have mixed blood, that's all. Michael Mansell, himself fiercely protective of his Aboriginal heritage, is among the most vocal campaigners on their behalf.

We met with Michael Mansell at a place called Regent Cove on a deserted stretch of Tasmania's coastline. It was here in 1804 that British troops had opened fire on a group of Aboriginals out hunting. No one knows exactly how many died, but the massacre of men, women and children is on record as one of the worst in the island's history. The land has subsequently been restored to the Aboriginal people.

Through his work as a lawyer, Michael Mansell spends his time fighting to improve the lot of his people, many of whom are young and disaffected. He represents juvenile offenders in court and runs a unique rehabilitation scheme designed to keep young Aboriginal law-breakers out of jail. As an alternative to prison he takes them off to a small and desolate island off the north-east coast of Tasmania, where they spend time living off the land and, hopefully, regaining some sense of self-worth. Sometimes his efforts succeed, sometimes not. He feels it is at least worth trying.

In Hawaii we had heard how the native people fare poorly in terms of health, jobs and education. It was a similar story among the Aboriginals of Tasmania. Unemployment among this minority is a massive sixty per cent, compared with around ten per cent among the white population. Michael Mansell pulls no punches when he accuses Australia of being a racist country. 'This country was built on racism,' he said. 'The rights of the Aboriginal people were ignored. Even today, leading politicians believe there is nothing wrong with being racist. That makes it very hard to say to people, *Don't you think Australia is a big country and there is enough room for two peoples to co-exist, so why should white people have the whole country?'*

He likens the discrimination suffered by Australia's Aboriginals to that experienced by blacks under the apartheid regime in South Africa. 'I remember my parents telling me that at Flinders Island in the north-east part of Tasmania they couldn't go into the hotel to obtain liquor. They had to remain in what was called the bull pit, which is where the blacks drink,' he said.

That was in the 1960s. Ten years later Neville Bonner, the first Aboriginal MP to be elected to the Federal Parliament, was refused service in a hotel in Queensland because he was black. Michael Mansell recalled a trip to Kimberley in north-western Australia where he found a hotel bar with a concrete and barbed wire barrier through the middle. On one side was a smart lounge for white customers, on the other was a bare room with a dirt floor for blacks. The year was 1994.

'Attitudes die hard in this country. Even though there are no formal laws, we practise apartheid,' he said.

The Whites always mean well when they take human fish out of the ocean and try to make them dry and warm and happy and comfortable in a chicken coop; but the kindest-hearted white man can always be depended on to prove himself inadequate when he deals with savages . . . if he had any wisdom he would know that his own civilization is a hell to the savage.
MARK TWAIN, *FOLLOWING THE EQUATOR*

ON A GREY AND CHILLY DAY we meet at an airfield to fly from Tasmania to Cape Barren, a small island located off the north-east coast. We are about to witness a remarkable homecoming.

One of the most tragic episodes in the history of the Aboriginal people happened comparitively recently. During the 1950s the authorities in Australia adopted a policy of forcibly removing Aboriginal children from their families and placing them within the white community. Over a period of twenty years tens of thousands of children were taken. The human cost of this misguided official policy of assimilation is immeasurable. Some of the families affected are still today trying to put their lives back together and mend broken relationships.

Among those families is the Peardons. It is more than forty years since the three youngest Peardon children were snatched from their mother. For more than twenty-five years Annette, the eldest of the three, has worked ceaselessly to reunite her fractured family. Now, as she prepares to return to Cape Barren, her younger brother Derek is with her. It is his first trip home since that fateful day forty-two years ago.

Derek Peardon was just four and a half when he was snatched by the authorities and placed in care. That same day seven-year-old Annette was also removed by welfare workers as she played with a friend. Neither child had a chance to say goodbye to their mother before they were bundled, confused, into separate vehicles and taken away. Theirs is a familiar story among Australia's stolen generation. Their baby sister, Dale, was also taken into care. Only one sister, ten-year-old Nola, who happened to be staying with relatives on the day the welfare officers called, was left behind.

When Derek Peardon was taken from Cape Barren it represented an irrevocable separation from his mother. He never spoke to her or saw her again. She died before there was an opportunity for reconciliation.

Cultures collide on the city streets where Aboriginal unemployment is rife: the paint and the instruments are all authentic; and yet there's something perturbing about using the tribal image, with all its living symbols, to busk for tourists.

His sadness and apprehension weighed heavy as he boarded a small aircraft for the short journey back to the home he barely remembers. 'I'm very nervous about going back,' he told us. 'Three nights in a row I've had very little sleep. I guess it's going to be very hard emotionally.' Were it not for Annette it is unlikely Derek would be making the journey at all. She has been the driving force in bringing her family together. Hers has not been a happy life but now, at last, she feels some measure of peace.

When Annette was summarily removed from Cape Barren she spent the rest of her childhood in an institution in Tasmania. Her little brother was growing up in a different children's home. Annette would regularly visit him, walking rather than catching a bus, spending the money she saved on sweets for Derek. He tells us, 'I think Cape Barren's changed since I was there. All the old houses long since gone. The only memories I have are of going to school and getting warm milk there. That's the only thing I remember. And day in, day out, kicking a little rubber football under the palm trees.'

On the short flight back both Annette and Derek appeared lost in thought. The drone of the engine filled the tiny aircraft and a light rain fell, casting a greyness over the landscape below. Annette had arranged for their sister, Nola, to meet them at the other end. Nola had not been told that Derek would be on the plane. When it touched down and the two were reunited he wept. 'Forty-two years,' he said, burying his face in her shoulder. 'It's a long time.'

The only one missing from the family reunion was Dale, the youngest, who had decided against resurrecting painful memories by going back. Despite her absence, Derek's homecoming represented a milestone for Annette. To have brought three siblings together on their home ground had taken a major effort.

'It's wonderful for me in the sense that I've nearly got our family back together, and that's very important to me,' she told us. There were no tears from Annette. 'I try not to show too much emotion. I've always felt that I'm the strong one within the family and I think I've proved that today.'

Derek remembers little about the day he was taken from his home but Annette has vivid memories. She and a friend were playing in an old car when two strangers tapped on the window. 'One asked me if I was Annette Elizabeth Peardon, and when I said yes they asked me to go with them. I looked at my friend and I remembered what I was taught – not to go with strangers. I can't really remember how I was enticed, but they just grabbed me and put me in a car. I was flown out to Launceston that day.'

It later emerged that her mother was sentenced to three months hard labour for neglecting her children. 'I don't think it was ever justified,' said Annette. 'I can't understand the reasons for any child to be removed from its parents. My personal opinion is that an injustice has been done to my mother, my family, and to any other Aboriginal child separated from its family.'

Annette grew up to be a rebellious teenager, moving from one institution to another. Throughout her childhood she struggled to come to terms with her background and a sense of being different from the white children she mixed with. She recalls sitting in a bath one day trying desperately to scrub her dark skin white. 'I don't feel resentful,' she told us. 'I've dealt with my pain and my hurt and anger. But I feel for the rest of the separated children.'

She also believes that her own children have suffered the legacy of her unhappy past. Annette proved to be a strict mother, running her home along the lines of the institutions she had known. 'I think the effect on my children has been very hard,' she said. 'I lost my son at the age of sixteen by suicide. He shot himself in the head. I do blame myself, but on the other hand I believe it was his choice. He was like me – very strong, but of course in our society there's the drug scene, the unemployment scene, and that would have played on his mind.

'I didn't give my children quality time and I have apologised to them. Unfortunately, I can't snap my fingers and be back in my own childhood in a loving family, and able to rear my children the same way.'

The rationale for removing Aboriginal children and placing them with white families was, ostensibly, to give them a better life. no one gave much thought to the emotional impact of sudden and unexplained separation. At one point Annette's mother came looking for her daughter. Annette, angry and resentful, shut the door in her face. Several years passed and a photo of Annette, who was then in her twenties and modelling, appeared in a local newspaper. Her mother saw it and wrote to her lost daughter, by then a more mellow individual and ready for reconciliation.

'I felt I needed to go home, to find my roots and find out who I am,' she said.

Derek meanwhile had turned out to be a gifted footballer, playing professionally in Melbourne for a number of years. He is a gentle giant of a man, a burly-looking character. Yet the memories stirred up by his return to Cape Barren were overwhelming him. He revisited his childhood haunts clutching a photo of his mother as a young woman, a gift from her sole surviving brother. At his mother's grave we hung back, respectful of his need for privacy. For several minutes he sat alone at the graveside mourning the woman he never knew. When he returned his face was wet with tears. He shook his head. 'Why couldn't I ever have met her?' Annette put a protective arm round him. 'Some things aren't meant to be,' she said.

Some time later we met with the Peardon family again. Annette had pulled off another triumph. For the first time all four siblings – including the shy Dale – had come together for a family photograph. There was enormous excitement, but some sadness too, that any family should have to wait until adulthood for the kind of snapshot most can take for granted. The four of them posed happily for the camera.

Annette was positively glowing. 'I feel very proud,' she told us. 'Today is probably the ultimate for me, to have my family together. Unfortunately, Mum passed away nine years ago, but I feel she is with us in spirit and that makes me feel even stronger in myself.'

They clustered round Sir Peter for more photos. 'I think your tenacity is absolutely extraordinary,' he told them. 'I've got one son and three daughters and I can imagine myself in the same position, having them taken away from me.'

A jubilant Annette was ready to celebrate. Clutching her glass of wine she declared that she just might get drunk.

'Really? Do you want me to take that away?' Sir Peter offered, reaching for her glass.

Annette hung onto it. 'Don't pass it to Nola,' she joked, 'she'll drink it!'

'What a family. What have you discovered?' Sir Peter said. 'You can have it back when the camera stops rolling!'

The Peardon family, together again for the first time in forty years: (left to right) Annette, Derek, Dale and Nola (seated).

The Peninsula is lofty, rocky, and densely clothed with scrub, or brush, or both. It is joined to the main by a low neck. At this junction was formerly a convict station called Port Arthur – a place hard to escape from. Behind it was the wilderness of scrub, in which a fugitive would soon starve; in front was the narrow neck, with a cordon of chained dogs across it, and a line of lanterns, and a fence of living guards, armed.
MARK TWAIN, *FOLLOWING THE EQUATOR*

---◆---

WE HEADED SOUTH on the road from Hobart to Port Arthur. It was here that one of the most brutal penal colonies in Australia was established in 1830. For almost fifty years, mainly white convicts were shipped out to this bleak spot to serve time in an atmosphere of hardship and austerity.

Port Arthur today serves as a carefully preserved and grim reminder of a sorry past. The once-feared institution survives as a popular tourist attraction, yet somehow there is an eerie despair about the place. It is almost as if the air is thick with the presence of those who endured the worst kind of punishment more than a century ago.

In recent years Port Arthur found itself the focus of world attention when a gunman drove to the old prison one afternoon in April 1996 and calmly opened fire, killing thirty-five people. Martin Bryant began his massacre in the Broad Arrow cafe, which was packed with tourists. In just thirty minutes a peaceful Sunday was transformed into a scene of utter devastation.

A simple wooden cross with the names of his victims now stands in the grounds of the jail. So great is the sensitivity about the tragedy that a pamphlet requests that visitors show respect to the bereaved and maintain a respectful silence on this painful subject when talking to the staff.

As we stood silently at the memorial a couple with a video camera approached. They filmed the cross and then moved closer, focusing on one particular name before walking away, their arms around each other. There are plenty of people in Port Arthur and beyond scarred forever by the inexplicable actions of one disturbed young man.

On the day we visited it was cold and grim and brought back unhappy memories for Sir Peter of his time as a private in the army. 'Like a bleak, empty parade ground, it brings it all back, the echoes of old screams and shouts,' he said. We wandered through the grounds past old workshops where prisoners once laboured, on past the guards' barracks and the stores. Even the flour mill had bars on the windows.

Over a fifty-year period around 13,000 convicts were shipped out to Port Arthur. They were all second offenders – regarded as heinous

Local historian Ken Lee leads Sir Peter through the stark ruins of the infamous Port Arthur penal colony.

villains – yet their crimes were often relatively mild. Records reveal that one man was transported to serve seven years for stealing two chickens, another sentenced to fourteen days with the Number Three chain gang for 'gross filthiness in Barracks Square'. Spelling obscene words in school resulted in forty-eight hours solitary confinement on bread and water for one offender, while 'sleeping under the same covering with George Meadowcroft in jail' led to three months with the Number One chain gang for another.

An attempt 'against the order of nature to commit with a ewe the detestable and abominable crime called buggery' brought one man a two-year jail term 'in separate treatment'. Food-related crime seemed to provoke harsh punishment – in one case, three days solitary confinement 'for eating a turnip at Port Arthur'. In another, a man was imprisoned for six months with hard labour 'for having 18 cabbages improperly in his possession'.

The prison stands in a desolate spot on the edge of a peninsula reached by a narrow causeway known as Eagle Neck. As the only means of access, the Neck was patrolled by warders with dogs day and night. Guard posts dotted around the neighbouring hills made escape practically impossible. In the entire history of the jail hardly any convicts managed to break out.

'One fellow tried to escape by putting a kangaroo skin over his shoulder and hopping across in front of the guards up at Eagle Neck,'

Between the dank rows of cells, where warmth never reaches, the solitary fire does little to lessen the gloom.

our guide, historian Ken Lee, told us.

He was unsuccessful. A hungry guard, tempted by the thought of a kangaroo steak, shot at him.

It is not surprising convicts were prepared to go to extraordinary lengths to escape. Port Arthur was infamous for its harsh regime. And those in solitary confinement were tested to the very bounds of endurance. The old cell block where solitary prisoners were held is still intact and serves as an example of the inhumanity of the jail. Wandering through the dank corridor which divides two rows of cells, we were all affected by the gloom and severity of the place. At one end of the block a fire burned. In the days when there were prisoners in the cells this was the only heat, and it was for the benefit of the warders. The inmates in their basic prison garb were left to shiver in bare, freezing cells.

The solitary block was run along the lines of a closed religious order. Communication between prisoners was forbidden and there was no idle chit-chat with warders. The only words the inmates were permitted to speak were *yes* and *no* when being questioned by a warder or prison doctor. Other than that there was total and utter silence. There was even straw on the stone floor to muffle the sound of the warders' footsteps and increase the isolation of their charges. Ken Lee led us past the cells, commenting, 'This is a place where they sent people crazy.'

We could imagine their madness, living in total isolation and deprived of the company and conversation of other men. Their only chance to make themselves heard came once a week at the Sunday service when they were permitted to sing. At one end of the block stands the old chapel, which was constructed so that the inmates' sense of isolation remained complete even during religious worship. Prisoners were led from their solitary cells one at a time up a wooden flight of stairs into the chapel, which had individual stalls in place of pews. For anyone accustomed to conventional churches it is indeed a bizarre place.

One by one the congregation would be shuttered in cramped wooden stalls so that each was obscured from the other. The tiered stalls faced the preacher, who stood in a simple, unadorned pulpit.

'Three-quarters of an hour of hellfire and damnation,' our guide said, stepping into one of the stalls to demonstrate how effectively it screened the prisoners, who remained on their feet throughout the service. 'The door would slam and there'd be a lock on it too. All you would see is the parson out front. You wouldn't be able to see anyone down below or on either side, or behind.'

The chapel was undoubtedly the barest and most depressing place of worship any of us had ever seen. No religious trappings, no icons, no altar with candles. Just cold, white walls.

'Can you imagine the roar, the release, the proof that people still had the capacity to talk and to sing words more complicated than yes and no?' said Sir Peter.

He gazed up at the stalls from the preacher's pulpit. 'This is extraordinary,' he said. 'It's a place calculated to degrade the human spirit, and it's made even worse because this is a chapel. It's atrocious in a sense, because its very simplicity suggests that the people who came here for enforced communion with some kind of God didn't deserve the merest trappings of bad taste associated with more conventional churches.'

Perhaps what Port Arthur demonstrates more clearly than anything is that, during the 1800s, when the white settlers in Tasmania were perpetrating great brutality on the Aboriginal people, they were also inflicting savage treatment on their own kind.

'It's a kind of saving grace that whatever other races or species of mankind suffered at the hands of the white invaders, the whites were as ruthless and as terrible with themselves at a certain time in history,' said Sir Peter. 'This to my mind is a symbol of all that is dilapidated and shabby in human nature and therefore, inevitably, in society.'

Even in chapel, the prisoners were denied the most basic human contact, locked in to individual cell-like pews which can still be seen today. (Bottom) The Usual Suspects: Sir Peter stands guard over the rest of the crew. Left to right: myself, Pratap Rughani, Matthew Fox, Mike Lax and Mike Fox.

◆

The convict life in Tasmania was so unendurable, and suicide so difficult to accomplish that once or twice despairing men got together and drew straws to determine which of them should kill another of the group . . .
MARK TWAIN, *FOLLOWING THE EQUATOR*

Australian history is almost always picturesque; indeed it is so curious and strange, that it is itself the chiefest novelty the country has to offer, and so it pushes the other novelties into second and third place. It does not read like history, but like the most beautiful lies. And all of a fresh new sort, no mouldy incongruities, and contradictions, and incredibilities; but they are all true, they all happened.

MARK TWAIN, FOLLOWING THE EQUATOR

◆

Everything about the Duke of Avram was bizarre, and his meeting with Sir Peter was no exception. The atmosphere and setting made it seem like something out of an episode of The Prisoner or The Avengers.

IT WAS QUITE BY CHANCE that I came across the Duke of Avram. I was on the road between Port Arthur and Hobart when I spotted an old election poster which grabbed my attention. It read, *Vote for John, The Duke of Avram*. At first I thought it might be a joke. As far as I knew there were no Dukes in Tasmania. However, the poster looked official enough. Swerving off the road and into a local garage I made a few enquiries. It seemed that the Duke of Avram was a real person who had indeed served as a member of the local parliament. He was a local estate agent in nearby Sorrell. Armed with directions, I went off to find him.

I couldn't help thinking we seemed to be encountering more than

our fair share of people who were not necessarily all they appeared. First there had been John Carter, the government chief whip in New Zealand, sacked for making a bogus call to a radio station in the guise of an unemployed Maori. Then there was Councillor Godfrey Bigot, formerly Brad Pedersen, in Manly. And now a man claiming to be a Duke. All three, curiously enough, involved in politics.

In Twain's day there had been an enormous scandal involving an Englishman called Arthur Orton, a butcher with a shop in the wonderfully named town of Wagga-Wagga. Arthur Orton rose to notoriety by dint of his claim to be Sir Roger Tichborne, heir to an estate in England. The case of the Tichborne Claimant became known all over the world. In *Following the Equator*, Twain had this to say about him: 'It was out of the midst of his humble collection of sausages and tripe that he soared up into the zenith of notoriety and hung there in the wastes of space and time, with the telescopes of all nations leveled at him in unappeasable curiosity.'

When I arrived at the modest offices of South East Real Estate I found the Duke, an unprepossessing character, poring over the usual paperwork associated with buying and selling property. The surroundings were rather less aristoctratic than I had hoped. Although I had no appointment he greeted me warmly, presenting me with a yellow and white business card on which both his photograph and his title featured prominently.

It seemed a slightly unusual combination, duke and realtor, not least in Tasmania which, as far as anyone knows, is devoid of dukes. Real ones at any rate. I probed as delicately as possible. 'Are you the Duke of Avram?'

'I am,' he said solemnly.

'But where is Avram?'

'Everywhere and anywhere,' came his response.

I sat in his office wondering if he would suddenly admit it was all a huge practical joke. As the minutes wore on, however, I realised he was entirely serious. In a country where identity raises many vexed questions John – the Duke – had transformed himself into the person he wanted to be, a titled gentleman; yet in a land where it is of virtually no advantage to claim nobility. As we spoke it emerged that he had once been an MP in the Tasmanian Parliament. His entry in the Parliamentary Yearbook reads 'John, The Duke of Avram'. Proof, if any were needed, that he is all he claims. Sadly, his tenure as an MP lasted one term before he lost his seat. Voters can be fickle.

He showed me a sheaf of photos of himself attending various events in his capacity as a Duke. Only recently he had been in Taiwan as the guest of honour at a prominent businessman's fiftieth birthday party. There he was, an official-looking chain around his neck, posing happily with his host. It occurred to me that perhaps, even to the Taiwanese

There was an air of unreality about the dapper suited figure swaying towards us on a chair-lift.

businessman, it is of no consequence whether or not he is a real duke. He *seems* to be one, which is probably all that matters in the end.

As I flipped through the pages of *Who's Who in the World* – a dubious publication – I found his entry, which listed a staggering array of titles, including His Holiness, Archbishop, Cardinal and Lord Rama. I felt that an encounter between John – not quite a real Duke – and Sir Peter – an authentic knight – might prove interesting.

A meeting was arranged in a desolate spot overlooking the town of Launceston in central Tasmania. We waited halfway up a hillside on a dull day for the Duke to arrive, finally spotting him, a dapper figure in a grey suit, suspended in mid-air on a chair-lift, the kind of thing you would normally expect to find in a ski resort. It was, as I had intended, suitably bizarre. He approached, swaying about precariously in the breeze.

'My goodness, what an entrance,' Sir Peter observed.

The self-styled Duke was in good spirits, beaming broadly as the chair lift shuddered to a halt beside us. He dug around in his pocket and produced a wallet full of credit cards, all in the name of the Duke of Avram.

'Anybody who can be a Duke in Tasmania deserves an enormous amount of respect,' Sir Peter told him. He was curious to know where Avram really is.

'It's more philosophical than territorial,' the Duke told him guardedly. His mobile phone rang. 'South East Real Estate,' he said, switching smoothly from aristocrat to businessman. There was an air of unreality about the entire proceedings.

'You say you are the Duke of Avram; and yet it's a creation of yours, but you think everybody has a right to be who they believe themselves to be,' said Sir Peter.

'You become what you think you are, what you want to become in your heart,' the Duke replied.

'I think we're very much more alike than you imagine,' Sir Peter said. 'There's only one difference between us –'

'You're famous and I'm not.'

'No – I'm not the Duke of Avram, and never will be . . .'

We watched him descend the hillside on the swaying chair-lift. Sir Peter muttered, 'I feel a kind of cold shudder that more and more eminent politicians are beginning to invade my profession, and becoming terribly good at impersonating others.'

*Back to Sydney. Blazing hot again. From the newspaper, and from the
map, I have made a collection of curious names of Australasian towns,
with the idea of making a poem out of them.*
MARK TWAIN, FOLLOWING THE EQUATOR.

◆

WE RETURNED TO SYDNEY, to our waterfront hotel with its view
across the harbour. When Twain had visited the city he had come up
with four things any visitor to Sydney should do – tour the harbour,
visit the Admiralty House, go shark-fishing, attend one of the
Governor's balls. I decided the modern-day equivalent of the
Governor's ball would be a first night at the opera. Kitted out in
tuxedos, we took a water taxi across the harbour for a performance of
Tchaikowsky's *Eugene Onegin*.

It was a beautiful evening. Sydney Harbour Bridge, awash in blue
light, arched elegantly across the bay. The white crests of the Opera
House – 'like nuns praying,' said Sir Peter – appeared luminous against

*The serene white roofs of the
Opera House are Sydney's most
distinctive landmark.*

the night sky. Sir Peter was to be a guest of the general manager of Opera Australia and his wife. Also in the party would be the chairman and his wife, the Russian Consul, and the novelist David Malouf.

The process of negotiating to film that night had brought back vivid memories of another chapter in my life. A year spent at the Royal Opera House in Covent Garden, making the BBC series, *The House*. It had been a fascinating undertaking, during which all manner of drama had been played out – both backstage and in the boardroom. Tonight the drama was rather more low-key.

In Sydney that night there were empty seats in the opera house,

Even en route to the opera, the camera case goes too!

which was unusual for a premiere. It was the day of Princess Diana's funeral and the cortège was due to begin its procession on the other side of the world as the curtain went up. It seemed that many people had chosen to mourn at home. Sir Peter made his way to his designated rendezvous point in the lobby – beside a portrait of Dame Joan Sutherland – to wait for his party. As if waiting incognito for an espionage encounter, holding up a ticket which revealed his seat number to be 00-something he said, 'I hate this sort of James Bond atmosphere in an opera house.'

Eugene Onegin is based on a Pushkin story about a girl from a small town who falls in love with a visiting nobleman. She pours out her heart in a letter, but he refuses her. Some years later the two meet again and this time he falls for her. But by now the girl, Tatyana, is married to a Prince and cannot abandon him. The lead in the Sydney production was being played by Elena Prokina, whom I had met while making *The House*. At that time she had spoken no English. Subsequently, she had learned a few words, but not enough to converse easily with Sir Peter, who went backstage after the performance to offer his congratulations. When he greeted her in Russian, she replied at length in her native tongue.

'My Russian is very bad,' he was forced to confess, 'but I'm going to get it back any minute!'

We took a taxi – by road this time – back to the hotel. The streets of Sydney were deserted. Our driver said he had never seen anything like it on a Saturday night. Princess Diana's funeral had cast a pall of sorrow over the entire city.

It was a sombre end to our stay. Next stop, India.

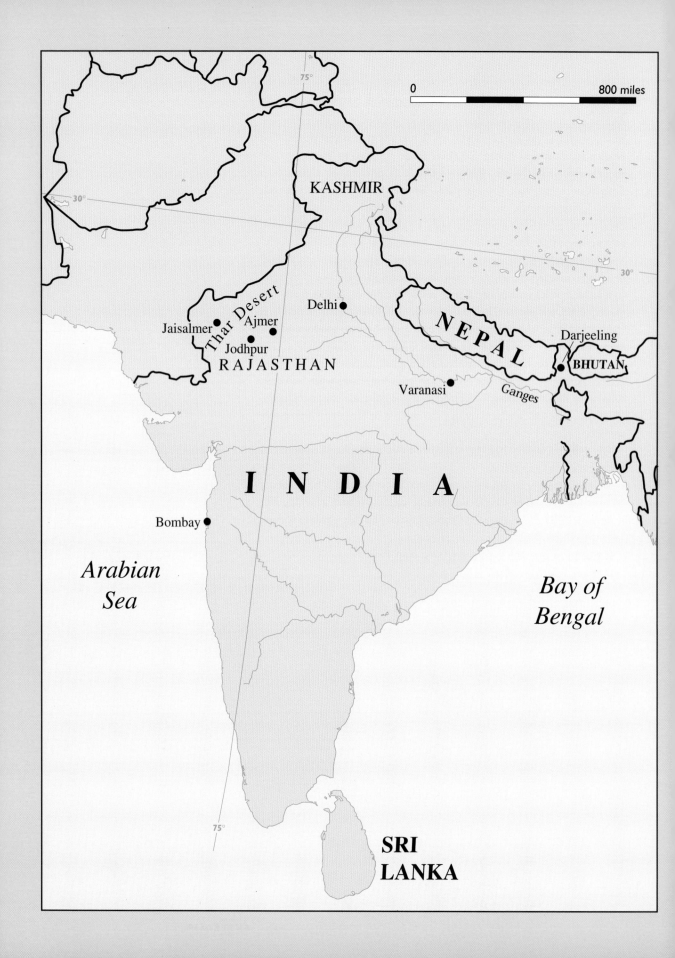

PART THREE

INDIA

INDIA

*When we arrived, the usual immense turmoil and confusion of a great
Indian station were in full blast. It was an immoderately long train, for all
the natives of India were going by it somewhither, and the native officials
were being pestered to frenzy by belated and anxious people.*
MARK TWAIN, FOLLOWING THE EQUATOR

◆

IT IS LATE, AFTER 10 P.M., when I arrive at the railway station just
outside Varanasi, in the northern plains of India, for the journey to
Darjeeling. Utter pandemonium. Platforms swarming with a mass of
bodies and baggage. The night train for Calcutta is boarding amid chaos
and confusion. Already, every carriage is packed to bursting.
Compartments intended to take six passengers swollen with at least
twenty, some squashed impossibly into the luggage racks above the seats.
Corridors so crammed that people can't even move their arms. They will
remain in this cramped state in their airless carriages for several hours.
Meanwhile, porters press themselves and their passengers against the
train's open doors in a ludicrous attempt to shoehorn yet more on board.

I find myself watching a family which has become separated in the
crush. A father and his two small sons are being shoved towards an
overflowing carriage by a porter who knows he will lose his tip unless
they can board. Already on board the train the mother and another
child, squeezed somehow into a carriage, are anxiously watching. There
is not the slightest chance her husband and sons will make it and, as the
train prepares to depart, mother and child are dragged roughly off the
carriage. They stand watching the train leave without them, the mother
rubbing an ankle twisted in the scramble to get off the moving train.

All those left behind settle down to sleep as best they can on the
station platform. They will repeat the performance the following night.
I witness all this from the relative comfort of the old station master's
office, a dusty room with shelves to the ceiling, piled high with years'
worth of records, stored in great, crumbling paper rolls. This is not
intended as a waiting room but no one asks me to move. A few minutes
go by and I realise I am not alone. A bundle of papers is rustling on the
floor. One at a time, three rats emerge and scurry off.

When it is time to board the Darjeeling train, my porter deftly
manoeuvres through the crowds, bearing my suitcase – all thirty-two
kilograms, marked HEAVY for the benefit of airport check-ins – on his
head. After the chaos of the Calcutta train I count myself fortunate to
have a reserved, air-conditioned sleeper car for my own overnight

The hustle and bustle of an Indian station. This one is Bombay, but the scene was the same as those we encountered wherever we went.

journey. Grateful to my porter, I tip him more than the going rate, although sixty rupees (around one pound sterling) still seems a small amount. In India, however, it is nearly a day's wage for an unskilled labourer.

En route to Darjeeling my thoughts return once more to the family struggling in vain to board the Calcutta train. For those low down in the pecking order of Indian society, life is invariably arduous, with little prospect of improvement. The country's caste system serves as an effective mechanism for determining one's social position for life. Once born into a lowly caste one's status is unlikely to change. Even through marriage it is practically impossible to advance oneself, since the Indian custom of arranged marriages almost always dictates a union based on equality of caste and class.

On our travels so far we had explored complicated issues of identity. In Hawaii we had spoken with local people whose official definition of self could be precisely measured in terms of how much pure native blood was in their veins. In Fiji we had met the descendants of Indians who – despite their heritage – proudly declared themselves Fijian. In Tasmania we had met the fierce pride of Aboriginals whom Twain and others had categorised as extinct. In India, however, it was questions of caste and class, rather than racial purity, which would intrigue us. We were keen to explore the arranged marriage, in which the quest for an appropriate partner, in terms of background and family, took priority over love and sexual compatibility. Perhaps more than anything, it is the arranged marriage which serves to maintain the established social order.

For outsiders like ourselves the caste system would prove a curious means of defining society. Even among Indians, there seems confusion as to the precise number of castes. Yet always at the bottom of the heap are the Untouchables – outcasts who do the lowliest of jobs, such as dealing with the bodies of dead animals. Mahatma Gandhi, moved by their suffering, called them *Harijans*, the Children of God. There are, of course, exceptions, sometimes dramatic ones. The current President of India, astonishingly, comes from the Untouchable caste.

There were other issues which had captured our imagination too. The Imperial legacy of the British Raj. The privileged royal families of Rajasthan. Bombay, teeming with its middle classes and swollen by migrants drawn by the prospect of work. The holy city of Varanasi, with its timeless charm. All contrasting pieces of a jigsaw which we hoped to assemble into a fascinating whole. 'So far as I am able to judge, nothing has been left undone, either by man or Nature, to make India the most extraordinary country that the sun visits on his round,' wrote Mark Twain in *Following the Equator* a century ago.

And so we began our exploration of this extraordinary land and its people.

AT JALPAIGURI STATION, the closest mainline stop to Darjeeling, I am met by a local guide, Jorden Norbhu, for the two and a half hour drive up the mountain to the Windamere Hotel. The Windamere – named after the English lake, despite the misleading spelling – has all the appearance of a building which has lain discreetly under dust sheets for the past sixty or so years. Everything is exactly as one would have expected it to be in the 1930s. Therein lies its unique faded charm.

Darjeeling itself has the appearance of a town indelibly marked by its days under the British Raj. The former hill station, chosen as an administrative centre by bureaucrats seeking to escape Calcutta's extreme heat and humidity, became so steeped in the habits and customs of the British that it seems unable to shake them off. Perhaps it has no desire to. Half a century after the British departed, the town retains its now faded colonial-style clubs where the new elite – now almost exclusively Indian – gathers.

It was a Sunday morning when I arrived at the Windamere to find the owner, 92-year-old Madame Tenduf-La, a small but awesome figure, engaged in a minor domestic drama. One of the servants had run off during the night with a married maid. Meanwhile, two other servants had reported clothing stolen from the washing line. It seemed convenient to point the finger at the runaways. Madame was not entirely convinced there had been any theft and suspected the missing couple were simply convenient scapegoats. She dismissed the complaints of the disgruntled servants, then turned to me and said, with an air of resignation, 'Whatever the truth, I shall have to buy them new clothes anyway – it doesn't do to have unhappy servants.'

Madame Tenduf-La, surprisingly sprightly in her bird-like appearance, is Tibetan, but has spent most of her life in Darjeeling. Her family moved there many years before the Chinese invaded their homeland. Although no longer actively running the hotel (her

Madame Tenduf-La, diminutive owner of Darjeeling's famous Windamere Hotel, still rules her hilltop empire with a will of iron.

son has taken over) Madame, with her long black hair plaited and coiled up on her head, her elegantly arched eyebrows, and her brightly painted nails, remains a familiar figure about the place. One has the impression she is as integral a part of the Windamere as cucumber sandwiches, white-gloved waiters, and the cocktail pianist playing 'Some Enchanted Evening' as the guests – mainly European – take afternoon tea.

Next morning I arrange to set off early for Tiger Hill, a vantage point which affords spectacular views over the surrounding Himalayas at sunrise. I had asked for someone to wake me with a knock at the door at 4.15 a.m., since one of the idiosyncracies of the Windamere is that the telephones in the bedrooms are purely decorative. A notice on the bedside table explains that 'when certain numbers are dialled three phones ring simultaneously in separate rooms, causing alarm to guests who value their repose. We have been keeping this deficiency in our intercom service under review and, meanwhile, crave your indulgence.' Put simply, they don't work.

At 3.45 a.m., after around two hours sleep, and a full thirty minutes before my wake-up call is due, there is an insistent knocking on my door. By 4.30 a.m. I set off in the dark for the forty-five-minute drive to Tiger Hill to witness the spectacle of the sun rising over the jutting peak of Kanchenjunga, at 28,169 feet the third highest mountain in the world. Just visible off to the west is Mount Everest. Despite the freezing cold there is enthusiastic applause from the small crowd which has assembled to watch as the sun makes its majestic ascent.

I am back at the hotel before breakfast, thawing out in a hot bath, which feels wonderful after the early morning chill. Later that day I check out some of the locations for filming prior to the arrival of Sir Peter and the crew, by now on their way from London to Delhi. The mountainous region of north-east India in which Darjeeling is situated is spectacular. On the steep green slopes of the tea plantations, women in saris are picking leaves for the world-famous Darjeeling tea. On their backs are large wicker baskets, held in place by a thick strap across the forehead. Selected leaves are thrown over the shoulder into the basket. As the women move along the rows of plants the sound of their voices – some chatting, some singing – carry in the cold morning air.

Looking down on Darjeeling from above it appears as a clutter of buildings, many crudely constructed in the style of shanty dwellings, wet clothing spread out to dry in the sun on uneven rooftops of corrugated metal. Car horns sound constantly. Although the sun is shining, it is cold in the foothills of the Himalayas.

As I contemplate the memorial stones at a small Anglican church, St Andrew's, a lump appears in my throat. One simple inscription catches my eye: *Forest Conservator, died 1884, aged 26*. Almost every stone seems to commemorate a life cut short; so many premature deaths summed up

in a few words. For some minutes, I stand in the church, imagining the many young colonialists whose dreams of new opportunities in a strange land far from home were tragically short-lived.

I head off to the Toy Train, a narrow-gauge steam railway which laboriously chugs its way the fifty-one miles uphill from Siliguri to Darjeeling, slowly but with charm. According to the timetable, the train runs two services daily. I had already been assured by our local guide it was running normally but, aware that Indian timetables are liable to change without notice, I decided to double check. At the station I found the station master's third deputy assistant, a toothless individual, who gave a nonchalant shrug when I enquired about the train.

'No trains,' he said. 'No coal.'

'When coal?' I asked.

'Tomorrow,' he said. I was not convinced.

I went in search of the second deputy station assistant. Two teeth but no less nonchalant. 'When coal?' I demanded.

'In three days,' came the reply.

Growing impatient, I found the first assistant, who boasted a full set of teeth but not the slightest idea of when the train might run again. By now suitably roused, I insisted the Station Master himself be found. It was early and I was told that he was sleeping, but I waited on the platform, and eventually he arrived.

The white-walled buildings of Darjeeling pile in a haphazard jumble of roofs and windows up the steep green hillsides.

'When was the last train?' I ask.

'Six days ago,' he says, predicting a wait of another six days before the next one, and bemoaning the lack of political clout of his superiors down the line when it came to getting coal supplies. I realise I am getting nowhere fast and head back to the hotel, where I place a call to the office of the Chairman of Indian Railways in Delhi. He is attending an emergency parliamentary committee meeting. I leave a message, hinting darkly that the honour of India depends on our being able to film Sir Peter on board the Toy Train. That afternoon a call comes back. The train will now run, especially for us, in two days' time. The manager of the hotel, who has witnessed all this, shakes his head, amused. 'Michael, I fear you have seriously affected the nation's economy to get the train running,' he says.

A bonus is that the powers that be have also agreed to wheel out one of their elderly engineless track inspection trolleys just for us. Since Twain had written about his trip careering down the mountain aboard just such a trolley, I was extremely pleased. Sir Peter, though, might need a little persuading.

The one land that ALL men desire to see, and having seen it once, by even a glimpse, would not give that glimpse for the shows of all the rest of the globe combined.
MARK TWAIN ON INDIA, FOLLOWING THE EQUATOR

◆

SIR PETER AND THE FILM CREW are due to arrive at Bagdogra, the closest airport to Darjeeling, on a flight from Delhi just before midday. My colleague Toby Follett sets off to meet them while I continue checking locations. It is a two and a half hour drive to Bagdogra on a rough road. Five four-wheel drive vehicles have assembled at the airport to transport the team and their gear back up to the Windamere. Meanwhile their flight from Delhi is still waiting to take off, delayed by thick fog, which clears only reluctantly.

Back at the Windamere I check my watch and grow concerned. Sir Peter's trek to Darjeeling had begun in New York, where he had presented the International Emmys – the US television industry's annual awards – and taken him via London, then on to Delhi for an overnight stop at a gloomy airport hotel, before the final hop to Bagdogra. I fear that being fog-bound for half the morning might have strained his patience; yet, when the convoy of vehicles finally arrives at the Windamere, he is in good spirits.

Madame Tenduf-La was on hand to supervise the arrival. She steered Sir Peter along a corridor whose walls were covered in old family photos.

'This is me as a little girl,' she said, gesturing with her walking stick at a framed portrait.

'Let me have a look. Oh yes, well you're still recognisable,' Sir Peter remarked.

'And that's my eldest brother dressed in Tibetan. He went with my father to Buckingham Palace to receive the King's Police Medal from George the Fifth.'

Sir Peter reached into a pocket. 'I just thought I'd amuse you because you've shown me so many interesting things.' He produced a photograph of himself with the Dalai Lama from his wallet and said, 'This just shows I'm in good hands on occasion. Do you recognise him?'

'I don't know this one, but that's the Dalai Lama,' she said, studying the picture.

'That's me,' Sir Peter said.

'Oh, really. Very nice picture.'

She nodded in the direction of another wall-mounted photo. 'That's in the dining room on Christmas Day. And this is my father with the King of Belgium, Albert.'

'Oh, I remember him, yes.'

Madame Tenduf-La appeared thoughtful for a moment. 'And in this very hotel my husband sometimes used to come home late, about two in the morning. I would ring Doctor Hurt – he was an American dentist here – and say, *Is my husband there?* He'd say, *Yes, but he's having a little fun*. I'd say, *It's two in the morning, would you kindly ask him to go home?* In those days there was no car, so he walked home.'

Sir Peter nodded. 'Difficult to imagine having fun with a dentist at two in the morning.'

Over tea Madame revealed that she had only recently returned to Darjeeling from a trip to see her daughter in California. 'I always have my maid to accompany me because now I'm ninety-two they're afraid I may fall – I've got weak knees. But I do these exercises for my limbs every day.'

'Really? I didn't come all this way from Europe to talk about my knees, but I would love a little help,' Sir Peter told her.

Madame Tenduf-La obligingly raised her arms in the air. 'They tell you to go up like this and then down again with the knees. Push up and down.'

'But where are you lying for this – on the ground?'

'On the bed. And as far as possible don't use a pillow. I use a very flat pillow because we all get spondylitis with old age.'

'I've never heard of it.'

'It's some nerve disease,' she said, tilting her head from side to side to indicate how to get some relief from the condition.

'Sounds like a Greek politician,' said Sir Peter.

Each afternoon the Windamere's guests drift into the lounge for afternoon tea, where wafer-thin cucumber sandwiches and dainty cakes are dispensed by waiters in turbans and gloves. Sir Peter spots a notice on the mantelpiece. 'Visitors are respectfully requested not to move around furniture in this room, in order that comfort may be shared in fair proportion by all. Also, visitors are requested not to take off their footwear, or put their feet on to the furniture, or lie supine on the hearth.' He raises an eyebrow. 'Or sleep behind the settees, lest unintended offence be given to others.' He glances about him. 'Is there anybody lying supine behind the settee, because if so we'd better tell the management . . .'

In a corner the hotel's resident pianist, Miss Chanrika Kanade, plays a selection of tunes, always beginning and ending with her signature, 'Roses of Picardy'. Not all the guests maintain a respectful silence during her performance. Applause is thin on the ground. One suspects that she, like the amusing notices and the white-gloved waiters, has become, not unintentionally, another quaint feature of the Windamere. After tea Sir Peter sought her out. 'I wonder if you mind a ripple of conversation, because it makes the music very background,' he said.

Miss Kanade appeared unperturbed. 'At the height of the season you find there is a buzz of conversation and there are just about two per cent who are really interested in listening. It can be quite disturbing, but then again it's not Carnegie Hall or the Festival Hall. It's just to create ambience in an hotel. You play a bit of this and a bit of that. It's not supposed to be pin-drop silence, so I suppose I've got used to it.'

'Which is a discipline of its own, and just shows that you're very professional,' he said.

'You do meet up with some characters here who are very loud; you know what I mean . . .'

'. . . I do.'

'Even my friends were quite disgusted, and wished they would go somewhere else instead of talking loudly and disturbing everyone else.'

'Well you won't find me talking through

In the genteel atmosphere of the Windamere lounge, pianist Miss Chanrika Kanade plays a daily selection to accompany afternoon tea. The strictures of polite behaviour as laid down to the Windamere's guests are endearingly arcane: it is clear from this shot that no one has had the temerity to lie supine behind the settee!

it,' Sir Peter assured her. 'Your playing brought back a very happy memory for me, because when I was kneeling before the Queen to get knighted, the military orchestra was playing, "I'm Going to Wash that Man right out of my Hair". Being a military orchestra I didn't recognise it until it was rather late. Da da da boom, shsh, boom, shsh, boom da da da – left, right, left, right!'

Miss Kanade dissolved in giggles.

'You wouldn't have recognised that interpretation.'

'That's from *South Pacific*.'

'Absolutely right.'

Miss Kanade was apologetic. 'Somehow I leave that piece out . . . I play "Bali Hai" and "Some Enchanted Evening".'

'Oh well, if you can master that piece I shall come back and listen to nothing but that, to stoke up happy memories.'

'What would be your favourite musical?'

'*Oklahoma* was a very good one.'

Inspired, Miss Kanade flexed her bony, ring-covered fingers and began to play.

'Oh what a beautiful morning,' Sir Peter boomed enthusiastically, and then promptly dried up. Miss Kanade played on, making a smooth transition into a lively rendition of 'The Surrey with a Fringe on Top'. Rodgers and Hammerstein might well have been turning in their graves, but Sir Peter closed his eyes in apparent rapture.

When Miss Kanade ended with a flourish, we applauded with a vigour we suspected was rarely to be found during her afternoon tea recitals.

After lecturing I went to the club that night, and that was a comfortable place. It is loftily situated, and looks out over a vast spread of scenery . . . Apparently, in every town and city in India the gentlemen of the British civil and military service have a club; sometimes it is a palatial one, always it is pleasant and homelike.
MARK TWAIN, FOLLOWING THE EQUATOR

IT WAS AT ONE OF DARJEELING'S once grand old clubs that we met up with Teddy Young, the last remaining British tea planter in the region; although he might baulk at this description, since he is fierce in his assertion that he is not truly British at all, but Indian.

'I was born in India, so I'm an Indian by birth,' he told us. 'I am proud

Appearances can be deceptive. He may look like the archetypal colonial, but Teddy Young, who was born in India and has lived there all his life, regards himself as Indian.

to be a person born in India.'

'I think you are very right,' Sir Peter told him. 'I am proud to be a person conceived in St Petersburg, although I was born in England.'

Teddy said, 'So you are really a Russian, and now you are a strange person like me, who's neither one thing nor the other.'

'I'm British now, by passport,' said Sir Peter.

'I'm British by passport too, but I'm not a citizen.'

As the last British tea planter in Darjeeling, it is probably no bad thing to emphasise one's sense of being a local. Our guide, Jorden, told us that the only other surviving British planter in the region had been murdered by his staff over a financial dispute. An entire family of tea planters ended up in a grinding machine, courtesy of their disgruntled workers. The tea industry can be surprisingly fraught with danger.

We had arrived at the Planter's Club, an institution which first opened its doors in 1868, in time for drinks on the verandah. One sensed that, whatever time we might have chosen to arrive, it would still have been cocktail hour. On a good day the mountains would have stood majestically, forming a spectacular vista before us. However, a cool mist had descended, draping itself so effectively around the distant peaks they were no longer visible.

Teddy, a gruff 74-year-old bachelor, clutching a glass of gin, and surrounded by local tea planters, summoned a waiter and ordered a fresh round. He was not the kind of man to allow anyone to refuse a drink. Sir Peter had already admitted he was not fond of champagne, leading Teddy to regard him suspiciously. 'Are you tee-tee?' he asked sharply.

'No, not tee-tee,' Sir Peter assured him.

Satisfied, Teddy summoned a waiter and ordered a gin and lime for his guest.

Gesturing about him he said, 'This is a wonderful place, wonderful people. You cannot get people like this anywhere in the world. They are most hospitable and kind. When I get old I shall never want for anything, whereas in England I would just be a bystander, the odd man out.'

One of the Indian planters teased, 'Sir Peter, as you can see, we've got him very effectively brainwashed.'

One suspects that Teddy Young's sense of belonging in a society in which he is undoubtedly the odd man out has much to do with the fact that he knows he could never adapt to life in England. He is one of a kind these days, a reminder of another time. Strikingly different in many respects from his Indian friends, yet somehow accepted. Teddy Young is reminiscent of another Darjeeling, when the British ran things.

'You're one of those very fortunate Englishmen who resembles a family portrait,' Sir Peter told him. 'One expects to see your face with a white wig and a lap dog.'

Somewhat bemused, Teddy said, 'I have completely reorientated my ways and I'm very much for the present.'

'Oh, I'm sure you are, but you can't help your physical features, which are marvellously eighteenth-century. You'd be wonderful as a sufferer of gout.'

Teddy Young stared into his glass for a moment. 'I've had too many gins,' he said, chuckling. Suddenly serious again he said, 'I believe you were in the Prime Minister's house at the time she was meeting her end . . . ?'

Sir Peter, accompanied by an Irish television team, had indeed been in the garden of Indira Gandhi's house waiting to interview her on the morning of her assassination in 1984. 'We heard three shots,' recalled Sir Peter, 'and the Indian cameraman said, *Oh, firecrackers.* Then there was a burst of machine-gun fire, and it was clear it wasn't a firecracker.'

Seven minutes later another burst of gunfire was heard. 'Soldiers rushed into the garden, aiming at everything and nothing, because they didn't know whether there were still some assassins hiding in the bushes,' recalled Sir Peter.

Within three minutes of the first shots being fired, Mrs Gandhi was being whisked away in an ambulance while Sir Peter and the crew remained marooned in the garden. It was six hours before they were allowed to leave. Several hours later a call came through from an official at the British High Commission. 'He said, "Er, Mr Ustinov, did you notice anything you think we ought to know?" I said, "No, I didn't notice anything I think you ought to know, but if I think of anything I think you ought to know I will certainly get in touch." "Would you do that . . . ?" A slight pause. "Oh, and would you be free for lunch with the High Commissioner tomorrow?"'

We had the impression that his account would be repeated over several more gins at the Planter's Club in the years to come.

Drinks on the verandah of the Planters Club: one British tradition, long since adopted by well-to-do Indians, that has hardly changed at all since the days of the Raj.

Plantations blanket the Darjeeling hills, where the combination of climate and terrain produces ideal conditions for growing tea. The leaves are picked by women whose faces (right, above and below) reflect the variety of ethnic backgrounds which can be found in this northwestern corner of India, tucked as it is between the borders of Nepal, Tibet and Bhutan.

The official school song of St Paul's School, Darjeeling.

WE MIGHT HAVE BEEN in one of England's more traditional public schools. The grand old buildings; the boys neatly turned out in navy blazers and well-pressed flannels, clustered in well-behaved groups around the quadrangle. The air of tradition and discipline. No wonder St Paul's School in Darjeeling is known as the Eton of the East. Founded in Calcutta 175 years ago, St Paul's moved to Darjeeling in 1864. One has the impression that little has changed over the years. The boys are impeccably polite. The authority of the masters is evident. According to the school Rector, Mr Howard, his pupils are a happy and balanced lot.

'What we try and do is give them a series of moral values which we hope will last a lifetime,' he told Sir Peter. 'Most of them come from business backgrounds and they need this sort of moral stiffening.'

A quiet pride emanates from the Rector, a proper and correctly spoken man, with a discreetly authoritarian manner. St Paul's attracts pupils from all over India, with a few from overseas. The boys, aged six to eighteen, come from a variety of religious backgrounds, but all accept the Anglican ethos on which the school was founded.

'We were strongly fashioned along the lines of Eton,' said the Rector. 'We used Eton collars and the hats for many years, before we gave them up.'

'I must say, that's one thing I resented as a boy, having to wear a stiff collar,' said Sir Peter. 'All our collars were covered in ink marks, and we struggled to shut them with those terrible studs which pressed into the Adam's apple and left a mark.'

The Rector said, 'Here it was far more practical. In a cold place like this, the only part of you that really gets dirty is the collar, so you just send that off to the laundry and the rest of it you can hold onto.'

A scene that wouldn't look out of place at any English public school: the boys of St Paul's take part in a carol service at the end of their Christmas term.

As the daylight faded the chapel bell began to toll. Christmas was less than a month away, and the boys were being summoned to the kind of carol service which would not have been out of place in an Anglican school in England. They streamed across the quad to the chapel. The masters, gowns fluttering around them, swept into the building in a solemn procession. A simple cross hung above the altar. Candles blazed. High up in the choir loft a soloist sang 'Once in Royal David's City', his voice clear and bold. Soft candlelight played on his features. There was a peculiar nobility to the proceedings, and an enthusiasm that was both inspiring and touching.

After the service there was supper, at which Sir Peter would have been Chief

Guest had it not been such a long and exhausting day. I agreed to act as his stand-in, not fully appreciating that this would entail handing out awards and making a little speech. I ad-libbed my way through an address, wondering if it was a major disappointment to the boys of St Paul's to be deprived of the famous Ustinov wit. Later, on my way back to the Windamere after a much-needed sherry with the Rector, my driver confessed that he had pressed his face to the hall window to watch the proceedings, and had witnessed the boys cheering and clapping – apparently in response to my speech. Perhaps it wasn't as bad as I had feared, after all.

And sure enough, he came, and I saw him – that object of the worship of millions. It was a strange sensation, and thrilling. I wish I could feel it stream through my veins again.
MARK TWAIN, *FOLLOWING THE EQUATOR*

SANGAG CHOLING MONASTERY, high on a rocky crag above Darjeeling. The monks, in dark burgundy robes, their heads shaved, gather for daily prayers. They sit cross-legged, some chanting, some rocking gently in silence, eyes closed, deep in contemplation. At one end of the hall, at the feet of a golden Buddha, is their spiritual leader. He sits alone on a dais, sipping tea from a tin cup, keenly observing the proceedings. He is Kyabje Thuksey Rinpoche II, an important and venerated figure in the Tibetan Buddhist community. Remarkably, he is just ten years old.

The Rinpoche was discovered in Ladakh, in the Western Himalayas, an area known as Moonland for its arid landscape. Buddhist disciples had spent three years searching for him, and believe him to be the reincarnation of one of their great spiritual teachers. I had visited the Tibetan monastery some weeks prior to filming, intrigued to meet this small boy, whom Twain might well have described as a 'living god'. When I arrived I was met by the secretary, Ngawang Tensing Gyatso, a serene and sweet man, who ushered me into his study. There, on the wall, was a photograph of the Rinpoche as a baby – at nineteen months old gazing solemnly at the camera, a finger in his mouth – taken just before his enthronement.

It was in 1959, when the Chinese invaded Tibet, that the country's people began crossing the border into India. The following year Kyabje Thuksey Rinpoche was offered a temple by the Sherpa people in Darjeeling and started to establish a community of Tibetan Buddhists. In 1971, under

the guidance of the Rinpoche, work began on the construction of the Sangag Choling Monastery, which now houses a community of around two hundred and its incarnate, the young Rinpoche.

'He is a very cute small boy, but he is one of our most important great teachers,' the secretary said. 'We all have a very strong faith and devotion to him.'

We were interrupted by the telephone. 'Hello. Oh – how are you? Are you still in Monaco?' the secretary said. 'The bank account number is . . .' and smoothly proceeded to reel off a series of numbers from memory to the caller – presumably a wealthy Monegasque benefactor wanting to make a donation. I suppressed a smile. So much for unworldly!

Opposite page and above:
We expected the Buddhist monastery of Sagang Choling to be serene, contemplative and silent. We found a place full of irrepressible joy, alive with laughter and joking, and young boys running to and fro between lessons.

When I returned to Choling with the film crew we spent some time observing the monks at prayer. Sir Peter tucked himself into a corner of the assembly hall with a cup of tea, which he left largely untouched. At one point I asked him to take a sip for the benefit of the camera. Later he wanted to know if I had tried it. 'I think it's made with condensed goat's milk, all brewed up together with lots of sugar.' He paused and grimaced. 'It's absolutely vile! I knew you were going to come and ask me to have another sip . . .'

His description of the tea was fairly accurate, although I suspected it was made with salt – even worse – rather than sugar. 'All in the cause of art,' I told him, carefully avoiding a cup myself. Sound recordist Alasdair Widgery and camera assistant Nemone Mercer, however, were more adventurous. Within twenty-four hours they would regret having taken tea with the monks.

We had an appointment to meet with the Rinpoche later in the day. First we caught up with his English teacher, nineteen-year-old Sam Irons (son of the actor, Jeremy), who was spending his gap year in India before starting his studies at Trinity College, Dublin.

'I came here expecting it to be very serene and peaceful – stereotypical monks – but it's like a boys' school. There's lots of joking and laughing,' he told us.

'I noticed two boys in the middle of prayers, one giggling and the other trying to look in the other direction until he couldn't bear it any more and he started laughing,' said Sir Peter.

'There's lots of teasing and a bit about girls, but it's not really serious.'

With his shaved head and gentle good-humour Sam, despite his Western clothes, had melted into the monastic community with ease.

'Are you a Buddhist?' asked Sir Peter.

He shook his head. 'Of all the religions Buddhism strikes me as the one that suits me best, but I haven't taken refuge in anything.'

'Well, I think sitting in there I felt more open to the spiritual door knocking at the inside,' said Sir Peter. 'It's very curious because they leave you alone. It's obviously something that's aimed at the individual, and other religions are aimed at the community. I was thinking of that long gap when nobody did anything but drink tea and sit in silence. I thought that was very impressive, because in any other church, everybody would think something had gone wrong – the lectern had broken or the clergyman had fallen down the stairs or something. But this was an absolutely unembarrassed silence.'

It may well have been that the monks were simply having a moment's respite before resuming the chanting of their mantra. In the space of a month they would chant a compassion mantra a hundred million times. Each monk's individual contribution would amount to around 1,800,000 repetitions.

'But who does the accountancy?' asked Sir Peter.

'The Discipline Master,' Sam told him. 'He was sitting next to you!'

That afternoon we were shown to the Rinpoche's quarters, high up at the top of the monastery, where he was to have his daily English lesson. Sir Peter was given a white silk scarf to present to the tiny deity, who sat in a corner, surrounded by the kind of paraphernalia any youngster might have. Fluffy toys perched in a row on a shelf. Among his books was a volume entitled *Great Sportscars of the World*. It was curious to think that this small boy with

. . . But there is serious ceremony as well. Here the senior monks make their formal arrival at prayers, accompanied by trumpets.

his childish tastes had already assumed the mantle of spiritual leader. He accepted the scarf and draped it round Sir Peter's neck in the customary greeting.

At our first meeting, on my earlier reconnaissance trip, the Rinpoche had been animated and giggly during his lesson. When Sam, in an exercise called *What do you do?*, had asked if he enjoyed being a monk, he had replied with a big grin, 'No – it's boring!' Sir Peter examined the toys on the desk in front of him. 'Is that yours?' he said, indicating a small telephone. The child beamed and nodded.

'A red telephone, like they have in the White House in America. Can you telephone on it?'

A shake of the head.

Sir Peter leafed through the exercise book. '*When I grow up I'm going to have a very big car*,' he read. '*Mercedes.*'

As the lesson progressed Sir Peter began to sketch a sleek saloon car. He presented it to the boy. 'There's another Mercedes for you,' he said. The drawing was carefully glued into the exercise book.

'What do you say to Peter?' said Sam.

With a beatific smile, the Rinpoche said, 'My best car!'

'I'm very touched,' Sir Peter told him.

'When I grow up I'm going to have a very big car . . .' Despite his exalted religious status, the 10-year-old Rinpoche, seen here with Sam Irons, his English tutor (right), is not so very different from other boys his age.

And so presently we took to the hand-car and went flying down the mountain again; flying and stopping, flying and stopping, till at last we were in the plain once more . . . That was the most enjoyable day I have spent in the earth. For rousing, tingling, rapturous pleasure there is no holiday trip that approaches the bird-flight down the Himalayas in a hand-car.

MARK TWAIN, FOLLOWING THE EQUATOR

◆

Among the many of Twain's experiences which Sir Peter sportingly agreed to repeat, sitting perched on the open front of a railway inspection trolley hurtling full tilt down the mountain was undoubtedly the most courageous . . .

IT WAS HARDLY THE MOST elegant form of transport. An old railway inspection trolley. No engine. Just a handbrake to prevent it from careering out of control, and two seats. Sir Peter appeared doubtful as a small crowd gathered around the trolley with its bright red canopy. In front of him the track sloped away and vanished round a bend in the hillside. Sir Peter had already done this journey uphill aboard the famous Toy Train, which had chugged through the hilly terrain in stately fashion. Thanks to the railway officials, who had been as good as their word, their original inspection trolley was now at our disposal.

A hundred years earlier Mark Twain had travelled along Darjeeling's twisting railway on an identical hand-car. He had found it an exhilarating experience. Despite the obvious shortcomings of the trolley, Sir Peter, with some trepidation, agreed to risk the ride. At his side was the driver, with one hand on the all-important brake. To the rear stood two rail employees, each clutching a red flag. Balanced precariously at the feet of the driver was cameraman Chris Cox. It was fortunate that he had refused the tea the previous day at Sangag Choling Monastery, since the less cautious members of the crew were clearly suffering the after-effects. They were our first casualties of the infamous Indian tummy trouble, although by no means our last. Supplies of Imodium were to become more and more essential as time wore on.

As the trolley moved off, conveying Sir Peter downhill, I felt a stab of concern as I heard

him say, 'This is very perilous.' He disappeared from view. The sound recordist and I chased after him, listening to the dialogue from his radio microphone.

'Mark Twain may have sat on this very trolley,' mused Sir Peter to his driver as the flag-bearers waved urgently at pedestrians loitering on the track. 'He found this the most exhilarating experience of his life. He must have lived a sheltered life. Of course, there was no bungee jumping in his day.'

We hurried on to catch up with him further along the track. The unfamiliar spectacle of the trolley, complete with its distinguished passenger, hurtling down the hillside drew looks of astonishment. A dog barked loudly as the strange contraption swept by. Sir Peter barked back. 'This is like a Harold Lloyd movie,' he said, looking alarmed. 'Here's a Jeep coming at us full tilt!'

He closed his eyes as it veered to one side to avoid a collision. I winced.

'I suppose it is exhilarating in a Victorian way,' said Sir Peter. In the distance the mountains, which had hidden shyly behind low cloud until then, showed themselves to be magnificent.

'I'm beginning to understand Mark Twain, but only just. It's not my cup of tea, I wouldn't want one of these – my garden's not big enough, thank God. *Aaaargh!*' With that he was gone again.

The full magnificence of Darjeeling's almost magical setting. In the distance, above even the level of the clouds, the majestic snow-covered peaks of the Himalayas soar breathtakingly into the sky.

Inside the great station, tides upon tides of rainbow-costumed natives swept along, this way and that, in massed and bewildering confusion, eager, anxious, belated, distressed; and washed up to the long trains and flowed into them with their packs and bundles, and disappeared, followed at once by the next wash, the next wave.
MARK TWAIN, *FOLLOWING THE EQUATOR*

◆

FROM COOL, MOUNTAINOUS Darjeeling we descended to the hot plains and flew from Bagdogra to Delhi, spending another night at the Centaur Airport Hotel, a modern four-star establishment. Air conditioning. Telephones in the rooms. Working ones at that. Yet somehow I had preferred the Windamere, in spite – or perhaps because – of its many shortcomings. There was something to be said for a hotel which provided hot water bottles and real, roaring fires in every guest's bedroom as a matter of course.

From Delhi it was to be on by train to Rajasthan – Land of the Princes – in western India. Next morning we were up before dawn for an early train, the Shatabdi Express to Ajmer. Even at 5.30 a.m. the station was throbbing with life. It came as no surprise to learn that Indian trains carry more than ten and a half million passengers every day.

Sir Peter progressed relatively smoothly through the station, up and down steps, over tracks, and onto the train. I had intended to film at least some of his trek through the crowds and positioned him at the top of a staircase awaiting his cue. Meanwhile, I asked cameraman Chris Cox to capture some of the scenes around us. Glancing back in the direction of Sir Peter I realised he was no longer where I had left him. My eyes searched the station. He was already making his way down the stairs. 'Stop!' I yelled at my startled cameraman. 'Start filming Sir Peter – now!'

Meanwhile, ensuring our small mountain of luggage was safely loaded proved a stressful affair. It seemed to take forever, and with half our belongings still on the platform as the train prepared to leave, I began to contemplate how best to hold it up. There were porters everywhere, and I seemed to be tipping everyone in sight in a frantic attempt to accelerate the loading process. Finally we were all on board with just minutes to spare. As the train began to move, Chris, having attempted simultaneously to film Sir Peter's arrival; our departure; grab general shots around the station; and keep one eye on his baggage, turned to me. 'This really is a one-take show,' he said.

We journeyed south-west in darkness, meeting the sun as it rose over a hazy plain, its orange light breaking through a landscape dotted with trees. As the morning grew hotter we dozed fitfully.

At Ajmer we were met by a posse of red-jacketed porters, keen to commandeer our excess of luggage. It all sat on the platform, a jumble of suitcases and bags, silver flight cases containing filming gear, and Sir Peter's colourful fold-up chair, which had by now been halfway round the world. The porters swarmed over our belongings, confidently piling delicate – and costly – equipment high on their heads. The camera assistant appeared frantic. We seemed unable to persuade them not to put more than one box on each head. As a flight case, several feet up in the air, began to wobble dangerously, I intervened. 'No,' I said, grabbing it. 'Not like that!'

They got the message and an air of bemused caution descended.

At the station a local representative from the tour company Cox and King's steered us to a waiting coach. Nine porters in single file followed. Much haggling over payment ensued. All of a sudden there were twelve porters, each one demanding 100 rupees. We left negotiations to the man from Cox and King's.

Our reason for stopping at Ajmer was the exclusive Mayo College, a fee-paying school originally founded for the sons of Maharajahs. It had a very different atmosphere to St Paul's in Darjeeling, its royal past conferring an air of genteel grandeur. Students, warming up for an end of term polo match, cantered about on glossy ponies. Handsomely turned out and exuding great style, they strolled confidently through the grounds, greeting us politely. There was an air of glamour and opulence about the place. Sir Peter had agreed to present prizes the next day – the final day of term.

We were due to have lunch at the Principal's residence with the Maharajah of Jodhpur, chairman of the school governors – himself Eton and Oxford educated. I found myself with an hour to spare and decided to tackle my expenses. The very act of sorting through various crumpled receipts merely made my head ache. They would have to wait. As had most of my expenses from Australia and New Zealand, Hawaii, Kiribati and Fiji. Composing in my head the memo to the accountants, I nodded off to sleep.

When the Maharajah appeared he was looking customarily suave and elegant in a sports jacket and open-necked shirt. He led us to the edge of the sports field where rows of chairs had been set out for the polo match between college Old Boys and present students. Off to one side the school band played 'A Bicycle Made for Two'.

I had met the Maharajah previously during my reconnaissance trip to India, when he had appeared in traditional Indian dress, worn with a Western cravat, and two small sausage dogs in smart coats yapping at his heels. The Maharajah of Jodhpur is very grand and not easy to contact. The meeting had been arranged partly through negotiation with his secretary, Sunder Singh, and partly through the efforts of one of his old friends, a Bombay banker named Deepak Vaidya. He had telephoned the Jodhpur royal residence in my presence.

The Maharajah of Jodhpur entertains Sir Peter to a polo match at Mayo College, Ajmer, an establishment originally founded exclusively to educate the sons of Indian royalty.

Wheeling their agile native horses on the dusty college polo fields, today's teenage students could have stepped straight out of one of the gilded paintings of Rajasthan's warrior history.

'I've just been telling Mr Waldman here how superior we Marathis are to you lot,' he said, in a reference to the renowned yeoman warriors of Maharashtra. After a moment he shouted into the phone, 'Not bald man – that's me! Waldman!' Laughing at the misunderstanding, he handed me the receiver, and I found myself listening to a voice dripping with privilege and culture. Smooth as chocolate, the royal voice agreed to receive me at his palace.

On meeting the Maharajah I had found his manner both charming and courteous. With his many minions, however, he was more businesslike. The merest click of the fingers would bring someone swiftly to his side. During that first meeting I became used to his habit of discreetly clearing his throat into a delicate golden spittoon. As we prepared to film the speech day ceremony at Mayo College I went to the royal guest quarters with the sound recordist, who was anxious to put a radio microphone on the Maharajah. His valet showed us into the princely bedroom where his master's clothes had been carefully laid out. We were asked to wait. All around was evidence of fine and exotic taste. Various tunics carefully draped on stands and, on the bed, next to a leather briefcase and a mobile phone, a pair of perfectly pressed underpants with the label just visible – Liberty's.

End of term prize-giving at Mayo College turned out to be a formal and proper affair. Prior to the ceremony the boys, in crisp white collarless jackets and black trousers, lined up on the lawn to have turbans in their house colours coiled expertly about their heads. Their dresser, an elderly man who had been at the college for forty years, worked his way through the queue with impressive speed, shaking out great swathes of starched orange fabric, which he deftly worked into a perfect turban. Each one took only around forty-five seconds. It was extraordinary to watch.

When Twain was in India he too had been fascinated by the skill of the turban winder. 'It seemed a simple art and easy,' he wrote in *Following the Equator.* 'But that was a deception. It is a piece of thin, delicate stuff a foot wide or more, and forty or fifty feet long; and the exhibitor of the art takes one end of it in his two hands, and winds it in and out intricately about his head, twisting it as he goes, and in a minute or two the thing is finished, and is neat and symmetrical and fits as snugly as a mould.'

Sir Peter appeared slightly self-conscious as the dresser turned to him and neatly wove a perfect turban around his head, teasing one end of the fabric into an elegant plume, which stood to attention. 'I've got absolutely no sensation at all in my head wearing this,' he said. 'I should be able to get good short-wave reception on the tip of the turban but I can't hear anything at the moment as one ear is covered. During the course of the day I know it's going to disintegrate slowly and make my speech all the more difficult, because it will cover my lips.'

So, regrettably, off it came. As the turban was carefully removed, Sir Peter was told he could keep it as a memento. 'I'll never be able to do it myself,' he said. 'Mark my diary, will you – visit to Bradford for turban tying!'

The prize-giving ceremony was indeed impressive. Hundreds of beturbaned boys streamed forward, one after another, under a glowering sky, to collect award after award after award. Academic accolades in all subjects, medals for football, cricket, hockey, tennis, basketball, swimming, cross country, squash. Best all-round sportsman, inter-house challenge cup, all-English debating cup, senior house shield for games. Sir Peter sat in a burnished throne next to the Maharajah, getting up to dispense the last and most important of these, warmly congratulating the procession of winners. He told his audience, 'It's that mixture of wisdom and humour and Olympian view of things which has characterised India and given everything I've seen a certain dimension which is lacking in many other countries. I personally appreciate very much being here.'

We were due to drive to Jodhpur that night to stay in sumptuous style at the Umaid Bhawan Palace. Part of the Palace, built by the Maharajah's grandfather, is still the royal residence, although much of the building has been converted into a luxury hotel. It is incredibly grand. The entire construction was begun in 1929 and took 3,000 workers around thirteen years to complete. At the time, the region was blighted by famine, and the Maharajah justified the lavish project as a means of providing employment for his stricken people. Once completed, the Palace was intended as a private residence – one of the largest family homes in the world – although the man whose vision it was died within three years of its completion.

We had been told it would take four hours from Ajmer to Jodhpur,

The skill and rapidity with which the turban winder transformed yards of flowing fabric into crisp sartorial elegance was truly astonishing.

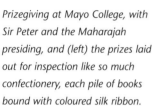

Prizegiving at Mayo College, with Sir Peter and the Maharajah presiding, and (left) the prizes laid out for inspection like so much confectionery, each pile of books bound with coloured silk ribbon.

although the Maharajah insisted it was no more than a three-hour trip. After we had been on the road for more than an hour I caught sight in the rear view mirror of a sleek black Mercedes with a distinctive numberplate approaching at speed. It was the Maharajah. The light was just beginning to fade and the road was busy with trucks, people, cows and camels drifting unconcerned across the highway. Overtaking was difficult, but the Mercedes shot past. His driver was clearly in a hurry. I waved at the Maharajah, who seemed slightly embarrassed. I could see why he was able to shave an hour off the journey!

The next afternoon we had arranged to meet with the Maharajah and his wife, the Maharani. Sir Peter made his way through the corridors of the Palace, through a vast reception room decorated with the heads of snarling tigers.

'What a most extraordinary building. When you come in you think you're in St Peter's in Rome. The dimension of the dome and everything is quite exceptional,' he remarked.

'It's said that the stone structure is interlocking,' replied the Maharajah. 'Technically, if you wanted to take it apart and put it up somewhere else you could do it.'

During the afternoon the couple's son, the Yuvraj, appeared. A handsome 21-year-old, he announced that he was taking a year off after completing his business studies course at Oxford Brookes University. 'I'm playing a lot of polo at the moment,' he said. He had long, long eyelashes. A fine patrician profile. The same dark good looks his father must have had at his age. Aesthetically, quite amazing to look at. Charming too. With those looks and that provenance no doubt many of those attending English polo matches had been captivated by the mere sight of him.

That evening we were invited to the wedding preparations of a distant cousin of the Maharajah. The groom, Brijraj Singh, was preparing for his send-off prior to embarking on a 400 kilometre journey for his marriage.

Opposite, bottom and this page, below:
The awesome grandeur of the Umaid Bhawan Palace of the Maharajahs of Jodhpur. When finally completed in the 1940s, it was among the largest private residences in the world.

India's princely families still honour their centuries-old traditions of pomp and ceremonial.
(Above) A dresser completes the final touches to the bridegroom's glittering costume, worth a king's ransom in jewels and gold.
(Right) The groom sets off at the head of a torchlit procession, mounted on a horse as richly caparisoned as himself.

'Is it an arranged marriage?' enquired Sir Peter. Like most Indian marriages – including the Maharajah's own – it was. No doubt an appropriate partner would also be found in due course for the Yuvraj.

Sir Peter was curious. 'But do they like one another?'

The Maharajah laughed. 'They are not averse to one another. It is not under duress,' he said.

I had met the bridegroom briefly once before and was fascinated to hear of his first encounter with his bride-to-be. To begin with, the prospective bride and groom were chaperoned by their parents. For a while the two families made conversation while the couple sat in their midst. Then it was suggested that the two young people go off and spend some time alone. It had been, he told me, a potentially awkward moment, which was rescued by the fact that they had a similar sense of humour.

I was intrigued. Had they been attracted to one another, I asked him.

He gave this some thought. Finally, he told me that they had not found each other unattractive. More importantly, the two families were ideally suited. The wedding plans had proceeded apace.

That night the groom was surrounded by relatives who chanted and prayed, anointed his hair and body with scented oils, and helped dress him in a glittering costume topped with a turban so heavily decorated in gold it had taken on the appearance of a crown. When we arrived it was so hectic it was impossible to grab more than a few words with him at a time.

'He doesn't want to talk,' said Sir Peter, as the bridegroom hurried past, preoccupied with a cufflink which refused to fasten. 'If it was me, before my wedding to someone I didn't know terribly well but approved of, I would be shy too.'

One of the groom's aunts approached to extol the virtues of the arranged marriage. 'Having a love marriage is quite taboo,' she said, adding that she had been happily married for fourteen years – to a partner arranged by her parents. 'And no problems so far,' she told Sir Peter, with a positive glint in her eye.

Finally, dressed in his splendid costume, and flanked by two servants who wafted huge fans made of ostrich feathers over him, the groom departed on a horse attired as richly as its rider. Accompanied by a band, which gamely played raucously out of tune, he headed off down the road on his mount for the ritual family send-off. Once out of sight, he left the horse behind and transferred to a car for the short ride to the home of a cousin, where he would spend the night before the long journey on to his wedding.

This is indeed India! The land of dreams and romances, of fabulous wealth and fabulous poverty, of splendor and rags, of palaces and hovels, of famine and pestilence, of genii and giants and Aladdin lamps, of tigers and elephants.

MARK TWAIN, *FOLLOWING THE EQUATOR*

VISITING RAJASTHAN ON THE reconnaissance trip I had found the region rich in stories and fascinating people. From Jodhpur I had headed off with my guide to Jaisalmer, in the Thar Desert, once the most important oasis for traders along the desert caravan routes. Today, the legacy of its prosperity is its fine old buildings – intricate temples and *havelis*, or mansions, built of local yellow sandstone. It was a six-hour drive from Jodhpur and we broke it with a lunch stop at a small, family-run restaurant in the middle of nowhere. A young boy, aged about eight, and accompanied by his father on small drums, danced exquisitely for us as we ate. Had I been an impresario, I would have signed him up on the spot.

It was dark by the time we arrived at Jaisalmer and checked into our hotel. A few people were on the lawn having drinks in the warm night air. Large quantities of whisky were being consumed, mostly by a fat man who wheezed and chain-smoked. He turned out to be the local Health Commissioner. A worse advert for his profession could hardly be imagined. He told me, 'We have no health problems here at all. They're all fit and strong, because they work hard and eat just fruit and chapatis. No malaria, no nothing!'

Next day I headed into town in search of some of the healthy locals and almost immediately bumped into a lively and loud character by the name of Bhagwan Singh. In an eye-catchingly bright turban and with his striking, dyed beard, he was not to be missed. As we talked, he touched his cheek, and announcing suddenly that he needed a shave, sprinted at once across the street and into a barber's chair. Two minutes later he was back. He told me he had come into town from his home in the desert to meet the Palace on Wheels, the tourist train which makes a three-hour stop there each week. Bhagwan Singh was occasionally their local guide.

He was keen to show us his home, and we agreed to have tea with him later that afternoon. I travelled in his car, with my guide following. All the way to the desert he drove like a madman. Once there we walked on the sand dunes and spoke about desert life. It was incredibly peaceful and beautiful. Correspondingly, his mood had calmed considerably. He was no longer the frenetic individual I had stumbled upon in Jaisalmer. We sat on the dunes, watching the sun set, and then headed back to his house, passing women in saris along the path, balancing hefty water containers on their heads with apparent ease.

As we sat outside his home in the darkness, Bhagwan's elderly father joined us. By the light of a full moon we watched the comings and goings of the desert people. In the distance, a small boy appeared in the road, herding cattle. As they drew near, Bhagwan's father began to call, individually and by name, to the animals. Each cow recognised its own call and wandered over to the old man to nuzzle him. It was quite extraordinary.

It seemed at every turn that Rajasthan was populated with exotic and intriguing individuals. In the still night air of the desert I considered the great golden sand dunes, like a shifting mountain range, and the old man at my side whispering to his cattle in a secret language. This alluring place with its echoes of a bygone age brought to mind Twain's impressions from a century before. 'You soon find your long-ago dreams of India rising in a sort of vague and luscious moonlight above the horizon-rim of your opaque consciousness,' he wrote in *Following the Equator*. 'And softly lighting up a thousand forgotten details which were parts of a vision that had once been vivid to you when you were a boy, and steeped your spirit in tales of the East.'

BACK IN JODHPUR WE WENT shopping in the marketplace, where Sir Peter succeeded in creating a minor stir. Just the sight of a large and elegant white gentleman browsing among the various stalls attracted a sizeable crowd. Before long he had taken on the appearance of a Pied Piper pursued by a chattering rabble of children.

He headed for a bookshop, so overflowing with merchandise it was almost impossible to get in. He paused at the entrance. 'You haven't got a Hindi/English phrasebook?' he called into the dim recesses of the shop.

The proprietor waved him inside and produced a chair for his customer while he rummaged among the stock, returning with an armful of books. A Ken Follett novel, Carrie Fisher's *Surrender the Pink*, *Roget's Thesaurus*, the *Oxford Concise English/Hindi Dictionary*.

'*Roget's Thesaurus* – well that's always useful,' Sir Peter remarked. 'But what about a phrasebook?' He was handed a well-thumbed English-language text book. 'Ah, that's it.' Flipping through the pages he began reading aloud.

'"A man is judged by his clothes. Do you have shirtings? It is the stitching that matters, not the cloth. Fast-coloured dresses in winter

An oasis of calm amidst the frantic scrum of traffic: a trader from the Thar Desert region rides his lofty camel through the streets of Jaisalmer.

alone. Tight dresses invite a number of diseases."' He paused. 'It would have to be very porous cloth, I imagine . . . and beautifully stitched. It's a wonderful book for non sequiturs – I'll take it.'

He was handed a business card. '*Pawan Book Depot,*' he read. '*Shop number 51, Clocktower. Available here all types of new and secandhand (sic) books.*'

He got to his feet and prepared to leave. 'I go out enriched now and able to speak English in a way in which it should be spoken,' he said, shaking hands with the proprietor. 'Now I think I shall go to shop number fifty.'

From a distance the neighbouring establishment looked like a particularly unkempt hardware shop. Lots of metal pipes in heaps, and shelves stacked with unfamiliar, industrial-looking objects. On closer inspection it turned out to be something far more sinister.

'Goodness,' said Sir Peter. 'These are bombs, aren't they? There's ammunition of all sorts, petrol to light buildings, the full equipment here for political activities. I don't think there's anything I could take away in my luggage. Certainly the bombs would be suspicious. I wouldn't get them through security.'

When I think of Bombay now, at this distance of time, I seem to have a kaleidoscope at my eye; and I hear the clash of the glass bits as the splendid figures change, and fall apart, and flash into new forms, figure after figure, and with the birth of each new form I feel my skin crinkle and my nerve-web tingle with a new thrill of wonder and delight.
MARK TWAIN, FOLLOWING THE EQUATOR

NEXT DAY WE FLEW TO BOMBAY, or Mumbai as it is now officially called, India's busiest and noisiest city. We were staying at the Taj Mahal Hotel and had been given rooms in the old part of the building. I remembered my previous stay a few weeks before when I had retired to my room early, exhausted, and had then lain in bed, unintentionally eavesdropping on a telephone conversation in progress in the adjoining room. Unintentionally in the beginning, at any rate. Once the illicit nature of the call became apparent, my curiosity got the better of me.

The disembodied voice of the man in Room 602 had filtered

through the locked adjoining door. 'I've been trying to make love to you for twenty-eight years!' he exclaimed. I woke up at once. 'Have you ever made love on a train?' he continued, playfully.

As the conversation – conducted loudly and indiscreetly on a speaker phone – progressed, it became apparent that he was talking to a married woman. Clearly, he was not her husband. I listened, amused, until overtaken by tiredness.

Our first stop in Bombay was Bollywood, the setting for the prolific Indian film industry. India produces hundreds of movies a year, many of them lavish productions, and all famously subject to strict rules which prohibit nudity and on-screen kisses. Interestingly, there are lots of shots of beautiful heroines in clinging wet clothing, which cleverly defy the no nakedness ruling and at the same time manage to be far more erotic for it.

The day we arrived at Film City, preparations were underway for a night shoot. An elaborate set had been constructed, depicting an Indian village on the edge of a man-made lake. In the background was a temple topped with fussy minarets. Marigold petals had been strewn prettily across a dance floor. The whole thing had been created from nothing in

The film sets of Bollywood feed a seemingly insatiable appetite for a mythic, romantic India, where handsome heroes and doe-eyed heroines overcome insurmountable odds to find true love.

Children sit in remarkably well-behaved rows in the mobile creche (above) while their mothers, among them Kamal Kate (below) do much of the heavy manual work on India's urban building sites.

just fifteen days. The leading lady was a dazzling beauty. Her leading man, all rippling muscles and classical good looks, was clearly sensitive about his thinning hair, which he and his dresser carefully teased into place between takes.

The popularity of the movies in India no doubt has something to do with the fact that for most people everyday life is harsh and onerous. There can be few jobs more tough than working on one of the many high-rise building sites to be found in booming Bombay. And it's a surprise to find that the basic work – carrying bricks and cement – tends to be done by women.

Across town we visited a mobile creche, established in 1969 to care for the children of Bombay's working mothers. There were babies barely two weeks old, whose mothers had already returned to work, most as labourers on the city's construction sites. When we arrived we found an informal lesson underway in the open air. Some of the younger children were indoors, cross-legged in rows, quietly feeding themselves curry and rice from tin plates on the floor in front of them. Around the walls were bright paintings produced by some of the youngsters. Facilities were basic, but there was a distinct joyousness about the place.

Without the creche, which moves from place to place in the shadow of the nomadic working mothers, most of the women would have no access to childcare. Much of the heavy, manual work on India's building sites is done by women. It is hard, physical, and poorly paid. And there is something slightly shocking to the Western eye about sari-clad women, bedecked in traditional jewellery, picking their way through rubble, a couple of large breeze blocks balanced on one shoulder.

We had arranged to film on one of Bombay's building sites, but when we arrived with Sir Peter and the crew we were turned away. The site foreman was not convinced we had the necessary permission. Some weeks before, myself and colleague Toby Follett had visited the site and followed the complicated procedures outlined for securing access to film. An impressive amount of paperwork had been submitted to the relevant authorities. As far as we knew, we had satisfied all the criteria. None of this cut any ice on the day, however, and I ended up dashing to the office of the man in charge – a retired Colonel – to try and clear up the confusion. Fortunately, our experience of India had taught us to allow extra time for just such eventualities. After some debate and a phone call to the Colonel's superiors, we were allowed to begin filming.

India's construction workers live an unsettled life, moving on each time a project is completed. We spoke to a woman, Kamal Kate, whose family had been uprooted more than fifty times in their search for employment.

'Is housing arranged for them?' Sir Peter asked our interpreter.

'No. The contractor gives them a plot of land and they have to build the house.'

'Goodness, that's really tough. But they build here, and then when this

work's finished they go somewhere else?'

The interpreter nodded. 'And again they have to build another house.'

'I don't know many people that would put up with that sort of thing. They'd collapse under the weight,' Sir Peter said.

The homes of the construction workers are tiny ramshackle structures, made from sheets of corrugated metal and rough timber. Plastic sheeting – intended as crude waterproofing – flaps in the breeze. There is no running water, no electricity. The shanty settlements contrast sharply with the high-rise buildings all around.

Kamal and her husband had so far built more than fifty different dwellings for themselves and their three children – a boy of fifteen, who also works as a labourer, their twelve-year-old daughter, and their youngest child, who is cared for by the mobile creche. She told us that for around ten hours work a day she earns between two and three hundred rupees (around five pounds sterling) a week. Speaking through an interpreter, she said that the work was hard, but that she had become accustomed to it.

'She says she wants her daughter to be educated. She definitely doesn't want her daughter to do the same kind of work that she is doing because there is a lot of physical turmoil. Her hands have become rough working all these years. She would definitely like her daughter to study and get a better job.'

Like most of the people we met in India, Kamal's marriage had been arranged. She was just fourteen when she became a bride. She had met

India's booming industry only masks the conditions of her poor: here a woman bathes her son in the shanty town which provides them with basic and temporary housing, while behind her loom the modern tower blocks which she and her fellow-workers build.

her husband only once before the wedding, but the union seemed to have been successful.

As far as we could tell, there was little evidence to suggest that the arranged marriage may be going out of fashion in India. Every so often, one discovers a love match. But these are comparatively rare. In the main, most Indians prefer their marriage to be arranged. Increasingly, however, traditional means of finding a suitable partner – where one family will approach another – are being usurped by more unconventional means.

At the offices of India's most popular English-language newspaper, the *Times of India*, we found the place teeming with men and women placing classified advertisements in the personal columns. The matrimonial classifieds, which account for twenty-five per cent of all classified ads in the paper, are booming.

We approached one man, Jaldeep, whose quest for a bride had so far brought more than a hundred replies. His ad had read, 'Smart, handsome 32-year-old. 5′ 8″, 70 kgs, highly educated, fun-loving and affectionate boy, senior manager in a multinational company, residing in posh locality in western suburbs of Bombay. Seeking attractive, tall, slim and well-educated girl below 29, fluent in English, modern outlook and traditional values. Write with recent photo.'

Sir Peter nodded. 'Well, that would certainly convince me if I was open,' he said. 'I think your description of yourself is very modest.' This was generous.

In the space of a month Jaldeep had met a girl he thought would make a suitable wife. Now he faced the task of replying to the many women who had unsuccessfully responded.

'I'm very thankful I'm not Indian,' Sir Peter told him. 'My wife and I could never have had an arranged marriage.'

In the offices of MK Anand, Senior Manager in charge of Classifieds at the newspaper, we discovered that the personal ads have spread beyond the newspaper and onto the Internet. The recently-launched *Times of India* website is attracting between fifteen and eighteen thousand 'hits' a day, many of them Indian expatriates in the United States and the United Kingdom.

Mr Anand demonstrated how it is possible to specify precisely the kind of partner you require – preferred age, religion, language, caste, and so on are fed into the computer which then searches for a suitable match. Sir Peter watched the process with a reluctant fascination. 'I never thought in modern times you'd send a mouse to search for your bride,' he said.

Even skin colour is unashamedly specified. 'The colour fair or very fair has a premium value in most Indian communities,' said Mr Anand. 'There are certain complexions you would not have heard of anywhere else . . . Wheatish–'

'Wheatish?'

'*Wheatish* and *dusky* are terms which are used to mention that the person is not too dark. Dark is me. But maybe if my mother had put in an ad she would have said "dusky boy".'

'Oh dear,' said Sir Peter. 'If I was doing an ad for myself, I would deliberately say "overweight, overage, flatulent old idiot, eager to find a widow of any age", and I'm sure I'd get hundreds of applicants which I would probably turn down.'

Mr Anand cast a professional eye over him. 'In your case I would describe you as very fair, well built, English speaking, convent educated–'

'Convent educated?'

'It means that the person is Anglicised.'

Unusually, Mr Anand's own marriage was not arranged. 'I didn't have to go through the matrimonials column,' he said. 'I found my wife when we were studying together.'

'That's very daring,' said Sir Peter. 'How did you find her?'

He laughed. 'She found me!'

His parents, however, were not happy. His bride-to-be was two years older, came from a different region, and was not a Hindu. Astrologically, too, the couple was far from well-matched. 'It took me two years to convince them,' he said.

Sir Peter said, 'As a parent I would never take the responsibility of forcing my children to do anything, simply because I think most people in this life are not doing the things they want to do. I think one's example is worth more than any amount of lectures or strictures.'

Sunday morning. Every week on this day the *Times of India* features several pages of matrimonial ads. We set off to meet a remarkable character who makes his living through an unconventional matchmaking service. Kavit Kirpalani – or KK, as he is known – describes himself as a senior marriage consultant. He specialises in cases most Indians would consider impossible – divorcees, the diseased, the disabled, the mentally ill. He operates from a stationery shop where he offers both personal and telephone counselling to his matrimonial clients in between over-the-counter sales of writing-paper and pens.

Because it was Sunday it took remarkably little time to get from the hotel to KK's base, Krips Stationers. 'It doesn't look like India at all,' remarks Sir Peter, 'because there's no one on the streets, and usually you're missing dogs, cows and people by inches.' He points to an advert for KK's services in that morning's paper. 'Any defects welcome,' it says.

We arrive at the stationery store-cum-marriage bureau to find KK waiting by his two telephones. Sunday is his busy day. At thirty-one years of age and single, he is not the most obvious candidate for the most delicate of matchmaking tasks. Yet forging successful unions between unlikely parties is something at which he clearly excels.

Under a makeshift awning to blot out the glaring sun, we set up our filming gear outside Krip's stationers, where marriage broker Kavit Kirpalani has his office.

Inside, KK wheels and deals on the telephone non-stop, priding himself on his skill at uniting even the most unlikely of couples in happily wedded bliss.

Solemn and direct, and full of a strange wisdom, he tells Sir Peter that he always wanted to do something unique in life.

'Our basic guidance for people is that they should go more on the qualities of the human being rather than on looks. We tell them that looks are temporary. Today a man looks handsome, tomorrow he may grow old or grey.'

He is interrupted by the telephone. 'Good morning to you, KK Matrimonial Services here . . .' The caller is enquiring about one of his female clients. 'Which caste? Shi'ite Muslims. What is the age of your cousin? Thirty-four. Married before? No. And what is he doing? He's staying in Bombay? Okay, so if I can have your contact number I will talk with the party and get back in touch.'

Throughout our meeting the phone rang regularly, mostly calls in response to KK's *Times of India* ads. His 'hopeless' cases were attracting a good deal of interest.

He began to tell us the story of a couple he had brought together against all odds. The woman, at forty-two and already with two failed marriages behind her, was not on the face of it a good marriage prospect. She was also hundreds of miles away in Delhi. But KK, undeterred, hatched a plot. He had a gentleman from Bombay in mind as a potential partner and decided to put the two together, to begin with through a series of phone calls.

'She had an advantage in that her voice was very attractive,' he told us. 'After a few conversations I took feedback from both parties and they said, yes, it's all going on very healthy.'

At that point KK revealed to the male suitor that the woman was badly scarred from burns. Despite this setback the relationship continued to blossom.

'One day I told him she's got one more problem . . .' said KK, revealing a hitherto unmentioned gynaecological matter. Still, her suitor remained keen.

'He wanted to meet her, and I said to be patient. First get to know each other and then we'll fix up a meeting.'

First, KK needed to have a heart to heart with his female client. There was something he hadn't yet told her about her charming telephone suitor. 'I said to her . . .'

Frustratingly, just then the phone rang. We were forced to wait for the revelation about the male client. Finally, hanging up, KK turned to Sir Peter once more. 'I told the lady there was some problem with the man – he's got a history of psychiatric illness. At one time he was suffering from schizophrenia.' By this time, however, the two had fallen for each other anyway, without even having met. KK's strategy had succeeded.

'What happened to them?' said Sir Peter.

'They are settled,' he said.

KK prides himself on his understanding of the human psyche and his unerring ability to weed out unsuitable candidates for marriage. His client list may be unconventional, but all are genuine in their pursuit of happiness. 'I do understand that sex is part of the life of a human being,' he says, his voice rising. 'But it is not the only thing in life. A man who totally goes only on the benefit of it is also likely to taste the further varieties after marriage.'

Sir Peter tells him, 'He'll have a much shorter life anyway.'

In between phone calls two young men turn up seeking a consultation. They have no appointment. One has recently arrived in Bombay and is looking for a bride – ideally a wealthy and independent woman with her own home in Bombay. 'Any defects will do, but she should be financially stable,' he says.

KK regards him with suspicion. He warns against becoming too dependent on any woman or her family. 'If they are rich people you have to become a puppet in their hands,' he says. 'Your self-respect goes away . . . your pride and ego might get hurt in the future.' His voice rises startlingly. 'I don't say it may happen to you but – they may even ask you to perform some outrageous sexual acts!'

The would-be client shifts uncomfortably in his seat. That would certainly be a high price to pay for a roof over his head.

THE NEXT DAY WE ARRIVE at the King Edward VII Memorial Hospital to observe the weekly clinic of eminent Bombay sexologist, Dr Prakash Khotari. Dr Khotari's public clinic is the only one of its kind in India, and demand for his services is high. In the past sixteen years or so more than 45,000 cases have been referred to him. The waiting area is packed, mainly with men. Dr Khotari himself is serene and endearing. In his casual, open-necked shirt he appears approachable and not in the least intimidating. He may have heard it all before, but his manner remains interested and sympathetic. And his patients seem at ease in disclosing the most intimate details of their dysfunctional sex lives.

A couple sits across the desk from him, explaining that their marriage is in difficulties because of the husband's sexual problems. Dr Khotari is matter-of-fact. Turning first to the husband, he says, 'Tell me what the complaints are.'

The man says, 'I am getting premature ejaculation.'

'I see. Just reply to these questions yes or no. Do you feel like sex? Do you get good erections? Do you penetrate?' He scribbles something on a pad. 'You think you are reaching orgasm early?'

His patient nods.

'Don't worry – this is something very simple.'

Uninhibited advertising: this street trader in Bombay who sells pills and potions for a wide range of sexual problems is not in the least bit coy about the services he offers.

After individual consultations, patients return to the waiting area where they are addressed en masse by the doctor. Assisted by slides he runs through a few basics before dispensing his advice. There are no magic potions offered – they can readily be bought on the streets of Bombay from vendors promising to help anything from 'sex weakness' to syphilis, and are dismissed by Dr Khotari as exploitation of the desperate. His own methods are more common sense than anything. Later, he takes us across town to his private consulting rooms, home to his prized collection of Indian and European erotica. Entering the building, we proceed along musty passages, to a dark and winding staircase, at the bottom of which is a higgledy-piggledy patchwork of professional notices on wooden boards – mostly for urologists and specialists in sexual diseases. There is dust, inches thick, everywhere. It is as far removed from the fashionable Beverly Hills sex doctor's practice as one could imagine.

Once inside his rooms, in pride of place, an ivory chess set modelled on various parts of the human anatomy. He hands Sir Peter a pair of pert ivory breasts. 'Look at the handicraft – the beautiful detail,' he enthuses. 'Until the thirteenth century sex education was given very freely here; but after the invasion of foreigners, sex became last on the agenda, and safety became first,' he says. 'But now the curtain is being raised. We advocate this on television. The government's attitude has changed.' In 1991 the doctor was one of the leading speakers at the first ever international conference on orgasm which, he says triumphantly, 'brought sex from the bedroom into the drawing room.'

The first time I had encountered Dr Khotari, some weeks earlier, he had told me that around one in ten of his patients had indulged in sexual activity with animals. He had reached for his in-tray and selected a file at random. 'There – with buffalo,' he said, pointing at the records. I noticed he had scribbled a note in the margin: 'And the buffalo enjoyed it', it read!

There is only one India! It is the only country that has a monopoly of grand and imposing specialities . . . Its marvels are its own; the patents cannot be infringed; imitations are not possible. And think of the size of them, the majesty of them, the weird and outlandish character of the most of them!'

MARK TWAIN, *FOLLOWING THE EQUATOR*

◆

PRIAYADARSHANI PARK, BOMBAY, at dawn. From a distance we observe a group of people who have gathered for a daily exercise class. Some of the women are in saris, some in leggings. Many of the men are in shorts and tee-shirts. To one side is the Arabian Sea, to the other the city's high-rise buildings, partly shrouded in a grey haze. The group forms a circle, arms in the air, and begins bending and stretching. Occasionally, a single jogger goes past. A chant goes up – Hee, hee, ha, ha! It appears to be a workout for the funny bone. Suddenly, on the count of three, the entire group erupts in raucous laughter.

This is no conventional exercise class. It is, in fact, a meeting of the All India International Laughter Club. Sir Peter, who has seated himself several yards away, shakes his head, utterly bemused. Quite how anyone can laugh at nothing is beyond him. 'I would laugh if I understood it,' he said, frowning as gales of laughter wafted towards him in the cool morning air. He appears both dubious and reluctant when I suggest he might like to join in. As he makes his way over to the group he is met with a chorus of welcoming chuckles. 'I've got to laugh at something,' he protested, surrounded by beaming faces.

'Mouth wide open, let's go for maximum sound,' instructs the group leader. Sir Peter stands obediently with his arms in the air, awaiting the signal to begin. I am far from certain he will warm to the idea of unprovoked laughter, yet, despite his misgivings, he is carried away. The activities of the laughter club are completely infectious. Afterwards, wiping a tear from his eye, he declared, 'That was good, very good.'

The group clustered around, keen to extol the advantages of their slightly bizarre morning constitutional. One man outlined a number of health benefits to be derived from a good laugh. By all accounts laughter is every bit as beneficial as more conventional exercise. 'When you laugh you

Laughter is the ideal medicine: the All India Laughter Club flex their glee muscles with the best of them.

release two chemicals in the brain, which relieve anxiety and tension,' we were told.

Apparently laughter enables the body to produce a natural analgesic and at the same time boost its immune system. A good hearty chuckle is said to be an excellent anti-stress measure, aiding relaxation, and thereby helping to prevent high blood pressure. When the All India International Laughter Club carried out a survey among its members recently, around eighty per cent reported some health benefits. One of the women in the group, casually turned out in leggings, and sporting a short, modern haircut, cheerfully told us that starting the day with a bout of shared laughter had helped her to temper her road rage. 'It changes our personal lives,' she said.

Sir Peter, renowned for his ready wit and ability to make people laugh, could see at least some of the merits of laughter which required nothing in the way of humour to set it in motion. 'I think people ought to laugh more at nothing,' he said. 'It would save a lot of trouble trying to make them laugh.'

Later, back at the hotel, he settled himself on a shady terrace and flipped through a handbook on laughter therapy. 'In a nutshell,' he read, 'it is not at all difficult to laugh without jokes if laughter is practised in a group.' He considered this for a moment. 'Which causes one to reflect how much less dangerous the Nuremberg Rally would have been if they had all gathered in order to laugh. *Sieg ha-ha, sieg ho-ho, seig hee-hee.* I think the history of the world would have been different.' A thought occurred to him. 'In which case – those people are right!'

A crow, perched on a ledge above, screeched. 'Haaaaa!'

Sir Peter swivelled round. 'Shut up,' he commanded. 'I will not be laughed at by a crow!'

WE HAVE A DATE LATER in the morning with Jaldeep, the lonely heart we had met a few days earlier at the *Times of India* offices. Having advertised for a wife in the matrimonial classifieds and been swamped with replies, he had found the woman he hoped to spend the rest of his life with. That day he planned to propose and had agreed to us witnessing it. We hoped he was not going to be turned down.

When we arrived at his home his fiancee-to-be, Angeline, was already there. Jaldeep's family knew what was coming. So did we. Angeline, however, had no idea. She thought we were simply making a film about life in Bombay and sat barefoot and unconcerned, slowly swinging back and forth on a chair suspended from the ceiling as we set up our camera in a corner of the apartment.

It was just ten days since the couple had first met. Four more meetings had ensued. That was enough to convince Jaldeep that he had found the right girl. Despite the brief time they had known one another there was a discernible chemistry between them. 'She has a good sense of humour,' Jaldeep told us, 'and I think both of us are pretty much mature and sensible people.' He smiled shyly. 'And of course she's pretty.'

Angeline grinned. 'He must have a sense of humour – he called me pretty!'

Before the two had met, Angeline's father had made his own assessment of Jaldeep. 'My father said he's a nice guy, not so good looking, wears spectacles, but he seems to be quite a confident guy.' Hardly love at first sight, but the relationship had blossomed rapidly.

That morning she had arrived at Jaldeep's home to meet the rest of the family. She was expecting neither a film crew, nor a proposal of marriage. When Jaldeep suddenly dropped to one knee, clutching a single red rose, and said, 'Will you marry me?' she was completely taken aback.

'Are you serious?' she said, taking the rose.

'Do you need time to think?'

'No,' she said.

'So will you – marry me?'

She smiled broadly. 'Yes.'

We watched, relieved. 'They are listening to us,' Jaldeep told her, nodding in our direction, halfway into the next room. The camera continued to roll. 'Not only listening – recording too,' he confessed. Angeline's eyes widened. 'You all knew about this except me?' she said, gazing around the room.

Jaldeep grinned sheepishly. 'Sorry for the surprise. They wanted to film me proposing to you.'

For a second or two we weren't sure how she was going to take this. She shook her head. 'You knew about this?' she repeated.

'I always do things in style,' Jaldeep joked. 'Now the whole world is going to watch.'

It was a dangerous moment, as Angeline considered the implications. An audience of millions for what should have been an intimate occasion. We braced ourselves, half expecting the rose she was clutching to be hurled back into her suitor's face. Instead, her expression softened. The sense of humour he had fallen for remained intact. He was forgiven. For the time being, anyway.

The Ganges front is the supreme show-place of Benares. Its tall bluffs
are solidly caked from water to summit, along a stretch of three miles,
with a splendid jumble of massive and picturesque masonry, a
bewildering and beautiful confusion of stone platforms, temples,
stair-flights, rich and stately palaces.
MARK TWAIN, *FOLLOWING THE EQUATOR*

◆

WE FLEW FROM BOMBAY to the sacred city of Varanasi, also known as
Benares, on the banks of the river Ganges. A hundred years before,
Twain had arrived here and met with a holy man whom he described
as a 'living god' – the guru Sri 108 Bhaskarananda Saraswati. 'As soon as
I had sobered down a little we got along very well together, and I found
him a most pleasant and friendly deity,' he wrote in *Following the Equator*.
A shrine to this revered figure now stands in the city.

The sacred River Ganges is the heart of Varanasi, India's most holy Hindu city.

Varanasi is the most sacred of all cities to the Hindus. Each year more
than a million pilgrims arrive, many to walk the road – known as
Panchakosi – which loops around the ancient city. Hindus believe that

to die in Varanasi is to achieve Nirvana, and therefore end the cycle of reincarnation.

I had been to Varanasi once before. On that occasion I was intrigued by one of my fellow passengers on the flight from Delhi. He was an Indian gentleman, impeccably dressed, clearly grand, and with the handsome looks of an actor. I assumed he was one of the Bollywood stars. When the plane landed and we headed for the arrivals hall a noisy mob of fifty or so went into a frenzy at the sight of him. As he slipped into the building, a soldier tried to bar the way of the other passengers. I squeezed past and therefore witnessed the ecstatic reception that this man received. I then discovered he was not an actor after all, but a powerful local politician. It was an impressive demonstration of the Indian tendency to deify political leaders.

As Twain had a century earlier, we found ourselves a guru in Varanasi, a holy man named H.M. Chatruvedi, or Guruji. Sharp-witted and voluble, he had entertained us during the reconnaissance trip with daring tales in which sex featured strongly. We were not surprised to learn that many of his disciples were attractive young women. His apparent obsession with sex was tempered by the devout aura in which he was shrouded. I envisaged a lively and entertaining exchange between him and Sir Peter.

On the appointed day for filming, we assembled at sunrise for a boat trip down the Ganges. Guruji was already in situ, straight-backed and serene in the soft morning light. We climbed on board beside him and began drifting slowly down river. In the shallows, close to the ghats — the stone steps at the water's edge — there were already people bathing, some immersing themselves fully clothed. All along the riverbank shrines and temples rose up, like great solid sentries standing guard over the holy waters.

Guruji seemed to have undergone a worrying transformation since our last meeting. For the benefit of the camera he had adopted a stiff and serious tone. Clearly, he was reluctant to commit himself to celluloid as the earthy, sexy individual we had first encountered. He had obviously decided it was more appropriate for a guru to project a wise

Twain described the 'massive and picturesque masonry', the 'confusion of stone platforms, temples . . . rich and stately palaces' that crowd the water's edge.

Guruji and his boatman.

image. As we drifted along he spoke in grave, measured tones, delivering long and incomprehensible monologues. I struggled to connect this solemn discourse with the vibrant character I remembered from a few weeks before. Sir Peter sat in dignified – and, I suspect, bored – silence.

In the background came the slap, slap, slap, of wet clothing being beaten against stone as the laundry wallahs did their washing, laying it out to dry on the steps at the edge of the water.

We had been rowing down river for almost an hour when Guruji said to Sir Peter, 'What is your opinion of sex?'

'I don't know what we'd do without it,' he replied.

'The size of your population suggests that you have discovered a lot of secrets which we may have lost or never had. But I think sex is something which is mystified too often. It used to be natural once but is getting more and more difficult.'

At the edge of the river we could see two bodies wrapped in bright orange cloth, awaiting cremation. We rowed over to the side and picked our way through the narrow passageway leading to the main cremation ghat, Jalsain.

Twain had also paused to watch the cremations, which take place round the clock. 'It is a dismal business,' he wrote in *Following the Equator.* 'The stokers did not sit down in idleness, but moved briskly about, punching up the fires with long poles and now and then adding fuel.'

Sir Peter made his way past towering piles of timber to speak with the man who for thirty years – beginning as a ten-year-old boy – has supervised the daily cremations. He sat cross-legged on the ground, a ring on every finger, an air of quiet piety about him. The smell of smoke was overwhelming.

Down below a body was burning under a stack of wood. Half a dozen dogs lay sleepily close by. Sir Peter wondered what attracted the animals – the heat, perhaps? Through our interpreter we learned that this was not the case. 'What happens, sometimes the body is not burnt and they eat the piece of meat . . .' he explained.

'Oh my God,' said Sir Peter. 'That's why they are queuing up. Well that's a part of the funeral procedure I had not envisaged, I must say.'

A steady procession of bodies, borne by family members, and accompanied by loud chanting, arrived at the ghat while we were there. Some draped in fabulous cloths, which betrayed the wealth of the deceased; others dotted with treasured possessions, which would be set alight along with the corpse.

We returned to the boat and the further pontifications of Guruji, who proceeded to tell us the story of a Yogi who had indulged in sex for an astonishing thirty-six hours. 'That's what we would call a marathon,' Sir Peter told him.

We rowed slowly on. At the Scindia Ghat dozens of people were bathing and soaping themselves on the steps. A saintly-looking old man stood alone, waist deep in the river, splashing his body with drops of the holy water in a ritualistic manner.

'Life is a gamble,' Guruji mused. 'And the stake is life itself.'

Sir Peter nodded in agreement. 'You've got to risk being unhappy in order to deserve happiness.'

Guruji considered this. 'Unless you are prepared to take the risk in life you can't achieve true happiness.'

Sir Peter said, 'We see very much eye to eye. I don't know whether

Above, left: Young and old alike, ordinary people bathe unselfconsciously in the cleansing waters of the river. Among them we saw many holy men (right) whose bodies clearly displayed the rigours of ascetic self-denial.

you've hypnotised me, or what's happened. Have you been cunningly hypnotising me all the way?'

Guruji smiled enigmatically. I had the distinct impression he was about to launch into another lengthy monologue. By now we had been drifting down the Ganges for more than two hours. I leapt in. 'I think we should stop there,' I said, much to everyone's relief.

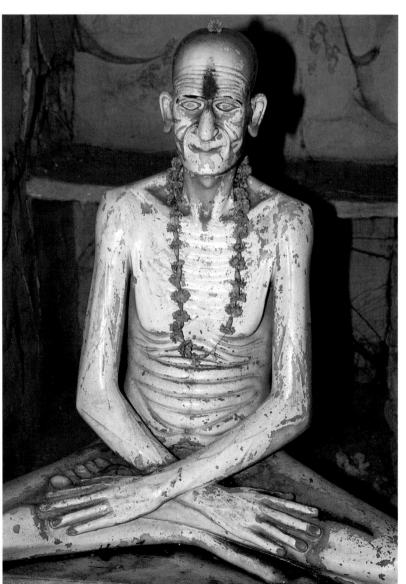

The striking image of Bhaskarananda Saraswati which dominates his shrine is undeniably both powerful and unsettling.

Back on dry land we met with a disciple of Bhaskarananda Saraswati, the 'living god' with whom Twain had been so impressed. Today the shrine to the guru features a remarkably lifelike statue of the man himself. As we approached it in the company of the disciple, Sir Peter was asked to remove his shoes as a sign of respect.

Our guide, Raman Shankar, explained that he had felt himself mysteriously called by the guru and had subsequently worshipped at the shrine and received blessings. 'I feel in my past life that I was one of his disciples,' he told us.

There is undoubtedly something charismatic about the effigy. It almost looks too real, not enough like the statue it is. At a glance it might almost be the man himself, a painfully thin figure, sitting cross-legged in meditation, his slender arms folded across his body. There is a smile on his lips. His eyes, dramatically outlined in black, appear startlingly penetrating.

Raman instructed Sir Peter to concentrate on the eyes of the figure before him. After a few moments he turned back to the disciple. 'When I move he appears to move, but I'm not steady on my feet,' he said.

'No, it's not that – even if I brought you a chair it would be the same,' Raman insisted.

When Twain had met Bhaskarananda he reported that his life of fasting and prayer had given him the appearance of someone older than his sixty years. The encounter had left a lasting impression. He wrote, 'He is utterly, utterly pure; nothing can desecrate this holiness or stain this purity; he is no longer of the earth, its concerns are matters foreign to him, its pains and griefs and troubles cannot reach him. When he dies, Nirvana is his.'

'It's uncanny to think that the guru is still having the effect on present generations that he did on Mark Twain,' said Sir Peter afterwards. 'I stared and stared and was not exactly touched by grace, but admired the quality of the sculpture. But if you stare long enough and hard enough, and don't eat and don't drink, I have a strange feeling that just before you die you can really believe anything they ask you to . . .'

The old part of Varanasi with its narrow, congested streets, struggles to cope with the traffic which pours in every day. Few motor vehicles attempt to negotiate the crowded roads, which throb with pedestrians, cycles, scooters, and the occasional cart drawn by a languid cow. Taxis comprising small, open rickshaws powered by men on bicycles weave dangerously through the packed streets. There is a constant toot, toot, tooting.

Having persuaded Sir Peter to ride on the inspection trolley of the Darjeeling-Himalayan Railway, I suspected he might be less than enthusiastic about a trip round town in an uncomfortable cycle rickshaw. All the same, he agreed. We chose a small and sprightly driver and Sir Peter climbed into the carriage. Within a few hundred yards,

Like some avuncular Pied Piper, Sir Peter attracts a crowd of curious followers in Varanasi's streets.

Opposite: Peace and tranquility
high in the hills: a moment of
relaxation snatched on a terrace
reminiscent of a scene from Jewel in
the Crown.

having bumped over a rough dust road, he begged for mercy. 'I can't do this,' he said.

'Fine,' I replied. 'Let's just get to the end of this road and see from there.'

There were obstacles and hazards at every turn. 'Now what?' I heard Sir Peter say. 'Are we going to get through?' The driver pressed forward and the rickshaw hit a pothole. 'Ooh! It's purgatory,' he muttered.

I could hear Lady Ustinov's admonition from a few months earlier – 'Michael, I hope you are not trying to kill my husband' – ringing once more in my ears. The driver dismounted and calmly steered his bicycle through a wall of people. Sir Peter slumped in his seat, resigned to his fate. A crowd began to follow him and a small, elderly man pushed forward, waving a pack of postcards. Sir Peter parted with 200 rupees for the lot. 'They're rather good, actually,' he said. Another vendor approached, a sack of wooden musical instruments over his shoulder. He stood at the side of the cycle rickshaw, playing sweetly.

'*The Magic Flute*!' declared Sir Peter. 'Beautiful.' He handed over 40 rupees and took possession of one. By now the rickshaw was surrounded by a sea of curious faces and the street was at a standstill. A third vendor appeared, a hooded man with an instrument constructed from a wooden pipe and a coconut, which produced a sound exactly like Scottish bagpipes.

'Oh, the Highlands! I can hear the skirl of the pipes!' said Sir Peter, taking one of the instruments and blowing into it. He hesitated. 'I'm tempted but I haven't room in my luggage.' Reluctantly, he handed it back. 'Lovely sound, but . . .'

The next night, I was glad he had turned down the Indian bagpipes, as I accompanied him and Lady Ustinov to Delhi airport for their flight to Thailand. As well as the usual mountain of suitcases, they had managed to acquire a large amount of hand-baggage during their stay in India. One more item might just have proved disastrous.

There was utter pandemonium at the airport, with staff refusing entry to anyone but passengers. With this very possibility in mind, I had brought my ticket with me for my flight to London the following day, and was allowed in. I waved the Ustinovs off for their Christmas break in Phuket and headed back to the hotel, finally falling into bed at around 1.30 a.m. Less than three hours later the alarm woke me with a start. Back to the airport, this time for the flight to London. Christmas was just three days away.

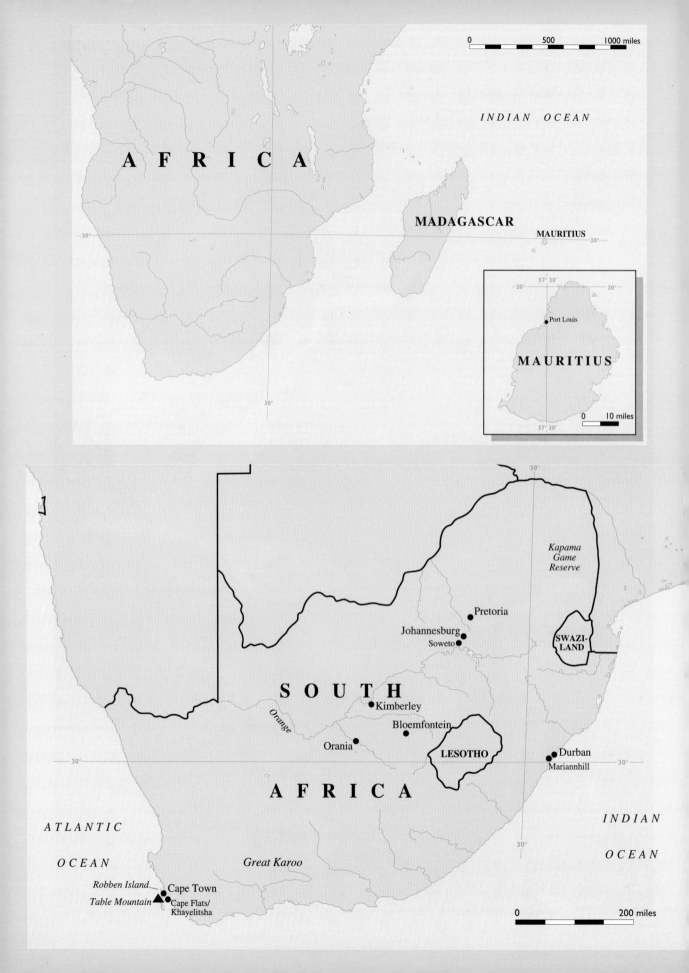

PART FOUR

MAURITIUS

·

SOUTH AFRICA

MAURITIUS

*From one citizen you gather the idea that Mauritius was made first, and
then heaven, and that heaven was copied after Mauritius.*
MARK TWAIN, FOLLOWING THE EQUATOR

◆

I LEFT LONDON FOR MAURITIUS a day ahead of everyone else, fondly
imagining that twenty-four hours on my own would provide valuable
thinking time before embarking on the final film in the series. However, as
had so often been the case, my plans went awry almost as soon as I stepped
off the Air Mauritius plane.

It was early morning and the day stretched luxuriously ahead of me. As I
strolled towards immigration control, I began to contemplate the tasks that
lay ahead. Nothing terribly onerous, as far as I could tell. A few phone calls.
A brief meeting. A final glance at the schedule. Perhaps there would be time
for a swim in the sparkling Indian Ocean.

The immigration officer interrupted my train of thought. 'What is your
business here?' he inquired in a tone which was impersonal and brusque. I
explained that I was about to make a documentary film. He was
unimpressed. 'Where is your onward ticket?' he said.

For reasons too complicated even to begin to explain, I didn't have one.
However, I did have a reservation with South African Airways for a flight to
Durban in South Africa in less than a week's time. This was not good
enough. A reservation is not the same as a ticket. Behind me, the queue
shuffled impatiently. The official impounded my passport while I went in
search of someone – anyone – who might be able to convince him to let
me into the country.

Finding the Air Mauritius desk unmanned, I threw myself on the mercy
of the local tourist board. Fortunately, the man in charge – an extremely
genial character named Iqbal – knew all about our plans to film on the
island. Together we returned to immigration where, after much discussion,
my passport was handed over. I hoped that Iqbal would be on hand the
following morning to repeat the process on behalf of Sir Peter and the crew,
due in on an early flight.

On arrival at the hotel I decided to double check our onward flights. SAA
calmly informed me that reservations were in place for Sir Peter and me.
They had no bookings, however, for the crew or assistant producer Pratap
Rughani. This was precisely the kind of news I did not want to hear. It was
just the beginning. In between wrangling with SAA, a call came through
from the series production office at Granada Television in London. Sound
recordist Mike Lax's passport was missing.

It emerged that he had sent it to the US Embassy with an application for

From the mountains the whole panoramic sweep of the island's western coastline was laid out at our feet.

a visa to cover a filming trip scheduled to follow our series. The Embassy had hung onto it for much longer than he had anticipated. Suddenly anxious, he endeavoured to trace it. The Embassy told him it was in the post. Two days went by and it failed to show up. On the Friday before his planned Monday flight to Mauritius, he alerted Sharon Thomas in our production office to his problem. Saturday's mail arrived. No passport. On the day of his flight he waited nervously for the post, which contained the usual bills and junk mail but, predictably, nothing from the US Embassy. The hours were now ticking by. He and the crew were booked on the Air Mauritius flight from Manchester to Paris, where they would connect with Sir Peter. It seemed increasingly unlikely that he would make it.

From my hotel I began to explore the possibility of finding a temporary replacement. The phone in my room rang constantly. Suddenly there appeared to be a number of crises looming: the getting Sir Peter and the crew into the country without onward tickets crisis, the SAA lack of reservations crisis, and the missing passport crisis. I called London and suggested badgering the US visa section one more time. If the passport was really nowhere to be found, perhaps an emergency replacement could be provided, and Mike could join us in Mauritius a day late. Meanwhile, the crew – minus sound recordist – were en route for Paris.

I hung up and the phone rang again almost at once. It was my South African contact with the Ministry of Tourism calling on his mobile phone from an international travel convention in Berlin. Apparently the Minister was now keen for President Mandela to meet with Sir Peter in South Africa, and would try to arrange an encounter. We spoke briefly and I promised to get back to him. Instantly, the phone rang again. Sharon in London. The missing passport had been located . . . in the basement of the US Embassy. A courier was at that moment speeding towards Heathrow, where an agitated Mike Lax was waiting to board a flight to Paris.

I gazed out of my hotel window at the ocean, glittering seductively in the sunlight. The view might have been created by the efforts of three of my favourite painters in collaboration. The exotic green flora beloved of Douanier Rousseau, the Hockneyesque blue and turquoise waters of the lagoon enclosed by the coral reef, all perfectly framed by a French window in the style of Matisse. For a few moments the phone was silent and I sat on the edge of my bed transfixed, yearning to be in the view rather than simply beholding it.

Then, using an American telephone credit card number, I called my South African contact in Berlin. My call – from Mauritius to a South African mobile number – went via the US. As I waited for the mobile phone to be answered thousands of miles away in Germany I pondered the quirks of late twentieth century communication. What on earth would Twain have made of it?

The next day I returned to the airport to meet Sir Peter and the crew, and made my way to the passport area – strictly off-limits to ordinary mortals like

Twain described the sea around Mauritius as 'just about the divinest color known to nature', and the view from our hotel gave us no reason whatever to contradict him.

me – by adopting an air of authority and determination. It worked. No one challenged me, even though I had no right to be in a restricted area.

Although the Mauritius Tourism Board had helpfully faxed passport control, requesting that our party be allowed into the country, I found myself faced with an official who insisted on written confirmation of our reservations from SAA. I explained that in two days' time we were intending to film the Independence Day celebrations, and that to turn us away would be potentially highly embarrassing for the government. This seemed to do the trick and, despite our lack of tickets (and dubious reservations) Sir Peter and the crew – who had yet to emerge from the flight – would be admitted to Mauritius.

First off the plane was a weary-looking Mike Lax, who trudged towards me and clasped me in a bear hug. Neither of us said anything. Sir Peter, seemingly immune to jet lag, emerged on his usual excellent form. He appeared in a wheelchair, a bag from the Duty Free shop in Paris on his knee. 'I'm sorry I'm so heavy,' he told the porter. 'It's too late to do anything about it now.'

When we arrived at our hotel, The Residence, he put on an act, pretending to be the Governor of Texas. The staff, gracious and charming, seemed entirely taken in. Since he both looked and sounded exactly as if he might indeed be the Governor of Texas, this was hardly surprising.

That afternoon I turned my attention to securing entry into the VIP enclosure at the forthcoming Independence Day festivities. Security for the event was predictably tight. As a genuine VIP, Sir Peter already had a ticket to the inner circle. The rest of us, however, had been excluded and shunted into the press area. In the course of the afternoon I found myself passed from one bureaucrat to another, none of whom was able to help. Finally, my persistence paid off. I managed to get through to the organiser of the event – the Minister of Arts and Culture. Perhaps flattered by the suggestion that we might want to interview him, he promised to see what he could do.

The following morning I am woken at 6 a.m. by a piercing and unpleasant ringing in my ears. It turns out to be my mobile phone. The driver who has been booked to chauffeur Sir Peter from location to location over the next few days has bad news.

'I can't come,' he says. 'I'm going to a funeral.'

'Well, we need a driver.'

He sounds genuinely surprised. 'You do?'

'Yes – please find a replacement!'

I manage a quick swim before ordering breakfast in my room. The receptionist cheerfully wishes me a happy birthday. I had forgotten all about it.

LATER THAT MORNING we set off for the capital, Port Louis, to meet Devinder Viraswamy, a champion of the Creole language, the French-sounding dialect widely spoken in Mauritius. We had arranged to meet Devinder in the capital's beautifully-preserved old theatre. Built in 1822, it is celebrated, somewhat bizarrely, for having been the setting for an early production of Mozart's *Don Giovanni*. No one was able to explain quite how this had come about.

According to Devinder, more than eighty per cent of the local population speak Creole as their first language. 'It is the language of Mauritius,' he tells us. 'The de facto national language.'

Yet, officially, it is not accorded the status of either English or French.

To the casual observer, Creole appears to be a close relation of French. The accent is similar, as is much of the vocabulary. Structurally and grammatically, however, it has little in common with textbook French, taking its influences instead mainly from English, Indian and African languages.

'The Creole language is a good example of how cultures from different parts of the world can blend and lead to the formation of something new,' explained Devinder.

Friends, Mauritians, countrymen . . . At Devinder Viraswamy's request Sir Peter declaims Mark Antony's famous speech from Julius Caesar in Creole.

A respected local theatre director, he has translated some of Shakespeare's plays into Creole in a bid to encourage its broader use. He was keen to school Sir Peter in a couple of passages from *Julius Caesar* à la Creole, beginning with the famous 'Friends, Romans, countrymen . . .' 'You know, the speech of Mark Antony after the death of Caesar,' Devinder explained. 'This grandiose speech. Mauritians love that, and it was very easy for me to get Shakespeare into Creole by maintaining that kind of forceful language. I will now ask you a favour, Sir Peter . . .'

Sir Peter, a fluent French speaker, was more than happy to have a go. In the centre of the stage, playing to an audience of one, he delivered his lines as if he had been speaking Creole all his life.

Devinder was delighted. 'Bravo,' he said, his applause echoing around the empty theatre. 'You are going to help us in our campaign to promote the language. If Sir Peter can speak Creole, it must be a good language . . .'

'Well, no,' came the modest reply. 'If Sir Peter can speak Creole, anybody can.'

We headed off for the Institute of Mauritius, where one of the island's original inhabitants has been as carefully preserved as the Port Louis theatre. Until the French first colonised it in 1715, Mauritius remained an unpopulated paradise. It was home, however, to the dodo, the flightless bird which has long been extinct. Inside a glass case in the museum is an example

Understandably, the dodo tends to look somewhat unhappy at its sudden extinction after thousands of years of undisturbed existence on Mauritius . . .

of one of these creatures, although to say it has been preserved is bending the truth somewhat. The exhibit actually consists of a reconstruction of a dodo on a real skeleton, although at a glance it appears authentic enough.

Apparently the dodo population began to dwindle once the first settlers arrived on the island. Not, as one might imagine, because they were hunted for their meat. In fact, there is nothing to suggest that they were palatable. Their demise stemmed from their habit of laying their eggs at ground level – a consequence of their inability to fly. Until the first settlers came, the eggs were safe. But the ships brought with them predators, in the shape of rats, which came ashore and found the eggs tasty. Increasingly vulnerable, and finding their once undisturbed environment changing, the lumbering birds eventually disappeared.

Sir Peter regarded the dodo in its glass case. 'It's not often one comes to a place and is faced with the original inhabitants – the only original inhabitant, in fact,' he declared. He studied its solemn countenance.

'It looks like an English judge. Probably more accurate in its assessments,' he mused. Two giant eggs caught his eye. 'You'd never be asked in a restaurant if you wanted more than one . . .'

What there is of Mauritius is beautiful . . . a ragged luxuriance of tropic vegetation of vivid greens of varying shades, a wild tangle of underbrush, with graceful tall palms lifting their crippled plumes high above it; and you have stretches of shady dense forest with limpid streams frollicking through them.
MARK TWAIN, FOLLOWING THE EQUATOR

WE WERE ON OUR WAY to visit an old, French colonial-style mansion called Eureka. The house, a long, low building dating back to the eighteenth century, nestles at the foot of a sheltering hill. A verandah runs all the way around the property, which is constructed in timber and painted white, its row of shuttered attic windows serving to accentuate its Frenchness.

All around lay lush, verdant scenery. At the side of the mansion a spectacular waterfall tumbled into a deep gorge. On the reconnaissance trip we had swum in the cool, crystal clear water.

The house has been carefully preserved (the theme of the day was rapidly becoming preservation) and today serves as both a family home and a museum. Its owner, Jacquie Maroussem, a descendant of the former French *noblesse* who once ruled the roost on Mauritius, guided us through the house with an air of undisguised pride. With its gleaming polished floors and its beautiful old furniture, it felt as if we were stepping back into a more genteel age. Yet while the atmosphere at Eureka is thick with the past, in other respects its owner has moved with the times.

In the days when the French ran things they regarded themselves as the white aristocracy of the island, even after the island was ceded to the British in the early nineteenth century. There was a definite sense of superiority among the Franco-Mauritian community, some of which lingered until fairly recently. 'We thought we were the best because we came from France,' said Jacquie with a Gallic shrug.

Now heavily outnumbered, the French have learned to be more tolerant, particularly towards the Indians, now in the majority, and governing the country.

'We are learning every single day from the Indian people,' explained Jacquie. 'When we got independence, we were scared of what was called in those days Indianisation. And we received the most fantastic lesson from

French colonialism has left some elegant legacies behind: Jacquie Maroussem's eighteenth-century house in its idyllic setting.

In common with many of the island's original French Mauritian families, Jacquie Maroussem (above) once had doubts about the new independent Mauritius. Now, however, he has become an enthusiastic convert to the vibrant, multicultural society that characterises this small nation.

those Indians who were the sons of liberals – who had been ill-treated by our grandfathers – asking us to come and work together and be part of a nation. We are losing our complex of superiority, slowly but surely.'

Jacquie Maroussem is a sixth generation French Mauritian. His wife is also French. And despite his newfound tolerance, Jacquie believes in the value of maintaining his sense of identity. His French roots matter enormously, which is why he is determined to keep Eureka as a monument to the past. 'You are now in a bastion of French colonialism,' he told Sir Peter, as they sipped vanilla tea on the verandah.

Over the years, Eureka has played host to a number of distinguished visitors to Mauritius. Jacquie recalled a lunch at which the Duke and Duchess of York were guests of honour. To commemorate the occasion he had compiled an album of photographs featuring examples of the island's architecture, which was to be presented to the royal couple.

'The pressure was immense that day,' he told us. 'Police here and police there.' In fact, he claimed with characteristic hyperbole, there was a police officer secreted behind every one of the mansion's 109 doors.

Two hours before the lunch he had inspected the commemorative album and, to his horror, discovered a potentially disastrous error in the inscription on the cover. 'Embossed with gold letters, "To their Royal Highnesses the Duck and Duchess of York". Can you imagine the scandal, the catastrophe?' he said.

The album was hurriedly whisked away and the inscription discreetly corrected before the Duke had a chance to see it.

'I regret that you were able to change it at all,' said Sir Peter. 'I think "Duck" is much better.'

Jacquie shook his head. 'On that day I was very embarrassed.'

'You might have been,' replied Sir Peter. 'But I think they all have a great sense of humour, and are dying to prove to everybody that they are human beings. They're not always given the chance. But with you and your printer there was a golden opportunity which was, unfortunately, missed because of your emergency tactics.'

NEXT MORNING WE RETURNED to Port Louis, where a crowd was already gathering behind the crush barriers lining the route for the Independence Day parade. A few Mauritian flags fluttered, and a selection of Elton John compositions, rearranged into easy-listening instrumentals, played over the public address system. Sir Peter and I were admitted without

The Island's Independence Day anniversary celebrations culminated in vibrant displays that lit up the night.

hesitation to the VIP enclosure. The crew, following in a separate vehicle and still without the promised VIP passes, were stopped. I had to go back and do some explaining before the police officers finally waved them through. Meanwhile, Sir Peter found his seat among the various dignitaries, many representing overseas governments. Unfortunately, he was obscured from our camera by a pillar. Mustering considerable gall I asked the Saudi Ambassador to swap seats to give Sir Peter – and our camera – a better view. Obligingly, he did so, and promptly vanished into obscurity.

It was a colourful event. A well-drilled military band – playing in tune for once – progressed down the road. The President of Mauritius swept up in a limousine. Everyone was dressed formally in suits and ties despite the stifling heat. A helicopter hovered noisily overhead, trailing a banner bearing a logo which marked the island's thirty years of independence. Drum majorettes in red jackets trimmed with silver, short white pleated skirts and calf-length boots twirled batons with aplomb.

A procession of brightly decorated floats bearing slightly ridiculous larger-than-life displays trundled down the road to polite applause.

'I particularly liked the mobile telephone float,' Sir Peter said. 'It took four hands to hold one phone. Let's hope they make a lighter model – one that only needs three hands to support it.'

Military bands, immaculate
majorettes and boisterous students
all joined forces to create the
carnival atmosphere of the
Independence Day parade.

That afternoon we went to the grandest hotel in Port Louis, hoping to take some scenic shots across the city from the roof. Not all rooftops are ideal for filming, and this one was a disappointment. We retreated indoors and identified two suites which would offer spectacular views. They were both occupied; one – the Presidential suite – by the visiting Indian Vice President. The suite directly below had been taken over by his security personnel. Somehow we persuaded them to give us access, although we clearly constituted a security risk. As we filmed, an anxious security man followed us around, glancing nervously up at the ceiling every few seconds.

Back in town we returned to the waterfront VIP area, where again the crew were refused entry. All we had in our possession was one rather grand, embossed invitation, made out to Sir Peter. I quickly scribbled on it in fairly illegible handwriting, so that it read *Sir Peter Ustinov, Michael Waldman, and the Granada TV crew*. Improbably, it did the trick. The police officer guarding the gate inspected it with a degree of scepticism, but allowed us in.

That night there was a fantastic fireworks display and a laser show. The '1812 Overture' boomed out in time with the pyrotechnics. As VIPs we had an excellent view. It was only later that we discovered how fortunate we had been. A French TV team, in Mauritius making an official film for the tourism authority, had been refused access. Understandably furious, they were forced to ask if they could borrow some of our footage.

As the festivities drew to a close, the dignitaries began to leave in strict order of protocol. First, the Mauritian President, who gave a low-key wave to the crowd as his motorcade swept by. Next, the Indian Vice President, who chose not to wave at all. Then the Mauritian Prime Minister, the *de facto* head of government, who raised his arms above his head, hustings-style, in a triumphant salute to his people. In response came a rather tepid ripple of applause.

The crowd of around 100,000, some still clutching their miniature flags, began to disperse. It had been a good-humoured celebration. Our own good humour waned somewhat when we returned to our vehicle, to find it completely gridlocked.

THE NEXT AFTERNOON FINDS US at the Prime Minister's residence to meet Mr Navin Rangoulam, who came to power following the elections in 1995. Before he arrives, we begin moving furniture around to create a suitable setting in which to film him in conversation with Sir Peter. As various heavy objects are being repositioned, I suddenly notice the PM striding purposefully past, seemingly unaware of the mild chaos being created on his terrace. Cameraman Mike Fox, assuming the grey-suited figure to be simply another Prime Ministerial aide, is about to ask him to lend a hand. I freeze, anticipating

an embarrassing exchange. Fortunately the PM is too quick for Mike, and vanishes before he can be press-ganged into helping.

Meanwhile, Sir Peter, sitting quietly in the background, is approached by a smiling aide. Imagining him to be Mr Rangoulam, he greets him warmly. 'I saw you on television last night. Very impressive.' I swiftly intervene to point out that this is not in fact the PM. Sir Peter, unfazed, salvages the situation smoothly. 'Television images are never very clear,' he tells the bemused official.

The Mauritian Prime Minister turns out to be a genial, softly-spoken character, who has spent much of his adult life overseas. Qualified as a doctor and lawyer, he spent long periods working in England and the United States. Although he grew up during a period of political change – his father was Prime Minister when Mauritius gained Independence – he told Sir Peter that he had had no serious ambitions to pursue a career in politics. In fact, at one stage his intention was to settle in the West Yorkshire town of Bingley, where he was working as a doctor. It was only when his mother died and his father became ill that he decided to return home. Gradually, he became more embroiled in the political scene.

Mr Rangoulam has enormous pride in his country's diversity of cultures. The cosmopolitan nature of the population had been evident in the crowds who had gathered in the main square of Port Louis for the celebrations the previous day. 'Instead of division, this can be a source of strength,' he told Sir Peter.

What is impressive about Mauritius is the manner in which the country's

Before he returned home and eventually took up the reins of power, the Prime Minister, Navin Rangoulam (left) practised as a doctor in the Yorkshire town of Bingley.

many different races on the whole happily co-exist. This no doubt owes much to the fact that there is no one ethnic group which can lay claim to having been there at the outset. Everyone came from somewhere else; unlike Hawaii, for instance, where the natives saw their rights and culture subsumed by the arrival of foreign invaders, or Fiji, where much of the racial tension had stemmed from the perception that the Indian immigrants were succeeding at the expense of the indigenous people. And in New Zealand and Australia we had seen how the native people had been exploited by dominant white settlers. Mauritius, on the other hand, had no indigenous people to begin with.

Even its white population is mixed. It was the Dutch who first discovered the island, but they decided not to settle there. In around 1715 Mauritius was occupied by the French, remaining a French colony until 1814, when the British assumed control until the country gained its independence in 1968.

When Twain was there a hundred years ago he remarked on the incredible diversity of the people. 'Went ashore in the forenoon at Port Louis, a little town, but with the largest varieties of nationalities and complexions we have encountered yet,' he wrote in *Following the Equator*. 'French, English, Chinese, Arabs, Africans with wool, blacks with straight hair, East Indians, half-white, quadroons – and great varieties of costumes and colours.'

Mr Rangoulam – himself an Indian Mauritian – is keen that no one is excluded when it comes to contributing to the success of the island and sharing in its prosperity. 'We are in the process of nation-building, and we want everybody to have a chance in life and to feel they are part of this country,' he said. 'I keep telling people, all of you have a contribution to make.'

Interview over, we carefully rearranged his furniture once more and, before leaving, relaxed on the cool terrace over a perfect English tea.

THAT EVENING WE HAD ARRANGED to meet a Catholic priest, Father Souchon, at his church in Port Louis. The flamboyant minister describes himself as 'culturally French, but terribly Mauritian.' His appeal is broad. He claims that more than 2,500 people pack into his church for mass on Sundays.

Father Souchon is well aware that he is preaching to a disparate congregation, drawn together in a common faith, perhaps, but with their own distinct sense of identity. In acknowledgement he has an impressive array of vestments which complement the different origins of his flock. He led Sir Peter to the sacristy and threw open the door of his wardrobe, to reveal a rail filled with exotic robes. Vestments in bright silk, embroidered in symbols evocative of the island's communities – Hindu, Mauritian, Chinese, African – shimmer exotically in the light. 'This is my treasure,' he declared.

'What a wardrobe – magnificent!' exclaimed Sir Peter.

'This is my very, very precious vestment,' continued Father Souchon, extracting a brilliantly decorated robe. 'This is when I go to the mosque for a wedding or for some prayer, and you see, in Arabic, this is the first phrase of the Koran.' He gazes at the vestment with delight. 'So I use these. This is Mauritius!'

He studies the rack of clothing. There are robes in exotic Oriental silk, in bright, vivid shades, decorated with complicated embroidery, painstakingly completed by hand.

'Long ago the police were allowed to wear pink just to say Christmas is coming, Easter is coming. I like the same symbolism of colour.' He picked out a robe in midnight blue trimmed in gold. He told us it was the vestment he had worn while celebrating an open air Christmas mass before five thousand people. 'I suppose I will wear this for mass tonight,' he mused.

'How long do you need to change?'

'Oh, it's a question of one minute.'

And a moment later, with the help of an altar boy, the dazzling robe has been slipped on and he is ready for mass.

'Before you escape into a divine world from a secular one,' Sir Peter asked him, 'How do you see the future of this country?'

'The future is bright. When I see what's happening all around the world, every day I say thank God we can live together – different religions, different races: Asia, Africa, Europe,' he replies. 'You see, in Mauritius we have no

Father Souchon's sumptuous range of vestments are designed to help him minister to all the island's diverse ethnic groups: Indian, Chinese and African as well as Catholic French.

colours, everything is in hues. Shading and mixing together. It's our *arc-en-ciel* – what do you call that?'

'Rainbow.'

'...What would be the future is very difficult to see. Will there be a mixture of races, and we are all Mauritians? Nobody white, no yellow, no black?' said the priest. 'You can either have a fruit salad, where you've got the different fruits keeping their own taste, but at the same time the juice tastes of all the fruits together. Or you can have marmalade, where everything is crushed and there is only one taste, of all the fruits combined. Personally, I prefer the fruit salad.'

WE WERE LEAVING MAURITIUS the next day, and had some time to ourselves in the morning. I badly needed to tackle my expenses, but was distracted by the view from my room. Sunlight sparkled on the still ocean. I was reminded of Twain sailing from Calcutta to Mauritius a century before, when he noted in *Following the Equator* that 'the sea is a Mediterranean blue; and I believe that that is about the divinest color known to nature.'

Leaving my expenses to one side, at last I went windsurfing.

I came back to find Sir Peter relaxing on the hotel's shaded wooden deck, overlooking the sea. Sipping at a local Green Island Rum, he studied the label on the bottle. On it was printed Twain's quotation from *Following the Equator,* that Mauritius was made first and then heaven, and heaven was copied after Mauritius.

'That's what an elderly native told him,' mused Sir Peter, 'and now it's attributed to Mark Twain himself, rather than the anonymous elderly native.'

He took another sip. 'Like all good rums, hardly in evidence until you've had your third glass, and you try to rise.' With that he began to sing, deliberately slurring as if the Green Island Rum had already – after no more than two or three wary sips – taken its toll.

It was with a sense of sadness that we checked out of The Residence, where everyone had made us so welcome. Mauritius had struck me as a near-perfect paradise island, with its beauty, its lack of racial tension, and its laid-back air. Twain, however, had not been so captivated. He felt it lacked a sense of the dramatic. 'That is Mauritius; and pretty enough,' he remarked in *Following the Equator*. 'The surfaces of one's spiritual deeps are pleasantly played upon, the deeps themselves are not reached, not stirred. Spaciousness, remote altitudes, the sense of mystery which haunts apparently inaccessible mountain domes and summits reposing in the sky – these are the things which exalt the spirit and move it to see visions and dream dreams.'

At the airport we picked up our one-way tickets to Durban. Sir Peter inspected his departure card. 'This makes a change from Malaysia,' he said, 'where I was given a visa which allowed me to perform, but not to sit out or dance with the audience. I asked what that meant, and they said "It's a measure we had to bring in to curb the activities of travelling prostitutes. Since you entered the country by aeroplane you fall into that category."'

He slipped the departure card into his passport. 'No one's said that to me here, and since I'm on my way out now I'm safe to dance with anyone I wish.'

Four hours after leaving Mauritius, we arrived in South Africa on the final leg of our trip. It was a Saturday night, and by the time we presented ourselves at the customs desk it was late. The official frowned. We were carrying one-way tickets? We were. He shook his head. Unless we could produce an onward ticket – proof of our intention to leave South Africa – we would not be admitted. It was the Mauritian experience all over again.

I glanced at Sir Peter, elegant and distinguished, a shining example of a law-abiding citizen, if ever there was one. Hardly the type to overstay his welcome and become a drain on the economy. The wrangling continued. The official was resolute. In the arrivals hall, the Mayor of Durban was waiting to greet us. Sir Peter surrendered his passport to the customs official and was allowed as far as the VIP lounge to meet the Mayor – by now severely embarrassed by our difficulties.

A taste of heaven distilled: Sir Peter, just like the rest of us, succumbs to the seductive spirit of Mauritius.

I produced evidence of the reservations which would ensure our departure from South Africa in three weeks' time. The official remained unmoved. He wanted to see our tickets, not reservations. But the last flight of the day had long since departed and the SAA desk was deserted. There was one other option – to deposit enough money to cover our flights. Fine. We had travellers' cheques or a credit card. Neither was acceptable. Only cash or a banker's draft would do.

In the background hovered a representative from the KwaZulu Natal Tourism Authority, appearing increasingly mortified as our negotiations wore on. An hour and a half went by before the Chief Immigration Officer, having consulted his superiors in Johannesburg and been given all sorts of guarantees by us, could finally be persuaded to allow us into South Africa.

SOUTH AFRICA

La Trappe must have known the human race well. The scheme which he invented hunts out everything that a man wants and values – and withholds it from him. Apparently, there is no detail that can help make life worth living that has not been carefully ascertained and placed out of the Trappist's reach. La Trappe must have known that there were men who would enjoy this kind of misery, but how did he find it out?
MARK TWAIN, FOLLOWING THE EQUATOR

◆

OUR FIRST NIGHT IN SOUTH AFRICA was to be spent in a monastery formerly run by the Trappist Order. Its original inhabitants endured extremes of hardship in the name of their faith. When Twain visited Mariannhill a hundred years ago, he was astonished at the conditions in which the monks existed. Living in utter austerity, they worked long hours, rising at 2 a.m. to begin the day's tasks, subsisting on meagre food. Their rigid code demanded that they observe a strict vow of silence. 'It is such a sweeping suppression of human instincts, such an extinction of the man as an individual,' observed Twain in *Following the Equator.*

Thankfully, the rules governing monastic life at Mariannhill had relaxed considerably by the time we got there. The accommodation was basic, but the welcome was warm. We were each given a simple room with a plain, wooden cross mounted on the wall for decoration. After our long wrangle at the airport I don't suppose any of us minded. We were just glad to have reached our destination and to have a place to sleep.

Next morning we were up early to attend the Zulu mass, which began at 6 a.m. Most of the congregation consisted of staff from the monastery. The priest who led the service – a German named Father Peter – addressed them fluently in their own tongue. The hymns were sung as if by a carefully rehearsed choir. Strong, clear voices in perfect harmony.

At one time all the monks at Mariannhill came from Europe – most of them from Germany. They were white missionaries who brought the word of their God to black Africans. Today, the monastery is a very different place. There are fewer white priests coming into Africa now, and those who are left – there are just a dozen at Mariannhill – are in the minority. A new breed of African missionaries is emerging: young black men from countries like Zimbabwe, Zambia and South Africa, convinced that they too have a vocation to spread the Christian message.

When I first visited the monastery, I had met with some of the novices, intrigued to hear what had drawn them to a life which to me – and to Twain, too, a century earlier – seemed so alien. I wanted to know how modern man coped with vows of poverty, celibacy and obedience.

I spoke with three very special young men, who were poised on the verge of a life which most of us could never contemplate, and was struck by their serenity and sincerity. To my surprise they told me it was not the vow of celibacy that they found the most difficult. It was harder, by far, to be obedient. Never to criticise or oppose that which they had vowed to accept.

We caught up with the same three once more after mass. Sir Peter spoke to them in the cloisters of the building. They perched on a low stone wall, dressed – despite the heat – in heavy black monastic robes, which reached to their ankles.

'You may have noticed I put a tie on this morning,' said Sir Peter. 'It's indicative of the kind of freedom I have preserved for a rather long time now – and which I'm rather jealously preserving. Every morning I can choose another tie and you can't. I want to know what it is about you that attracted you towards this life you're about to embark on.'

'It comes from the bottom of the heart. It is a decision that one can't make easily,' Ivo told him. Collins, twenty-two, said simply, 'We are trying to live the best way we can.' John, just twenty years old, told Sir Peter that they had put themselves at the disposal of whichever elements of the community needs them; and that since they are not tied by commitments to a wife or family, they are free to go wherever they might be required. Their first responsibility at all times is to God.

There is still time, however, for them to address any doubts they may have. First they make their temporary vows. Then, after another three years, their final vows. In the meantime they can reflect on whether they are, after all, suited to a monastic life.

When I had met these same novice monks a few weeks earlier I had been surprised and moved by their willingness openly to express their reservations about the religious life they were pursuing. It seemed important to them to articulate their concerns.

Sir Peter clearly had the same impression. 'You're feeling your way towards the inevitable,' he said.

'With the help of God,' said Ivo, 'we hope to achieve what we came here for.'

'Presumably you can go either way,' said Sir Peter. 'Either take vows and continue in this life of rarefied but intense help for others; or you can also do something completely different, but maintain the same precepts and the same goals. So that the abandonment of vows doesn't seem to me to be an automatic end to the kind of feelings you have for your fellow man.'

At Mariannhill there is a perceptible gulf between the old – epitomised by the senior German monks – and these newly-arrived young Africans. 'We had to look at the community – are we acceptable, are we going to fit in?' said Collins. 'These are the older ones, and in some ways you find there are differences in understanding, because we are young.' Yet the company of older monks, had, he admitted, deepened his understanding and helped him grow.

'We really should have respect for each other, in order to be able to speak on equal terms,' said Sir Peter.

Occasionally, however, the generation gap can lead to disagreement. The vow of obedience means that there is no room for debate, no opportunity for the novice to disagree with his superior. 'If you find that your ideas are not acceptable, you have to bend to the rules, because they are the ones implementing the rules,' said Collins.

'But wait another ten years and present your ideas again, and you will see that the resistance will have suffered a bit because the world moves forward, you can't stop it,' said Sir Peter. 'I believe nothing is absolutely permanent, nothing.'

As the lunch bell rang out, the monks streamed in to the dining hall. All stood while grace was said aloud. Sir Peter was formally welcomed. Despite their cloistered life, they had managed to see a film he had made in the Vatican. How much had changed since Twain's day, when simple conversation was forbidden and there was strictly no entertainment at Mariannhill.

Over lunch, Father George explained how the early Trappists in South Africa had been presented with a choice by Pope Pious X: to continue with their strict ascetic life or to become missionaries.

These three earnest young monks in the cloisters of Mariannhill (left to right, John, Collins and Ivo) made a deep impression on us with their frankness, faith and sincerity.

'Surely it's difficult to have contact with people on the outside when you're so rigid inside,' asked Sir Peter. 'There must be a barrier.'

'There was,' said the priest.

'Would you have coped with such a stricture?'

Father George was unambiguous. 'No. I became a missionary. I didn't want a contemplative order.'

That evening, in complete contrast to the serenity of Mariannhill, we went into Durban, where one of South Africa's sharpest satirists, Pieter-Dirk Uys, was performing at the city's Playhouse Theatre.

I had met him once before in the quaintly-named town of Darling, a couple of hours drive from Cape Town, where he has his own tiny theatre.

Over the years he has built such a substantial following that even the Cape Town sophisticates are prepared to leave their fashionable city and travel to remote Darling to see him.

His audience at the Playhouse comprised mainly white, middle class South Africans. He told them, 'I come to you this evening a rare – but no longer protected – species. A white Calvinist Afrikaner.'

For many years Pieter-Dirk Uys was a thorn in the side of the apartheid government in South Africa. Through his one-man shows, he fearlessly and hilariously attacked the powerful elite who divided the country on the basis of colour. The National Party politicians, seemingly devoid of humour, proved perfect targets for his savage brand of satire. A talented mimic, Pieter-Dirk donned make-up, a dress and high heels to transform himself into his best-known character, Evita Bezuidenhout, and mercilessly sent up South Africa's rulers. Unwittingly, they provided him with the titles for his shows, among them *Adapt or Die*, *Total Onslaught*, and *Beyond the Rubicon*.

One might have thought that the coming of the new South Africa would have robbed Pieter-Dirk Uys of material. Yet he has bounced back with a new show which now opens with him transforming himself on stage into a passable Nelson Mandela. Later, as himself, he tells the audience, 'Since the tenth of May, 1994, I'm just a South African who happens to be not black. And I'm alive – now, how's that for an achievement for a South African today, considering what's out there waiting for us – the hijackers, the murderers, the muggers, the thieves . . .'

Indeed today, in the new crime-ridden South Africa, where the murder rate continues to rise, his show is appropriately entitled *Live!* As he wryly points out, in a society where fear of crime borders on paranoia and where the tendency is to remain safely locked indoors after dark, it is increasingly difficult to persuade people to venture out to the theatre at all.

Crime has become a major preoccupation among white South Africans, who go to enormous lengths to ensure their personal security. Their cars boast the latest in anti-hijacking devices. At night they drive through red lights for fear of being attacked if they stop, even briefly. Their homes are surrounded by high walls. Their windows have burglar bars. There are electric fences and alarm systems wired up to round-the-clock armed response units. Snarling dogs roam about the walled-off grounds, barking at cars and passers-by.

Pieter-Dirk Uys regards his audience with an amused air. 'Look at us. It's Sunday and we're sitting in the theatre. Live! Do you know what it takes to get you here? We have to start the show at six p.m. so you don't get murdered on the way home,' he tells them.

'We know you don't want to leave your homes, especially at night, because that means you've got to pick up your security keys again – and probably get a hernia because they're so heavy. You unlock the twenty-five locks on the sitting room door just to get out. You open the door and the passage is covered in laser beams. You step over the laser beams, but don't touch the walls because of the panic buttons. Then you get to the front door, and you've got to open your front door, and your verandah is covered with barbed wire.

'Your little Pekinese dog is . . .' He pauses, pulls a face, and draws his hand ominously across his throat. '. . . and the walls are getting higher and higher and higher.'

His audience, for whom this dire lifestyle is horribly real, fall about with helpless laughter. South Africa may well be experiencing an appalling crime wave, Johannesburg may have one of the worst murder rates in the world; but the people have not lost their sense of humour.

Afterwards, we crowd into the dressing room where Pieter-Dirk, who has left the stage in the guise of Evita Bezuidenhout, is removing his make-up. A pair of gaudy gold high heels and a handbag sit conspicuously on the shelf beneath his mirror.

'Nelson loves Evita,' he told us, expertly peeling off a false eyelash. 'I have met him four times recently, each time dressed as Evita. The last time I said to him, *President Mandela, we can't go on meeting like this. Every time I meet you I'm wearing a dress.* He said, *Don't worry Pieter, I know you're inside!'*

He describes the New South Africa as 'optimistic but still fraught with problems'. At least, he believes, they are problems which can be solved.

'We didn't know how it was all going to end,' he says, referring to apartheid. 'Everybody said, *One day you are going to be punished*, and I think the irony is we are still waiting. I mean, is it possible we got away with all that?' He is genuinely incredulous.

In the run-up to the election in 1994, many white South Africans believed that democracy would bring bloody revolution. Many were gripped by siege mentality, stocking up on tinned food to see them through the imagined dreadful times to come, as they huddled behind their high walls. Instead, against the odds, the transition was peaceful.

'It is quite extraordinary,' says Pieter-Dirk Uys. 'And of course no one can avenge themselves on anybody, because Nelson didn't do so. What an example.'

On with the motley . . . Pieter-Dirk Uys – still half in the guise of his most famous stage creation, Evita Bezuidenhout – and Sir Peter mess about with makeup in his dressing-room at Durban's Playhouse Theatre.

Afterwards, we returned to the monastery at Mariannhill for our last night in Durban. I found it hard to say goodbye to the three young novices, John, Collins and Ivo. It seemed that in a short space of time a connection had been forged between us. From the expressions on their faces as we took our leave, I suspected that our presence had deeply affected them – perhaps unsettled them. They too had similarly affected us, and we drove away in silence.

At this point the puzzles and riddles and confusions begin to flock in.
You have arrived at a place which you cannot quite understand.
MARK TWAIN, FOLLOWING THE EQUATOR

◆

WE FLEW NORTH FROM DURBAN to Bloemfontein and from there drove through an awesome thunderstorm to Kimberley, in the Northern Cape. On the map, the whole of this region appears empty. The province has the largest land mass in South Africa, but is the most barren and underpopulated region of the country. The road from Bloemfontein to Kimberley forms an unbroken line through the flat, desolate landscape. Ahead of us the road stretched into the distance, straight and clear. It was eerily quiet.

Above, the thunder began to rumble ominously. To the west the sun shone bright while to the east dark clouds glowered. Great flashes of lightning cleaved the sky spectacularly as we sped through the rain.

Sir Peter, sitting in the back of the car, was transfixed. 'It's like Tiepolo, with a touch of Caspar David Friedrich,' he remarked.

We sped on. I suspected he would have liked to rest, but the combination of the extraordinary natural phenomena overhead and the speed of my driving kept him wide awake throughout the journey. That night we stayed at the Kimberley Club, an old colonial establishment once favoured by Cecil Rhodes. It's a place that hangs determinedly on to its past. Ties must be worn in the bar – which refuses to admit women. Sir Peter was given the Cecil Rhodes suite.

Next morning we went to Orania, a small town built on the banks of the Orange River, home to a community of around 600 Afrikaners, who see it as the starting point for a new fatherland. They are attempting to make it the self-declared *Volkstaat* of the Afrikaner people, who make up just seven per cent of South Africa's population.

Sunset and thunderstorm: the vast skies of South Africa make for some truly spectacular weather.

It is bizarre to find such a community living in the middle of nowhere, committed to the ideal of establishing their own nation state. Over the past five years they have encouraged other Afrikaans people – Boers – to uproot and come to Orania. Those already established believe that they are creating a paradise out here in the remote Karoo desert.

Orania sits uneasily in the new South Africa. Since the

1994 elections, when Nelson Mandela's African National Congress took control, many Afrikaners – the so-called white tribe – have complained of feeling powerless. Where elsewhere there is talk of integration and reconciliation, Orania harks self-consciously back to the old days, although any suggestion that they are reconstructing an apartheid system is strenuously denied. However, Orania is a whites-only community – designed to exist without black workers – and its people are fiercely protective of their culture, history and language, all of which they believe are threatened by the new democracy. They have withdrawn into themselves. Just as South Africa has emerged from isolation, here is a people who crave their own isolation from the new order. It is a curious notion. In a country where previously segregated peoples are learning to live together, Orania resolutely chooses to be apart.

We had arranged to meet with the founder of the community, Professor Boshoff, whose wife is the daughter of Hendrick Verwoerd, the former prime minister and architect of apartheid who was assassinated in 1966. The couple's son, Karel, an articulate and persuasive young man, had also chosen to settle in Orania.

The Professor, a softly spoken man, explained how Orania came to be. It was, he told us, the only way in which the Afrikaner people could ensure that their identity would survive. He cleverly uses the political language of oppressed minorities.

'We came to the decision that the only way to survive in Africa is to have some kind of self-determination; but we also need a territory, an area where it's possible to come together and put up a new state, to build up from scratch something new.'

In some respects, the idea that Afrikaners should move on and re-establish themselves is nothing out of the ordinary. They have a history of doing just that; trekking north from the Western Cape, deep into the interior, following the arrival of the British in South Africa. To seek out fresh territory and start anew is at the very heart of the Afrikaner's psyche.

Orania in many respects was the perfect location. Once owned by the Department of Water Affairs, it was used as a base during the construction of an irrigation system. When the work was completed, the town was abandoned, standing empty until Professor Boshoff chose it as the site to fulfil his dream.

Today, Orania has about it a feeling of still being the deserted town it once was. It is incredibly peaceful. Too peaceful, perhaps. One of the main objectives is to attract more people into the community. The Boshoffs are confident that in time the people will come. They cite Israel as an example of a state which began in a small way and today has a population of four and a half million.

The Professor said, 'The point is this. We have been subjected to very fierce ways of Anglicisation earlier in the century, so that now we are especially worried about Afrikaans, about our language.'

Carved from the same unmistakable stock as the old Boer pioneers, Professor Boshoff's dream is to forge a new Afrikaner homeland out of the inhospitable desert.

Karel added, 'The most expedient way for a community to look after its affairs is to have its own state.'

And yet this hardly seems a practical solution. One cannot help but wonder where South Africa would be if all its various tribes took a similar stance.

'The Afrikaner nation is not dead; and it's not dying, and it's not planning to disappear,' insisted the Professor. 'It's planning to survive, and taking all the prerequisites for survival. It has chosen this option of establishing its own state. And therefore it's up to the will of the Afrikaner to prove the possibility of this.'

We met with one man who had travelled the world, yet had chosen to settle in Orania. John Huyser, a big, muscular individual in his forties, spoke passionately about creating an Afrikaner fatherland for the future.

'We are moving into our own country,' he told us with enthusiasm. 'It is our country, our own government, our own language, our own national flag.'

What brought John to Orania was a heartfelt desire to be part of a new Afrikaner nation. He is wholly committed to the idea of an Afrikaner *Volkstaat*. Yet at the same time, he passionately refutes any suggestion of racism.

'I would say to everybody that I am not a racist, and none of us living in this little town are racist,' he said. 'Lots of people in the outside world think we are, but we are not. The only thing we want is our own country. That's it. Nothing else. We are willing to live in peace. Not *willing* to live – we *want* to live in peace with everybody around us.'

It is in Orania that Betsy Verwoerd, the widow of Hendrick Verwoerd chooses to live. She, like all the others in Orania, wants to keep the New South Africa firmly at arm's length, and yet she welcomed President Mandela when he visited the town in one of his typically conciliatory gestures. The light was fading by the time we were taken to meet her. At ninety-seven years old she is a frail woman, who moves slowly and with difficulty. All day a strong wind had blown through the arid landscape. One sudden gust could have swept this fragile, stooped figure away.

'You have to speak English now,' her daughter instructed her, steering her out onto the *stoep*, or verandah, at the front of the house.

Sir Peter offered her his arm and helped her into a seat. She seemed composed and at ease, smiling, one hand clutching her walking stick, her silver hair pinned up into a neat bun.

'So you live in the middle of Orania?' said Sir Peter. 'Surrounded by your own.'

Mrs Verwoerd was candid. 'It's quiet, and we haven't got the other people with us. We are all whites. Everything is white. So that makes it easy for us and safe, very safe.'

One senses that she may have been equally frank when President Mandela arrived to take tea with her.

She went on, 'I am so pleased I came here. It was the best thing I could have done. They tried to keep me from it. *What are you going to do? It's a place*

John Huyser has travelled the world, but he too has chosen to make Orania his home.

that's terribly cold and terribly hot. So I said, well I was born in the Karoo. I'm really a Karoo person.'

'And you had Mr Mandela to tea, I gather,' said Sir Peter.

'I prepared everything for him. After all, he was – what do you call it – an important person. And I was pleased to receive him and took out my best cups and saucers and things.'

We had been chatting for only a few moments but it was clearly tiring for Mrs Verwoerd. In the background, her daughter intervened. 'I think that's enough.'

'There's no reason why I shouldn't receive him,' she told Sir Peter, still speaking of Mandela.

'Of course not,' he replied, as she was helped to her feet. Before she vanished into the house her voice trailed back over her shoulder. 'You can see the people are very happy.' The door closed firmly behind her. Frail, certainly; but with her ideas and principles as unbending as ever.

That night some of the residents of Orania gathered for a barbecue. It was a formal affair, with a warm greeting extended to Sir Peter by both the Professor and Karel. Flags of the old South Africa hung in the background.

'We are glad that you are here. We are glad that we could use the chance to put our ideas and goals to you and through you to the wider world,' said Karel.

'We came in here today without passports, and we were very grateful for it,' said Sir Peter. 'Mandela came here and had tea with Mrs Verwoerd. I hope these symptoms of openness continue, because they are the mark of maturity, which is what you deserve after such a long trek.'

But one cannot help thinking that the reality of Orania has so far failed to live up to the dream. In eight years, only a few hundred Afrikaners have moved to the settlement. The hope is that in time there will be a million people living there; that there will be bustling cities and prosperity. It seems unlikely. The apparent determination to create a *Volkstaat* at Orania is clearly crazy, if only on a practical level. The Afrikaner vision of a thriving and prosperous fatherland in this barren place in post-apartheid South Africa seems utterly misguided.

'We are all whites . . .' Ninety-seven years old, Betsy Verwoerd is clearly determined to live out the rest of her life surrounded by her own.

Professor Boshoff relaxes with his wife, Anna and their son, Karel (left), outside their modest home.

And now we do kung fu . . . No visitors are allowed in to the diamond mines at Kimberley without elaborate safety precautions and proper protective clothing.

It is worth while to journey around the globe to see anything which can truthfully be called a novelty, and the diamond mine is the greatest and most select and restricted novelty which the globe has in stock.
MARK TWAIN, FOLLOWING THE EQUATOR

SIR PETER SETTLED HIMSELF on a bench in the workers' changing room at the De Beers diamond mine in Kimberley. Before going underground he must put on the clothing provided for him by the company. As he began to undress he said, 'The last time this happened to me was in New Zealand, going into a pool with a load of Maoris.'

He stepped into a pair of voluminous white overalls with a huge red cross on the back. Someone removed his shoes and socks and replaced them with official De Beers footwear.

He turned to us, his normal sartorial elegance obscured. 'And now we do kung fu?' he joked.

A blue hard hat completed his outfit. Similarly attired, we followed our guide to the lift which would take us deep into the earth. 'If we're not back in three hours, move on to the next location,' remarked Sir Peter, stepping into the deepest-running Otis elevator in the world (and possibly the biggest: all mine vehicles and equipment are transported – upended – in it). A siren wailed as the lift doors closed and we began to hurtle downwards.

When the lift stopped it was rather like stepping on to the elaborate set of a James Bond film. We emerged into a noisy, vast and brightly-lit cavern. Jeeps drove past. A miniature cargo train filled with debris from the diamond face rattled by. Someone handed us earplugs and an alarm rang out. Three explosions, one after another, boomed through the rock chamber. I imagined one of the Bond villains in just such a setting, hatching a plot to take over the world. There was something futuristic and otherworldly about the whole place.

In the employees' rest area we had arranged to meet with a former miner, Manne Dipico, now Premier of the Northern Cape province. Manne once worked at Kimberley and is fondly remembered there. As word spreads that he is in the mine, workers appear to greet him with hugs and elaborate African handshakes. A big, jovial character, he reacts with delight to be back on his old stomping ground. Manne may now be one of the leading politicians in South Africa, but he remains refreshingly down to earth.

He began to tell us how his life had unfolded. The eldest of four children, he was a bright student. He won a place at a private Catholic school where he passed his matric — the South African equivalent of A-levels. University beckoned, but he was unable to continue with his studies since his mother, a single parent struggling to raise her family on the wages from her job as a hospital cleaner, could not afford to continue supporting him.

At nineteen, his studies abandoned, Manne landed a job at Finch Mine, about 140 kilometres from Kimberley, before later moving to the Kimberley mine itself. It was an eye-opening experience for the teenager, who found himself living in a hostel, in difficult and degrading conditions. His education counted for nothing. He was simply another black mineworker.

'Feeling that you are nothing, and seeing that you have to call someone, not by his name, but to show he is a *baas* — that he is a boss to you. That was very difficult,' he told Sir Peter.

It was a baptism of fire. Soon he was involved in organising the disgruntled workers.

'There were no unions at that time in the mine, and the workers came together. We were not happy about the wages. It ended up in a strike, organised not by force but by a feeling of togetherness. Within two weeks we were all dismissed and I lost my job.'

He managed to find another job cleaning toilets, saved hard, and was able to go to university the following year. His experience in the mine led him to study industrial psychology and sociology, in the hope that he would be able to apply his knowledge to improving the lot of the mineworkers. Expelled from university for his activism, he joined the newly formed National Union of Mineworkers. His first task was to organise the workers of the diamond fields in the Northern Cape.

'I have worked with them since 1985, dealing with issues which affect them — even issues beyond the mine, issues which affect their family, issues which affect where they stay in the community, issues which affect their political aspirations of seeing South Africa free. All that was intertwined. One had to be involved in all those issues.' For his trade union activities he was sentenced to five years in prison.

'That's a fantastic story,' said Sir Peter. 'And recalled with such pleasure, all sorts of things that can't have been pleasurable at the time. Opposition to all sorts of things. And now you're Premier of the whole province.'

Now one of South Africa's most influential politicians, Manne Dipico was a mineworker — and a spirited union activist — for many years.

The buildings of Kimberley outlined against the skyline give some idea of the size of the eponymous Big Hole.

On the fringes of the diamond fields prospectors dig laboriously by hand, scraping a meagre living in the hope that one day they will find a stone that will make them rich.

Opposite page: Kimberley above ground and below. The massive pithead silhouetted against the sky lowers one of the world's largest and deepest lifts. While mining will always remain a relatively high-risk occupation, conditions underground in the diamond industry – for the majority of workers, at least – are a great deal less hazardous than some.

With a big smile, Manne Dipico then gave a splendid rendition of the mineworkers' song, the one which they used to sing to keep up their morale. With it ringing in our ears we ascended – nearly one kilometre in three minutes – into the brilliant sunlight.

———————◆———————

They are beautiful things, those diamonds in their native state. They are of various shapes; they have flat surfaces, rounded borders, and never a sharp edge. They are of all colors and shades of color, from dewdrop white to actual black; and their smooth and rounded surfaces and contours, variety of color, and transparent limpidity make them look like piles of assorted candies.
MARK TWAIN, FOLLOWING THE EQUATOR

———————◆———————

WHEN TWAIN WAS IN KIMBERLEY a hundred years earlier, he had visited the offices of De Beers to see how the diamonds were sorted and graded. Security surrounding this process has always been tight.

'An unknown and unaccredited person cannot get into that place,' he wrote in *Following the Equator*, 'and it seemed apparent from the generous supply of warning and protective and prohibitory signs that were posted all about that not even the known and accredited can steal diamonds there without inconvenience.'

The modern headquarters, Harry Oppenheimer House, were opened in 1974. A tall, austere building, it has no windows on its southern side – just a sheer brick face looming skywards. Only authorised personnel are admitted. There are heavy metal grilles on the doors, which are kept locked. It is rather like a prison in appearance.

Staff are routinely searched to ensure that diamonds are not being stolen. Trouser pockets must be kept sewn up. Security cameras, inside and out, keep permanent watch. Sir Peter is intrigued. 'They wanted to sew up my trousers,' he says as he is led to the north side of the building, which has windows, and where the diamond sorters work. He asks if we can go to the side without windows.

Inside the sorting office, workers sit silently at tables, sifting with tweezers through small mounds of what looks like grey silt. It is painstaking work. Some wear enormous goggles as they concentrate on their task. The windows in front of them are angled to provide the best possible lighting. Some of the diamonds are tiny and, in their raw state, dull and discoloured.

In all there are 14,000 categories of diamond, depending on size, colour and quality. De Beers have ninety-five people permanently sifting and sorting. Our guide – a senior member of the De Beers team who, for security purposes, was wearing trousers with useless pockets – showed us a fist-sized diamond mined in Kimberley in 1974. Known as the Six One Six, it is the single largest octahedron (eight-sided) diamond in the world and a source of great pride to De Beers. It is impossible to say how much it would be worth on the open market – millions of pounds, no doubt.

Sir Peter examines it. It is not the sparkler one might imagine. It looks like an ice cube and feels cold to the touch. Ironically, to polish the stone would undoubtedly diminish its size, so there is little chance of the Six One Six ever becoming a truly dazzling diamond.

Before we left Kimberley we visited the old De Beers boardroom. It was here in 1888, two years before he became Prime Minister of South Africa, that Cecil Rhodes established the consortium which became De Beers. By 1891 the company owned ninety per cent of the world's diamonds.

We went on to see a giant crater, the result of the mining activities. Known as Big Hole, it is the largest hand-dug crater in the world. It was nearby, on the banks of the Orange River, that in 1866 Erasmus Jacobs found the first diamond in South Africa. The stone was dubbed Eureka. Five years later, diamonds were discovered on a small hillock called Colesberg Kopje. Prospectors working with picks and shovels demolished it. Where the *kopje* once stood there is now Big Hole, which covers seventeen hectares and measures 1.6 kilometres around its circumference. Over the years 22,500,000 tons of earth was excavated from the site. Around three large bucketloads of diamonds were extracted. Sir Peter stood at the edge and peered down. 'Thousands worked here; died here,' he said. 'It seems a meagre harvest for forty-three years of sweat, tears, and all the inconveniences a diamond rush in those days represented.'

Looking for all the world like a common or garden ice cube, the Six One Six is the largest single diamond of its kind.

Natives must not be out after the curfew bell without a pass. In Natal there are ten blacks to one white.
MARK TWAIN, FOLLOWING THE EQUATOR

◆

IT WAS DURING THE RECONNAISSANCE trip that I first encountered Sandra Laing in Johannesburg. Hers was a terrible and tragic story, which first made international headlines thirty years ago.

Under South Africa's old apartheid regime everyone was classified according to colour. Sandra Laing, born to white Afrikaner parents, grew up among the rural white community with her two brothers. But Sandra was different. As a result of some genetic throwback, her skin was darker than the rest of her family. Her features were similar to those of a coloured person.

In 1966, at the age of eleven, she was called out of her class at boarding school one day to be told she had visitors. A police officer was waiting for her. Without explanation, Sandra was escorted home. She never returned to her school. The authorities had reclassified her as coloured and, under the country's strict racial segregation laws, Sandra could no longer be taught alongside white pupils. The implications for the child and her family were terrible.

Fifteen months later the authorities had a change of heart and reclassified Sandra as white. Her parents struggled to find a school that would take her. Finally, she was offered a place at a convent school. But by then the damage was done. She was insecure and confused; no longer certain where she belonged. At her new school she met the man who was to become her husband. They absconded, and since then she has lived among the black and coloured communities.

Thirty years ago Sandra Laing's story was met with shock and disbelief around the world. Among the most moving accounts of her plight was a documentary film, *In Search of Sandra Laing*, made by the British writer and director Anthony Thomas when Sandra was twenty.

I was introduced to Sandra through a local journalist, Amina Frense, who had managed to get hold of a copy of the Thomas film. Sandra was about to see it for the first time. I asked her if she would wait until we returned with Sir Peter and the crew. Sandra, who had already waited half her life to see the film, agreed that another few weeks would not matter.

When we returned to film with Sandra, we arranged to meet her at a petrol station on the edge of the township outside Johannesburg where she now lives with her second husband and their children.

Amina acted as our guide, and explained some of the background to Sir Peter as they sat under parasols on the garage forecourt, waiting for Sandra to arrive.

'This is the sad part – her family rejected her,' said Amina. 'There was shame. Her father didn't want to have anything to do with her. Her father has since died, and she only found out two or three years later. She doesn't know if her mother's alive. She would like to take care of her mother and, of course, to ask her mother what happened.

'Her children are confused. They know they have white grandparents, but they have no evidence, not even a photo. Now they will see this video made twenty years ago.'

Estranged from her white family, Sandra Laing found acceptance – and happiness – among the black and coloured community. Here she shares a loving moment with her son.

In the distance we could see Sandra walking towards us. When she arrived, she told Sir Peter that the last time she had seen her family was in 1971. 'I wish that I could see my brothers or my mother. I heard my father died in 1986,' she said.

Amina asked, 'How did you feel about the family not wanting to be in touch with you?'

'I was hurt at first, but now I don't worry any more. I've got my own family now.'

We went with Sandra to her home, a modest brick-built property where her children were waiting to see the film which told their mother's story. Everyone crowded into the small room. As the first images of her old family home in Panbult appeared, Sandra's face crumpled and her tears began to fall. Her mother and father appeared in grainy black-and-white newsreel, an ordinary couple with their young family. Pictures of a smiling Sandra filled the screen. She watched, weeping softly. The narrator explained how her parents had moved to a new area in an effort to avoid scandal, and how her father had insisted he wanted no more contact with Sandra.

Her first husband, Petrus, appeared. 'What they did was bad, but that's not my business,' he said. 'All I can say is thank you for giving me my wife.'

Sandra refuses to be bitter about the manner in which she was treated under the old apartheid regime. A woman of few words, she simply told us she was happy to have her own family, although she remains deeply curious about the mother and brother she no longer sees.

Amina said, 'The question of identity is still bugging people today. Some people are asking, *Where do we fit in?* There is a lot of confusion. We had apartheid, we have a democratic South Africa. We are a so-called 'Rainbow

Nation' but there is still a lot of confusion. People have been severely traumatised.'

On the day we visited Sandra it was her son's eighteenth birthday, and the family gathered outside in the sunshine to give him presents. Although her life has been undeniably difficult and there is sadness etched on her face, Sandra had, in extreme circumstances, managed to find equanimity. And at last, her children had found answers to at least some of the questions concerning their past.

Perhaps one day there would be a reconciliation with her white family. In the new South Africa, anything is possible.

IN THE CENTRE OF JOHANNESBURG is a small, curious shop which sells muti – the herbs and potions used in traditional medicine. Strange, exotic scents fill the air. An elderly man sits quietly in a corner, pounding unidentified substances with a pestle. Animal skins hang from the low ceiling. The atmosphere is gloomy. At one time traditional medicine was shunned by the whites in South Africa. Now, such is the interest in traditional healing that the *muti* shop in downtown Jo'burg doubles up as a musuem.

Trained in western medicine, Nomsa is also a sangoma – a traditional healer – of considerable presence and power.

South Africa abounds with traditional healers. Often their homes are identified by colourful flags fluttering outside. Increasingly, they are respected and accepted throughout society. In the near future, it is quite possible that medical aid schemes will treat bills for traditional healing in the same way as those for conventional medicine.

It was in Soweto, the sprawling black township outside Johannesburg, that we encountered a practitioner of this traditional craft – a *sangoma* – called Nomsa. An intelligent and humorous woman, she treats all manner of ailments, working in tandem with conventional medicine. A trained nurse, she is happy to refer patients for western treatment where appropriate.

A striking figure dressed in scarlet, her long hair falling over her shoulders, the *sangoma* welcomed Sir Peter into her consulting rooms. She sank to the ground, a small fur pouch in her hands. Inside was a collection of bones which she would cast onto a mat on the floor in order to diagnose whatever complaints Sir Peter might have. As Nomsa put it, the pattern the bones form as they fall presents her with an 'X-ray'. All around is a fascinating collection of animal skins, ornaments and mementoes associated with her ancestors. A saddle to remind her of her grandfather, who used to ride everywhere. A chair which also belonged to her grandfather. The skin of the goat which was slaughtered for her while she was training in her craft.

Every so often in South Africa, a story will emerge of body parts being offered for sale or stolen. One man was arrested trying to sell a pair of eyes outside a Johannesburg shopping mall. Another scandal centred upon a police mortuary in the city, where organs were mysteriously vanishing. 'There is nothing like medicine to build up rumours, and the *sangomas* have a good reputation, on the whole,' said Sir Peter, 'but there are people who say that branches of it use dead people's limbs in the diagnosis and treatment of diseases. Is that nonsense?'

'That's nonsense,' Nomsa confirmed, 'because you cannot use any human flesh or bones whatever. Healing is something that is very clean, which you cannot mix with something that is evil. Those people using that kind of thing we call witches.'

'Exactly. Witch doctors.'

The sangoma's traditional equipment occupies much of the room where Nomsa gives her consultations.

Nomsa lights candles and murmurs into the fur pouch before handing it to Sir Peter. She instructs him to blow into it and ask his ancestors to provide the answers he seeks. Then she casts the bones onto the floor.

She studies the arrangement. 'Your heart is so big to help people get what they want in life,' she tells him. 'Sometimes you feel so exhausted, so tired. I cannot say you are sick, although you have sicknesses in your body which are caused by age.' Her brow creases in concentration. Candlelight flickers on her skin. Her voice is firm. Sir Peter must rest. In the background, I thought about the punishing filming schedule he had been following with impressive stoicism in recent months. The boats onto which he had clambered. The flights of stairs he had been forced to negotiate in Indian railway stations. The endless travelling, the jet lag, the lack of sleep. There had been precious little rest for any of us. But Sir Peter, who had turned seventy-seven during the making of the series, must at times have felt it keenly.

Nomsa told him, 'I can see you are a very strong person, a person who can take any pain.' Even so, she said, his knees and feet were a cause for concern. Her 'X-ray' had revealed some stiffness in the neck, too.

'You speak exactly like my wife, and she knows me much better than you do,' Sir Peter replied, impressed.

'You feel like a young boy sometimes. You feel so strong that you can work. You can cope with the pain. Sometimes when you have those aching bones and joints you still feel you can do it. You don't like to be told.'

'No, I think that's the best cure, perhaps.'

She knelt forward, studying the bones. 'Keep from overworking yourself. Try to relax,' she said.

'Yes, well, I hope my colleagues hear all this.'

Nomsa went on to tell him that his grandmother on his father's side was watching over him. 'She was the person who was a light in all you are doing. That is why you became so successful in life.'

She told Sir Peter that he was suffering from water retention, and made up a prescription comprising two herbs to be mixed in boiling water and drunk morning and evening. As she measured the herbs into bags and gave him precise instructions on how they should be administered, Sir Peter gazed about him. Her diagnosis and the room with its clutter of belongings, each one significant to Nomsa, had clearly touched him.

'It's all very interesting, because it shows the deep roots that the Africans have,' he said. 'How they care for their families when they are alive, and when they're dead they are living people still. I think it's your enormous strength, and that's something the white populations have really lost completely.'

Before we left, cameraman Mike Fox slipped into the consulting room for a private word with Nomsa. Emerging some minutes later, a herbal prescription in his possession, he declared himself amazed at some of the things she had told him. He was in no doubt about her psychic and healing abilities. Sir Peter too was impressed. I was not so sure. It was clear that Nomsa was an excellent healer, both knowledgeable and genuine. But as to whether or not she possessed any real clairvoyance, I had still to be persuaded.

Several long journeys gave us experience of the Cape Colony railways; easy riding, fine cars; all the conveniences; thorough cleanliness; comfortable beds furnished for the night trains . . . spinning along all day in the cars it was ecstasy to breathe the bracing air and gaze out over the vast brown solitudes of the velvet plains.
MARK TWAIN, FOLLOWING THE EQUATOR

◆

NEXT DAY WE DROVE TO PRETORIA to board the famous Blue Train for the journey to Cape Town.

The Blue Train is the most luxurious means of covering the thousand miles to the Cape. It cuts a majestic swathe through the landscape, with its distinctive royal blue livery. It is a far cry from the dull grey and yellow crowded commuter trains which carry workers into the city from the townships each day. In comparison, the Blue Train provides unhurried, spacious, untroubled travel. It is all elegance and opulence. The uniformed staff are courteous and attentive. It unashamedly harks back to an earlier, more privileged era. These days it is mainly foreign tourists who sample the delights of the Blue Train. Few locals can afford such luxury.

On the morning of our departure, porters in immaculate blue jackets wheeled a trolley piled high with Sir Peter's and Lady Ustinov's baggage through the station. We all trooped on board, anxious as usual to see how the porters proposed to accommodate the luggage within the confines of a railway compartment. Somehow, they managed it. By the time Sir Peter and Lady Ustinov boarded the train, their cases were arranged in neat and unobtrusive rows at either end of their berth.

'Fantastique, c'est charmant,' was Lady Ustinov's reaction on seeing the dark wood panelled walls of the compartment. 'Et toutes les valises!' she exclaimed at the sight of the suitcases.

Sir Peter settled himself in an armchair beside the window. 'Now we can really

The train retains all the formal trappings of comfortable, cossetted travel.

If it wasn't for the fact you can see the landscape going by outside the windows it would be hard to believe that a bar this size could be part of a passenger train!

make ourselves at home,' he said in his most convincing American accent. 'Most of the people on this train are Stateside. I've been talking to them – just fine people. I look forward to making their acquaintance, exchanging addresses, and forming a lifelong relationship. You know what I'm saying?'

Lady Ustinov smiled. Indeed she did.

The beauty of the Blue Train is that it is a sedate means of reaching Cape Town. None of the hurly burly of the airport check-in. For the next thirty-six hours we could enjoy a rare breathing space. Relax, and enjoy some of the South African landscape, too.

Unlike every other train I had ever travelled on, this one's corridors were covered in soft, thick carpet. There was a bar. A lounge dotted with soft, squashy sofas and comfortable armchairs. A restaurant with superb service and fine food. Each compartment had its own bathroom; most with a shower, some with a bath. The prospect of luxuriating in a hot bath on a train seemed to me bliss beyond belief.

That night as I made my way to dinner I found a Dior lipstick in the corridor, its expensive gold case glinting up at me. Rather than handing it straightaway to the steward, I showed it first to Sir Peter. Putting on his best Belgian accent, he reprised his role as detective Hercule Poirot as he addressed our fellow passengers in the lounge: 'A murder may have been committed. Already my moustache has been stolen. And outside my room I found this lipstick . . .'

By dawn next day we were travelling through the wine country of the Cape. The summer rains had left the landscape a healthy shade of green. On we went, drawing level with a road at one point, the train keeping pace with an open truck packed with workers who waved enthusiastically at us. The contrast in our modes of transport could not have been greater.

At Cape Town station, the butler from the Mount Nelson Hotel was waiting on the platform. He made a quick assessment of our luggage and summoned two porters and trolleys. It was a bright and sunny day: Table Mountain presided over the city, solid and magnificent, a blanket of cloud sitting prettily on its flat top. Cape Town was preparing for the arrival of President Clinton, who was due to address parliament that afternoon, having arrived in South Africa on the most important leg of his African tour. Evidence of the American presence was all around. There was a large contingent of police, some routinely armed with 9mm pistols in holsters strapped to their waists, others with more heavy duty automatic weapons. Some roads were already blocked to assure the smooth progress of the presidential motorcade.

At the Mount Nelson, a grand old hotel painted a delicate shade of pink, the Stars and Stripes flapped in the breeze. It emerged that most of the rooms were occupied by members of the US press corps, which numbered several hundred. A conservative estimate put the US entourage at more than a thousand, including aides, advisors, and press. President Clinton himself had commandeered the more easily secured harbourfront Cape Grace Hotel.

We retired to the terrace, where a stiff breeze – the famous Cape Town south-east wind – blew through the grounds, ruffling the feathery fronds of the palm trees. Behind us stood Table Mountain, solid and silvery in the sunlight.

Sir Peter smiled conspiratorially. 'You didn't notice, because I'm very good at this kind of thing, but I snaffled this at reception when I was getting my key.' He unfolded a piece of paper. 'I don't know what its contents are, but it looked important and that's why I stole it.'

He began to read in an American accent: 'Attention White Press Corps – reimbursement of tax. Please bring all receipts for the purchase of goods and proof of identification to the Cape Grace Hotel, Room 119, between the hours of 1900 and 0100.' Sir Peter paused. 'My God, it doesn't say here – it must be on another piece of paper – which I shall steal on the way out – what happens to people who bring their receipts and proof of identity after oh-one-hundred.'

A waiter placed a sandwich and a pot of tea in front of him. He picked up the sandwich and regarded it with dismay. 'Does this constitute a purchase? It's no fun to be a suspect oneself, you know. And what does the White Press Corps mean? Don't they know that apartheid is over?' As he folded up the paper and secreted it in his pocket, he said, 'I feel like swallowing this now I've read it.'

Life in South Africa has yet to improve a great deal in the townships, where too many people still face a daily grind of unemployment, poverty and deprivation. Yet there is genuine optimism in the faces of these Soweto children.

NEXT MORNING WE HEADED OFF to Khayelitsha in the Cape Flats where we were scheduled to visit a school. The Flats are notorious as a place of poverty and violence. There is a huge drugs problem. Gangs vie for control, and daub their slogans across walls throughout the neighbourhood. The Hard Livings. The Sexy Girls. There has been considerable tension of late between the gangs and an organisation called People Against Gangsters and Drugs (PAGAD). In one ugly incident, a gangster was set alight and executed as police officers stood by, apparently helpless to intervene.

Life in the Flats is often nasty, brutish and short. All too often youngsters growing up in a culture of drugs and gangsters are likely to end up in trouble. Yet in Khayelitsha we came upon a school choir which was both inspirational and exceptional in its talent.

Sixty young people performed magnificently for us in a classroom, their voices attracting curious students who pressed their faces against the window to watch a remarkable and informal concert. We sat spellbound while they performed a repertoire of traditional African folk songs, ending with the national anthem.

The choir had been brought together by a music teacher, Solomon Mutshekwane, a former student at the University of Cape Town. He had been one of only two black students studying music at UCT, and was constantly being approached by youngsters wanting help with choral music.

'Choral music in South Africa counts well compared to instrumental music,' he told us. 'We have instrumental music, we have orchestral and opera.

Education cuts mean that he may not have a job next term, but in the meantime music teacher Solomon Mutshekwane (far right) puts his heart and soul into the choir he runs for the disadvantaged pupils of Khayelitsha's school.

Agnes Jibilikah (bottom row, right) is one of Solomon's star singers.

Agnes graciously took us to visit the house where she lives with her family of seven.

In the Western Cape we've got the best opera house, the best symphony orchestra, the best choir; but only a few people are able to use those facilities. What about the rest of the peninsula? So they rely on choral music in their churches, in their adult choirs at home, at the workplace, at school . . . You will be surprised that even at a school like this there are no facilities. The only facilities I have are the voices.'

Sir Peter sympathised. 'I heard that the problem is that there is really no money for anything. It's already a miracle that this beautiful building exists in the middle of a shanty town.'

Indeed, South Africa's great difficulty is finding the money to do all it needs to bring opportunity to its disadvantaged people. Already, there have been huge cuts in education. Thousands of teachers have been made redundant, with thousands more redundancies to come. Teachers like Solomon have no idea if they will be asked to leave the profession in the next wave of cuts. 'What about the fate of the children?' he asks.

At the end of the school day we leave with one of the choristers, sixteen-year-old Agnes, who has agreed to be interviewed at home. Agnes normally catches the train, but when it arrives we realise that there is no chance of us all getting on. Every carriage is packed, and there are people hanging out of the open doors. Some wedge themselves precariously in between the carriages. We watch helplessly as a mad scramble to get on ensues, and decide it would be safer if we all went in a taxi.

When we finally arrive at the three-room house that Agnes shares with seven others, it is filled with curious cousins. Agnes ushers us into the living room, which also serves as kitchen, dining room and bedroom. It is simply furnished and the walls have been papered with the bright pink wrappers of Lux soap. Agnes, who has spent the morning singing her heart out, offers us a seat and then – under the gaze of her cousins – becomes suddenly tongue-tied.

Sir Peter tries gamely to coax her into chatting but she remains resolutely monosyllabic. He tells her. 'I think between you and me you speak three languages – English, Xhosa, and silence. I'm coming to all sorts of conclusions about you. When you're not singing, you're silent.'

Three small boys sitting side by side at the table grin broadly. One manages to smile and stick out his tongue at the same time. Agnes remains self-consciously tight-lipped.

Sir Peter admits defeat. 'You've obviously got to recuperate after you've spent all morning singing beautifully for my benefit,' he tells her. 'I've applauded you until I'm blue in the face, and now you deserve a rest.'

I was in South Africa some little time. When I arrived there the political pot was boiling fiercely.
MARK TWAIN, FOLLOWING THE EQUATOR

Those were wonderfully interesting days for a stranger, and I was glad to be in the thick of the excitement. Everybody was talking, and I expected to understand the whole of one side of it in a very little while.
MARK TWAIN, FOLLOWING THE EQUATOR

◆

THE TRANSITION FROM OLD TO NEW South Africa was indeed remarkable. Instead of the violent revolution feared by some, the new democracy slipped gracefully and without fuss into place. And, despite the human rights abuses perpetrated against them during the dark days of apartheid, South Africa's formerly oppressed people are, largely, moving forward in a spirit of reconciliation.

Sir Peter listens attentively to the proceedings of the controversial Truth and Reconcilation Commission, under the chairmanship of Archbishop Desmond Tutu.

Even so, the past cannot simply be swept aside. There were too many unexplained deaths and disappearances. At least ninety black leaders were murdered or disappeared during the apartheid era. And all too often, those guilty of subverting justice were the police and security services. Now they are being called to account for their actions.

Since 1996, a roving Truth and Reconciliation Commission under the chairmanship of Archbishop Desmond Tutu has been hearing accounts of some of the atrocities which went unpunished in the old South Africa; and considering pleas for amnesty by those responsible. To date, more than 7,000 cases have been heard.

In Cape Town, under a banner which read, *Truth – The Road To Reconciliation*, we heard former police sergeant Gideon Nieuwoudt describe the events leading up to the death of Steve Biko in police custody in the Eastern Cape in 1977. Four other officers had already, separately, applied for amnesty. It was Biko's story which inspired the film, *Cry Freedom*. In 1997, twenty years after his death, President Mandela described him as 'a great man who stood head and shoulders above his peers.'

Nieuwoudt gave his testimony, describing how there had been a struggle. How he had beaten Biko with a length of hosepipe, and how during the struggle Biko's head had hit the wall.

'He fell, fell down to the floor, and at that stage he seemed to me to be confused and dazed,' said the applicant, who gave his testimony in Afrikaans.

As in so many cases to come before the TRC, the former officer insisted that he had merely been following orders. Steve Biko's widow and son listened while Nieuwoudt gave his evidence. In July 1996, the family lost their battle in the Constitutional Court in Johannesburg to prevent apartheid killers from being pardoned if they confessed.

Clearly, not everyone agrees that the Commission is the right way to deal with past human rights violations. But Archibishop Tutu believes the hearings have proved cathartic, and that to deal openly with the wounds of the past is the only way in which they will properly heal. Trials, rather than commissions, would have proved counterproductive, he believes.

He told us, 'What happened in this country is that the world, for all sorts of reasons, has focused a fair degree of attention as a result of the anti-apartheid struggle. We have a concentration of loving, of praying. I don't think there is any other country in the world that has been prayed for as much as South Africa has, or for so long. Nor do I know of any other issue that has captured the imagination of so many for so long as the anti-apartheid issue. And so because of these exigencies of history, when the time came for a transition to happen here we could not have a Nuremberg-type of trial, nor could we have amnesia – those who were saying let bygones be bygones. You are forced into talking rather than shooting and killing.'

He went on, 'We speak of something called *ubuntu*, which is very difficult to put into any Western language, but it asks that you speak about the essence of being human. That I am because you are.

'*Ubuntu* means you are caring, hospitable, gentle, a warm and welcoming person, which is an attribute that is highly prized. And it is because of *ubuntu* to some extent that people show this willingness to forgive, because *ubuntu* sets high store by communal harmony. Revenge, anger, resentment are corrosive of this harmony, and destructive, because when one person is dehumanised, diminished inexorably, I am diminished. I am dehumanised.'

The TRC is in its own way remarkable, given the history of South Africa. But, as Archbishop Tutu pointed out, there are many extraordinary things happening in the new South Africa. 'Sometimes you have to keep pinching yourself and saying, *are we awake? Are we dreaming?*' he said. 'When President Clinton was addressing our national assembly the people sitting there, many of them – starting with our President – had just four or five years ago been terrorists. Most of those chaps were people who were on the run, and now they're making the laws of this country. It's incredible.'

Sir Peter said, 'It shows that everybody is redeemable, everybody can change. Why in this world is it so bad to change your mind? You're regarded as abandoning convictions. I believe doubts are more important than convictions. I believe doubts are the spur to all thoughts, because doubts unite people, and convictions separate them.'

'You have got some beautiful ways of saying profound things,' said the Archbishop with a smile. 'We have come to realise that forgiveness is not something nebulous, is not something ethereal for religious people. It is actually deeply pragmatic. It is part of real politics, because you come up to the realisation that without forgiveness there is no future.'

*. . . towering above us was Table Mountain — a reminder that we had
now seen each and all of the great features of South Africa except Mr
Cecil Rhodes.*

MARK TWAIN, FOLLOWING THE EQUATOR

◆

*David Abromawitz (below, on his
yacht) also runs a ferry service to
Robben Island with an enterprising
consortium of ex-political prisoners.*

IT WAS A FINE DAY WHEN WE SET OFF for Robben Island, once home to the top security prison which numbered among its inmates Nelson Mandela, and now a national monument. We sailed on a 54-foot yacht named *Independence*, cutting through the sparkling blue water of Table Bay, white sails billowing above our heads. Its skipper, David Abromawitz, also runs a regular public ferry service on a high-speed passenger boat, taking visitors from Cape Town to and from the island. In partnership with him are ten ex-political prisoners each of whom served time on Robben Island.

As we sailed into the island's harbour our guide, former prisoner Lionel Davis, was waiting on the quay for us. He led us into the old jail, across a highly polished floor and into a narrow corridor leading to the wing which housed the political prisoners, stopping at cell number five, where Nelson Mandela spent eighteen years. The tiny cell — around two metres square and three metres high — offered few home comforts. Not even a bed in the early days. Prisoners were given a mat to sleep on and blankets for warmth — three in the bitterly cold winter and two in summer. As we stepped into the cell with its pale blue walls and bars on the windows, Sir Peter remarked, 'We're on hallowed territory now.'

I imagined Mandela sitting in this cell for much of his time, allowed out only for brief periods of exercise or a shift of hard labour crushing stones. In the distance, he would have been able to see Table Mountain, tantalisingly close, but impossible to reach. Visitors were rare and mail was restricted. Just one letter of five hundred words written and received every six months.

It was while imprisoned on Robben Island that Mandela began his autobiography, *Long Walk to Freedom*, documenting his story on toilet paper in tiny script. Bit by bit it was transcribed and eventually spirited away to England by former prisoner Mac Maharaj, now the Minister of Transport. The original manuscripts, which were hidden in plastic bottles and buried in the grounds, have subsequently been unearthed.

Lionel Davis spent seven years on the same wing as Mandela. Today he chooses to live on the island with his wife and child. 'Conditions were pretty grim. In those early days they used to bury political prisoners up to their necks in sand and the warders would urinate on their heads. They were all white warders and all black, male prisoners. I saw political prisoners being beaten up. When we first came here, we found political prisoners with broken arms and wounds across their bodies.

Criminals were thrashed all the time with batons and pickaxe handles. So it was tough.'

As he described what life had been like on Robben Island, Lionel spoke without bitterness. What he was describing was in the past. Not to be forgotten; but his level tone of voice made it clear that there was no resentment buried inside. He told tales of food being withheld as a punishment, of 'spare diet' during which only meagre rations of boiled maize, rice and water were served. There was brutality, solitary confinement. Like the rest of South Africa, the prison authorities discriminated on the basis of colour. Coloured and Indian prisoners were given certain privileges, while

In this claustrophobic cell, with only the barest of necessities, Nelson Mandela spent eighteen years.

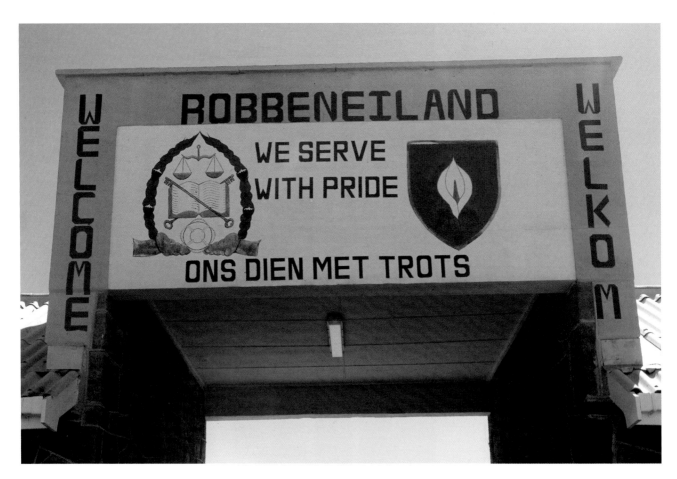

WELCOME

ROBBENEILAND

WE SERVE
WITH PRIDE

ONS DIEN MET TROTS

WELKOM

In post-apartheid South Africa the motto over Robben Island's gateway possesses a terrible irony . . .

Lionel Davies still lives on Robben Island, working as a guide alongside those who were once his jailers.

the black prisoners had the worst food and the most basic clothing. Astonishingly, some of the old prison warders have also chosen to settle on Robben Island. They too are working at the museum.

'Sworn enemies now sitting together in meetings and planning ways of raising money so that we can buy equipment, we can have dances, we can live like human beings,' said Lionel with a smile. 'I think we will set a wonderful example for the rest of South Africa, because our society is still very divided.'

'So it's really a microcosm of your whole society,' said Sir Peter. 'I'm terribly impressed, not only with what has been achieved but with the potential which is still to be achieved. I think this is wonderfully symbolic, and it has a strange serenity about it.'

'My focus is primarily to speak to South Africans about the necessity to change, the necessity to cast off baggage, to start learning to trust and to love and to be peaceful,' Lionel told us.

THROUGHOUT OUR TRIP I had been trying to secure an encounter between President Mandela and Sir Peter. It was not proving easy. The Presidential diary is always packed with important meetings. His time is precious. Still, I persisted. Our contact in the President's Office, Priscilla Naidoo, was doing her best on our behalf; but she was also accommodating the needs of the Clinton people, who clearly took precedence.

Just the sheer scale of Clinton's entourage made him a force to be reckoned with. In addition to the thousand people who went everywhere with him, two US transport planes had flown in an impressive range of essential hardware, including helicopters and the motorcade. In terms of access to Mandela, we were undoubtedly trumped by the US President.

Twice I wrote to President Mandela, hoping to persuade him to spare us a few minutes of his precious time. We would change our schedule if necessary. If an interview was out of the question, then perhaps a photo-call might be possible? And so on. Meanwhile, various people, including the Ministry of Tourism, lobbied on our behalf.

Finally, word came back that the President would be attending a dinner on board the *QE2*, which had cruised from Durban to Cape Town, and was now docked in the harbour. We could have five minutes with him. We were overjoyed.

For the rest of the day we took a cable car to the top of Table Mountain. Mist swirled about, obscuring the view of Cape Town below. We watched the cable car set off on its descent and vanish into the cloud. Sir Peter

perched on a wall and was soon swallowed up by a dense white fog. Every now and then it would clear for a few seconds, and we would see the city and the *QE2* at anchor far below.

That night we boarded the liner in high spirits and went straight to the appointed suite, where we had been told we could have our five minutes with the President at 6 p.m. precisely. We got ourselves ready and settled down to wait. Security guards stood at the door, occasionally speaking into microphones concealed up their sleeves. A stills photographer appeared. The minutes ticked past. By 6.20 I was becoming anxious. There was no sign of the President. A sudden flurry of walkie-talkie activity saw the departure of the security people. Everything went quiet. Clearly there had been a change of plan and Mandela would not be coming after all.

Sir Peter had been invited to stay for dinner, a charity event in aid of the Nelson Mandela Children's Fund, and was seated on the next table to the President's. We decided we might as well film Mandela's arrival and speech anyway. When he appeared, dressed in his usual floral shirt, a choir formed a lively guard of honour. In customary style, he boogied his way into the room, followed by his companion, Graca Machel – now his wife – who swayed along in her formal evening gown.

As the dinner progressed, I approached the organiser and explained that our interview had fallen through at the last moment. I wondered if he might speak to the President on our behalf . . . He slipped away and moments later was seen in conversation with Mandela. I held my breath. He returned

triumphant. We could have five minutes in the President's suite after dinner. This time we decided not to go on ahead and set up. Instead, we asked if we could film Mandela on his way from the dinner to the suite.

During dinner he rose to deliver a speech in which he explained that he had established the fund, to which he gives one third of his salary, after encountering some of Cape Town's street children.

'That night I couldn't sleep peacefully and I kept turning over and over because I was haunted by the expression of anxiety and insecurity that was written across the face of each and every one of them,' he said.

He then embarked on a long and fascinating discussion about his concerns for his country. The longer he spoke, the more it became clear that he was departing from the text of his speech. I could see the look of alarm on the

At last we managed to snatch a brief few moments out of the President's hectic schedule.

faces of his aides, as the time approached 8.40 p.m. He was due in town at another meeting within half an hour and there was still no sign that he was about to wind it up. When at last he did so, he was running extremely late. We began filming as he and Graca Machel left the dining room, followed by Sir Peter and Lady Ustinov. There was mild confusion as he left. Various security people spoke urgently into the mikes concealed up their sleeves. One, unaware that we had permission from the Head of Protocol to film, stepped in front of the lens and tried to stop us. A hurried explanation followed and we were allowed to continue. It was all rather fraught.

Finally, we made it to the Presidential suite, where Mandela was in relaxed mood. It soon emerged that he was rather a fan of Sir Peter's. While imprisoned on Robben Island, he had managed to see some films in which Sir Peter had featured.

'You really gave us a lot of strength and hope. I would like you to know,' said Mandela.

'That's too good of you,' replied Sir Peter.

They spoke briefly about the President's plans for his children's fund.

'Your fund is very close to any thinking person's heart,' said Sir Peter. 'I have just finished thirty years with UNICEF, and therefore I have seen that the architecture of poverty is the same everywhere.'

President Mandela agreed. 'One of the most serious challenges to humanity – it is a time bomb – is the question of poverty, of hunger, of ignorance and illness. Without attending to such questions, democracy counts for nothing,' he said.

In the background we were aware of the presidential aides trying to hurry things along. Their carefully prepared schedule was already in disarray, and there were still more engagements to fulfil before the end of the evening. Finally, the President announced he would have to leave. 'We are rushing because tomorrow we must be in Mozambique, and we must leave very early,' he said with a hint of regret.

'I do understand ... I am gratified you could see us, and if there is anything I can do for your children's fund just tell me,' said Sir Peter.

The two shook hands. 'I can assure you, I am not going to wash my hand for some time,' said the President.

'Well, I think I'll follow your example,' Sir Peter replied.

And with that he rose to leave. On the way out he spotted camera assistant, Matthew Fox, who stands 6 feet 7 inches tall. 'We need you in our basketball team,' he told him. Then he paused to shake hands with the rest of us before being ushered off to his next meeting.

To me the veldt, in its sober winter garb, was surpassingly beautiful. There were unlevel stretches where it was rolling and swelling, and rising and subsiding, and sweeping superbly on and on, and still on and on like an ocean, toward the faraway horizon, its pale brown deepening by delicately graduated shades to rich orange, and finally to purple and crimson where it washed against the wooded hills and naked red crags at the base of the sky.
MARK TWAIN, FOLLOWING THE EQUATOR

◆

OUR FINAL DESTINATION in South Africa was the Kapama Game Reserve in the old Eastern Transvaal, now renamed Mpumalanga. The reserve is owned by one of the country's most successful businessmen, an Afrikaner named Johan Roode. He had made his fortune from flour, and recently won the contract to supply all the bread buns to McDonald's in South Africa.

Mr Roode was an example of someone who had survived the political change in South Africa and gone on to even greater economic success. Having spotted the potential in the tourist market, he had built Kapama on land once farmed by his wife's family. A last-minute, multi-million rand deal meant he was unable to join us at the reserve, but he had sent his right-hand man, Rob Smith, in his place. Two private planes were waiting to convey us to the reserve.

Alongside our jet at Johannesburg International was one of Clinton's transport planes. The nose of the aircraft was open to reveal a cavernous interior. I suspected we could have probably taxied straight in and been swallowed up.

It was a short flight out to Hoedspruit with its private airport – also owned by Roode. Once a major military airbase, with the changing priorities of the new South Africa Hoedspruit has been scaled down, and now sees more tourists than air force activity. The heat hit us as we stepped off the plane. A member of the airport staff stepped forward to shake Sir Peter's hand.

'I met you many years ago, at the Kruger,' she told him. 'You actually drew a little picture for me.' Sir Peter appeared nonplussed. 'At Skukuza, in the Kruger National Park,' she added.

'I've never been here before,' Sir Peter told her.

She was undeterred. 'You look like a gentleman who was.'

'I'm glad he did a little picture. I'm willing to do another one,' said Sir Peter obligingly.

'You look very much like that man,' she persisted. 'Must be your brother.'

'Oh, really? That's alarming – I grew up as a single child.'

Next morning we had some time off. Although my neglected expenses were beginning to prey on my mind, I found I could not face them. Instead, for

the first time in my life, I went fishing. Assistant cameraman Matthew Fox, Rob Smith, Tom – our ranger – and I sat in a small boat on a nearby lake hoping the worms on the end of our rods would attract something. As the morning went by none of us had anything to show for our efforts. Suddenly bubbles appeared on the surface of the water in front of us and we became briefly optimistic. Tom studied the water for a few seconds then smartly reversed the boat away. A couple of minutes later a hippo surfaced. It had been right beneath us. We watched, fascinated. And we'd been lucky. Apparently more people are killed by hippos than any other animal in Africa, mainly as a result of the hippos accidently overturning boats as they surface. These massive creatures are certainly a force to be reckoned with. I had encountered a hippo on the reconnaissance trip a few weeks earlier and had watched as a pride of lions had approached the edge of a water hole to drink at dusk. The hippo, clearly feeling territorial, had made plain its displeasure and the lions backed off.

In the late afternoon, Tom took us out in an open Jeep. On the front of the vehicle was our tracker, Laurence, who had grown up in the area and had an incredible knowledge of the terrain and the wildlife. Laurence had been taught as a child about the medicinal properties of the plants on the reserve. He had proof of their efficacy. Indeed, he told me he had managed to cure

No trip to South Africa would be complete without a safari. Tom, our ranger, is driving and our tracker, Laurence, is poised on the specially adapted platform.

his brother of gonorrhoea using a herbal remedy!

It emerged that Laurence's wife and two sons – the wonderfully named Divine and Excellent – lived around sixty miles away. Laurence stayed on the reserve most of the time, going home every fifth week. His ambition was to become a ranger – at one time, in the old South Africa, an impossible dream since there were no black rangers, but today a real possibility.

I was fascinated by the names he had given his children. One day, twenty years from now, I would love to return to find out how Excellent – born just as the nation was changing – has fared, and if his life lives up to his name.

On our game drive we encountered plenty of animals. A group of rhino with a young calf. Giraffes. A herd of elephants, which crossed the dust road right in front of us. And lions, which stretched out sleepily in the shade.

We settled down to watch a dominant male lion which lay half asleep and seemed completely unperturbed by the close proximity of our vehicle. Sir Peter closed his eyes and began to mimic the sleepy predator. 'What happens when night falls?' he said. 'I've got to get active and dominant. What rubbish.' He sighed and stole a glance at the camera. 'Still there?' he said. 'It's so dry in this reserve and to think I've got to get to the water hole and I can't think of any females to do it for me . . .'

On he went in this vein. 'I've another two or three years to go and then I'll be out in the cold, ignored by everybody.' He glanced at us again. 'Oh go away,' he growled. 'I'm exhausted again.'

There was something touching about this impromptu performance. That Sir Peter, who had so often proved himself a lion of a man, should secretly wish to steal away and find peace and solitude. Perhaps the sleeping lion had the right idea after all.

He opened one eye. 'Oh, that was nice. I had a dream I was two years old again and beginning to grow a mane. Oh boy, now I've got to wake up and find it's an illusion and they're still here in that Jeep.' He shook his head. 'I thought I recognised David Attenborough – they never tire of looking at lazy lions.'

The next morning we flew back to Johannesburg. It was the end of a long and exhausting trip. The real end this time. We would not all be meeting up in some far flung place a few weeks down the line. It was strange, somehow, to think it was all about to be over. From the very beginning we had moved inexorably towards this point. The finality suddenly hit me. Like it or not, we were about to go our separate ways. Sir Peter and Lady Ustinov to Geneva. The crew to London. I was staying on for a week's break in Namibia.

I felt a surge of protectiveness as the Ustinovs, laden with presents, headed off to the departure lounge at Johannesburg International Airport. Sir Peter was clearly worn out from all the travelling. The *sangoma*'s words echoed in my head. *You must rest.* Perhaps now there would be an opportunity.

I went off to find the crew checking in for their flight home, and we said our goodbyes. It was all rather subdued. Watching their departing backs, I

thought, *is that it?* It seemed a long time since we had jubilantly crossed the equator on board a ramshackle ferry deep in the south Pacific. That had been the beginning. In the space of a few short months we had journeyed around the world. A hundred years earlier it had taken Mark Twain more than a year to make the same trip. Perhaps we should be feeling more pleased with ourselves than we seemed to be.

I turned to the final page of my battered copy of *Following the Equator* for inspiration. When Twain had sailed into Southampton at the end of his trip, he had written, 'It seemed a fine thing to have accomplished. The circumnavigation of this great globe in that little time, and I was privately proud of it. For a moment.

'Then came one of those vanity-snubbing reports from the Observatory people, whereby it appeared that another great body of light had lately flamed up in the remotenesses of space which was traveling at a gait which would enable it to do all that I had done in a minute and a half. Human pride is not worthwhile; there is always something lying in wait to take the wind out of it.'

Indeed.

The watchers watched . . . Now I've got to wake up and find it's an illusion, and they're still there in that Jeep . . .'

EPILOGUE

WHY NOT A PROLOGUE? Well, first of all this book speaks for itself. Secondly, I wanted to read it before reacting to its contents. Having done so, I am full of admiration for Michael Waldman's recollection of events, as well as his more than deft handling of those administrative nightmares which were spared me as I was pushed, pulled, levered, coaxed, lifted, dropped down, up, onto, into, along railway lines, steps, small boats, large boats, flimsy aircraft, lifts, palanquins and hot springs. He has a light, often ironic reporter's touch, not so very different from that of Mark Twain himself, without perhaps the voluptuous attention to foliage and cloud formations which were generic to Mark Twain's period, and more of a social sense, which is the hallmark of ours.

This is not to say that Mark Twain was indifferent to horrible conditions of life or lacking in outrage at the presence of injustice. There were merely fewer possibilities of dealing with such atrocities at the time. Suffice it to say that the modernity of Mark Twain's outlook is almost brutally expressed in his claim that there is not an inch of soil on this planet which has not, at sometime or other, been stolen.

Since I was extremely honoured to have been chosen to be the link between the great man of the last century and ours, and consequently, as it were, the guiding spirit of the 're-run', there are not surprisingly quite a few references to my presence by Michael Waldman, frequently adding such grace notes as 'with his customary wit'. In the nature of things what is described as customary wit rarely survives the hazardous journey from utterance to printed page without involuntary damage, and the friendlier the pen, the more the ephemeral quality of the wit is exposed. This is not terribly important, but I did not wish to leave the impression that I had accompanied my colleagues on this incredible journey merely to seek to brighten their waking hours with badinage. The journey had a profound effect on my comprehension of all kinds of tides and undertows at the end of a century of unique contrasts in both violence and understanding.

Kiribati was an example of a new nation so seemingly unimportant in the past that it was left more-or-less to its own devices, squadrons of kamikaze mosquitoes notwithstanding. Today it has taken its own destiny in hand by changing the dateline to make functional survival possible, and is the proud possessor of a sparkling and disproportionately large Chinese embassy. Limousines smartly aligned under car ports are a consequence of its efforts to attract attention to its new aspirations.

Fiji is an exception to Mark Twain's observation about the totality of land on this earth having been stolen at some time or another. Mark you, it must have been continually stolen in antiquity, as tribes took turns to lord it over others. But in modern times it is an unique example of a nation given voluntarily to another in the hope of avoiding the interference of a third. Fiji gave itself to Queen Victoria's Britain on condition the British paid the considerable American debt then owing. This extraordinary espousal of British manners explains why the Union Jack is part of independent Fiji's flag, and why portraits of British royalty are on display in the Presidential Palace and in many government offices to this day.

It may well have been the sight of neighbouring Hawaii gradually foundering under the weight of American creature comforts that warned Fiji of the dangers of less experienced Empire builders. Today, Hawaii, after the destruction of its monarchy and the undermining of its health, is a revitalised 50th state; its body, beautiful as ever, its face practically indistinguishable from Miami. As for its soul – there lies the catch. A language has survived, and with it a people, not quite pure in every case perhaps, but accepted as a valid minority. Back in the twenties, the US congress decreed that land claims would be granted according to the percentage of unadulterated Hawaiian blood in an applicant's veins, a solution which would be the joy of any Balkan apostle of ethnic cleansing. Today, there remains an impure but unrepentant minority for whom emotional Hawaiianess is more important than blood counts, and who are as difficult for a state-of-the-art democracy to assimilate as are the resolutely backward-looking patriots in Quebec.

New Zealand presented a different problem, the Maoris being a fiercely independent and evolved race who impressed the early British settlers to the extent that the British Government allowed the Treaty of Waitangi to be signed in both languages, English and Maori, in 1841. Now, English is a marvellous language, rich in nuance and allusion and therefore in imprecision. To the gratification of lawyers, the language of Shakespeare is the only one, to my knowledge, to possess the phrase 'the interpretation of the law'. The law as formulated in English is in permanent need of (highly paid) interpreters. Other, poorer languages have the advantage for the law, if not for lawyers, of being precise, often to the point of dullness. Well, in the Maoris the British met their match in longevity of memory, respect for ritual, and endless patience. The result is that landclaims and fishing rights of considerable size are now being conceded to various Maori tribes with a commendable sense of fair play.

Australia's problems are different again, the Aboriginal people being more artistic than warlike, and slower to develop in a social sense than the Maoris. Their backgrounds are entirely different, the Maoris being a maritime people, whose language is understood all across the Pacific Ocean, while the Aborigines are believed to be the inheritors of the landlocked traditions of India. Be that as it may, the Aborigines have found a voice in the contemporary world, often to draw attention to their appalling treatment in the past. That a politician like Ms Pauline Hanson should exist and be an embarrassment to thinking Australians, is an indication of the fact that this wonderful country has not fully come to terms with the inevitability of its geographical position and the nature of its heritage which, far from being meekly accepted, is being forged with every passing day.

We were in India before the success of their five nuclear tests and the consequent delirious dancing in the streets, an event which would have made Mahatma Gandhi turn in his grave. We all knew that India was an extremely old civilisation; we had no idea it was also an extremely old-fashioned one. It would, no doubt, have changed one's appreciation of the country's progress into the next millennium if one had been eye-witnesses to the popular jubilation as the solemn announcement of success was pronounced – tantamount to a declaration that a lottery had been won, first prize, an indecent sum, but in a worthless currency. A few days later, there was gleeful dancing in Pakistan. Now, both countries have sobered up in the realisation that something much more constructive could have been done with the money.

Mauritius is memorable for being the only independent nation where the French language has won over English in common usage, and where the growth of the Indian population has produced few of the tensions noticeable in Fiji. It is, in fact, an island paradise, perhaps because, once again, it has defied Twain's law by having been stolen from the Dodo, its only original inhabitant.

South Africa provided the greater challenge of the trip by providing a kind of urgency not noticeable elsewhere. It is, obviously, a country in transition, with a growing crime problem, but with a powerful and audible pulse. In a sense, it is the Mecca of Africa, in matters of technical advancement, industrial power and energy. That many outsiders flock to South Africa, just as many from Central America surge to the United States, adds fuel to the crime wave, but also underlines the country's primordial position in its area. But most important, with the extraordinary ascension of Nelson Mandela to power after twenty-seven years in prison, and the luminous clairvoyance of Archbishop Desmond Tutu by his side, there is a sudden surge of purely African wisdom, which is already showing its effect on the larger stage of the world. And let us not forget that Mahatma Gandhi, a previous purveyor of wisdom, cut his teeth on the obtuseness of apartheid before he ever returned to Mother India.

Today, Kofi Annan, the Ghanaian Secretary General of the United Nations, succeeded, from a position of weakness, to deflect a waiting Armada from committing another lightning incursion into the Gulf, with the resultant deaths of many innocents in the remote hope of destroying the guilty. This is not the way of truth or of reconciliation. What is the way then? Perhaps the realisation that what hope we express in the new millennium will be conditional on how much we are allowed to forget compared to what we are incited to remember.

SIR PETER USTINOV, AUGUST 1998